Spotted Pony Casino Mystery Series

Poker Face
House Edge
Double Down
The Squeeze
The Pinch
Down and Dirty

Crapshoot

Spotted Pony Casino Mystery

Book 7

Paty Jager

Windtree Press

Corvallis, OR

CRAPSHOOT

Contact information: info@windtreepress.com

Windtree Press
Corvallis Oregon
http://windtreepress.com

Cover Art by Covers by Karen

PUBLISHING HISTORY
Published in the United States of America
ISBN 978-1943601-68-4

Special Thanks to:

The Confederated Tribes of the Umatilla Family Violence Services Department.

About the Book

This series is set in and around a fictional casino on The Confederated Tribes of the Umatilla Reservation in NE Oregon. The reservations is real. I have researched and while I've made up people and where they live, I will try to stay true to the life people live on the reservation.

Chapter One

"Is it just me or does Kaydee seem jumpy tonight?" Dela asked her friend, Rosie, who sat beside her in the basket weaving class.

"I noticed a bruise on her left arm when she pulled her sleeve up to grab the reeds out of the tub of water," Rosie whispered.

Dela didn't like the thoughts that were bumping around in her head. She and Rosie had been taking basket weaving classes from Kaydee for six months. The classes didn't usually go that long. They'd been stretched out longer than the usual three months because many of the meetings were canceled due to Kaydee being sick. After digging and asking questions to see if they needed to help with medical bills, Dela discovered Kaydee hadn't been sick, just too bruised to go out in public.

"I think it's time we had a talk with her husband," Dela whispered.

Rosie shook her head as she wove a reed into the

struts of the six-inch basket she was making. "That will only cause her more trouble. I say we go to Public Safety. Talk to someone in the Family Violence department."

Dela liked to do things herself, which had put her in harm's way more times than she cared to think about. Partly due to her Army training and because she'd been brought up by a strong woman who had kept them fed, clothed, and a roof over their heads without a man being in her life.

"Someone is coming to the casino tomorrow from Public Safety to talk about spousal abuse. I'll sit in on the talk and see what the person has to say about intervening for Kaydee." Dela knew who the speaker was. Marion Shumack. A woman she'd never met, but whose brother she highly respected.

"That's a good idea. In the meantime, it wouldn't hurt to let Heath know your concerns." Rosie clamped her mouth shut as Kaydee walked over to their table to inspect the baskets they'd been working on.

"How are you two coming along?" Kaydee asked. Her voice didn't have the happy lilt it had when they'd started the class.

"I'm still struggling with the twist on the twining," Dela said, frowning at the uneven twists on her basket.

"It will become natural the more you do it. Concentrate on the direction you need to twist as you turn the basket and work up." Kaydee shifted her gaze to Rosie's basket. "That looks like you've been doing this your whole life."

Rosie's cheeks were a shade darker than usual when Dela glanced over at her friend. Dropping her gaze to Rosie's basket, she stared in awe. It did look like a basket that had been woven by an elder.

"I told you, you'd be a natural at this," Dela said, wondering if she'd ever get to the same level as her friend in basketry.

"I did a little basket weaving as a child with my grandmother. She made the most beautiful things." Rosie picked up another tule reed and began working on the basket.

"I've seen some of your grandmother's work in Tamástslikt," Kaydee said with reverence.

"I need to go through the museum again," Dela said, poking at the end of a reed sticking out of the middle of her weaving. An idea struck. "Would you have time to meet me there tomorrow afternoon around three?" she asked Kaydee. "Maybe having you explain the baskets and their weaving process would help me better understand what I'm doing."

The other woman's eyes sparkled for a moment before she shuttered them with her lashes. "I'm not sure I can make it. I love seeing the old baskets and discussing their methods. Can I call you, say at noon, and let you know?"

"That works." Dela pulled a tule out of the pile on the table in front of her and Rosie. She sprayed it with the water bottle to moisten and make the reed more flexible.

Kaydee moved on to the next table of two weavers.

"That's a good idea," Rosie whispered. "Maybe you can work the conversation around to how she has been getting all the bruises."

Dela nodded and held the tip of her tongue between her teeth as she twisted and twined the tule around her foot-wide basket. She never did anything in a small way.

♠ ♣ ♥ ♦

Thursday morning, Dela arrived at the Spotted Pony Casino conference area as the attendees to the Violence Against Women event waited for the speaker to appear. She sat in the back of the auditorium.

A tall, good-looking woman with long dark hair and eyes that matched Trooper Hawke's stepped onto the stage. She had a microphone hanging from a lanyard around her neck. She stood in front of six chairs with microphones on stands in front of them.

"Welcome to the Violence Against Women conference. I'm Marion Shumack. I work for the Family Violence Services." She gave a brief bio of being a lawyer and now being an advocate for women. She continued, "This conference is to help you identify when someone needs help and then how to go about getting help for them. We have a panel that will talk about the different aspects of this. There will be time for questions at the end of our discussion."

Dela was impressed with how well the woman spoke and the information the conference planned to cover. She sat back and listened as the panel members were introduced. Mimi Shumack, one of the speakers and Trooper Hawke's mother, was the last person introduced. The crowd clapped loudest for her. The other members of the panel had been people who worked for Public Safety and the Tribal Police. She was surprised Heath hadn't said anything about the police presence when she'd mentioned attending the event this morning.

But then he had other issues on his mind. Tribal police had learned there was fentanyl flowing through the reservation. One teen had died from it already. They were working around the clock to find out where it was coming from before there was another death.

Dela sat through the whole morning's talks. The information would help her when dealing with Kaydee and her circumstances. It also shed light on a couple of the casino employees she'd noticed acting out of character.

When the morning session broke up, she made her way over to the mother and daughter.

"Dela, it's good to see you," Mimi said, reaching out and taking her hand.

Surprised that the woman remembered her, Dela felt her cheeks heating. "Mimi, it was good to hear your perspective on this topic and how the MMIW movement has been pushing to get more agencies involved in finding more missing women and children."

"It is a good movement and one that I will be a part of until I'm gone from this earth. Too many good people have become nothing more than the memories and sorrow of their loved ones." Mimi nodded, her eyes glistening with unshed tears.

"Dela, I believe we've never met. But I hear about you quite often." Marion held out her hand to shake.

Dela took her hand and was pleased by the firm handshake. "I was hoping to get some time with you today. Is now a good time or should I wait until the afternoon session is over?"

"We were just going to the buffet to get lunch. Sit with us," Mimi said, walking out of the auditorium.

Dela fell in step with Marion as the older woman led the way along the gaming tables to the buffet. Other women who had been in the morning session stood in line waiting for a table. Dela hadn't clocked in, but as she walked through the casino, she took in where the security personnel were and whether or not they were doing their job. As head of security for the casino, she didn't keep certain hours to be at work. It kept her employees on their toes, never knowing when she'd show up.

As she walked, she noted two guards talking in the corner when they should have had their eyes on the slot machines and people playing them. She mentally made a note of the two and then smiled at Marion and answered her question. "I do enjoy my job. I'm helping to keep the tribal members and members of the public safe."

Marion smiled and nodded. "I have heard a lot about you from Quinn. You two have a history that goes back to when you were both in the military." The woman studied her.

Not one to show her emotions, Dela tamped down the urge to tell the woman about Quinn's highhandedness while working special forces and she was military police. But she wanted the woman to help her with Kaydee, so she smiled and said, "Yes, our jobs had us bumping into one another fairly often. He caught prisoners of war, and I made sure they stayed locked up."

Mimi now stood in line, talking to the two younger women in front of them. Dela recognized them from a self-defense class she helped Heath give at the Yellow Hawk Health Center.

Both women noticed her at the same time.

"Dela, I wouldn't think you'd be interested in violence toward women. You have that handsome

Tribal at your beck and call," the taller woman said.

Smiling and gritting her teeth, Dela replied, "I thought as head of security for the casino, it would be good for me to know the signs of abuse. My security might be able to help save someone."

"That's a good idea. I'm sure this is a good place for a man to get away with being abusive. There's so much noise and confusion," the shorter of the two said.

Mimi put her arm around Dela's shoulders. "She and my son saved two women from Nixyáawii who were stolen for human trafficking."

The two women ducked their heads and murmured as they were led to a table.

"You didn't have to tell them that," Dela said, feeling self-conscious. She didn't help people to be lauded as a hero. She knew many on this reservation, and off, didn't have someone looking out for them. Especially, Indigenous women, children, and two spirits. While the community believed she was half Hispanic and white, she knew in her heart that her father was Umatilla and from this reservation. She just hadn't found all the evidence to prove it and didn't want to ask her mom, having discovered he may have been in prison for a heinous crime.

"Dela, you are special. You and your mom were sent to us for a reason. Your mother to love and teach our children and raise you here. And you to protect." Mimi ushered them behind the hostess.

Following the tall, proud stature of Marion, Dela thought, *You don't know how much I belong here.*

Chapter Two

After they had filled their plates through the buffet lines and were seated, Dela cleared her throat and said, "I was hoping you could give me some advice."

Marion and Mimi both stopped eating and peered at her.

"Both of us?" Mimi asked.

"I think Marion can help me, but I'd love your advice as well." Dela took a drink of her iced tea and started. "I've been taking basket weaving classes from Kaydee Wadass. She's canceled half of the classes, saying she was sick. But when we, Rosie and I, checked up on her, she hadn't been sick. She was bruised. We tried to find out what happened, but she wouldn't talk about it. We think her husband has been abusing her. What steps do we need to take to help her?"

"Talking to me is a start," Marion said. "I can drop by their home and visit with her when I know her husband isn't there. Do they have children?"

"Two that are too young for school. Her auntie

watches the kids while she teaches the classes." Dela had discovered all the info she needed for Marion by investigating Kaydee's family to figure out how to intercede. "Her husband works for Johnson Towing. I haven't been able to figure out if he works regular hours or is just on call."

Marion's left eyebrow raised. "You've done your homework. I can find out when he works." She winked. "I have my sources, too."

Dela knew she meant her lover in the FBI- Quinn Pierce. "Do you ask him questions about the tribal members you investigate?" Dela asked, wondering how much information she had gathered from the FBI and how much they had on the tribal members.

Marion glanced at her mom and then leaned toward Dela. "I'm only telling you this because Quinn trusts you. He's been keeping an eye on that particular towing company. I thought you knew because your boyfriend has been working with Quinn on finding out where the fentanyl's been coming from."

Dela leaned back and stared at Marion. Heath hadn't said a word to her about working with Quinn or that they were interested in Johnson Towing. She thought he would have said something, knowing her concern about Kaydee.

"I take it he hasn't told you." Marion muttered something under her breath, and Mimi put a hand on her arm.

"That's okay. With me worrying about Kaydee, he must have known I'd get caught up in whatever he's doing." Dela tried to make light of what she'd learned, but it hurt to know that Heath had kept this information from her.

They finished eating, talking about the people they collectively knew. As they stood to return to the seminar, Dela excused herself.

"I need to get to work. Thank you for the insightful discussions this morning and for looking into Kaydee."

"You don't want to sit in on the afternoon discussions?" Mimi asked.

"I wish I could, but this isn't one of my days off. I need to get scheduling done and check in on everyone." She turned to Marion. "It was a pleasure meeting you in person."

"I'll let you know what I learn." Marion smiled and then followed her mother out of the buffet.

Dela stood a moment, still stunned that Heath hadn't said a word about investigating the towing company.

"You're growing roots," a voice behind her said.

Dela turned and peered into the smiling face of the waitress. "Sorry about that. I better get to work before I'm fired."

The young woman laughed. "Like they are going to fire you. Have a good day."

"Thanks. You too." Dela walked out of the buffet with a smile and past the deli.

"Hey!" Rosie called from behind the counter.

Dela changed her direction and walked into the deli, stopping at the end of the counter.

"Did you learn anything this morning?" Rosie asked.

"Yes. Marion Shumack of the Family Violence Department is going to do a check, and I learned some interesting things that make me think we have a couple of employees here at the casino who may need someone to talk to."

Rosie studied her for several seconds. "How are you going to do that?"

Dela grinned. "By telling you who they are. You can start a conversation with them when you see them. You seem to be able to get people to talk to you better than I can. Then when they happen to tell you what's going on at home, you can slip them Marion's card. Which I'll get from her before she leaves today." She came up with the idea on the fly, but it sounded solid.

"You really think they'll open up to me and then follow through with talking to Marion?" The way Rosie's round face scrunched, Dela had a feeling she would punch a hole in her idea.

"Why wouldn't it work?"

"First, what if they think I'm prying? And second, how will we know if they followed through and went to see Marion?"

"You don't pry. You are a very good listener. Ask them about their kids or something you know about them. I'm sure you or they will work the conversation around to what is going on at home. We won't know for sure if they see her, but we are at least giving them the option of doing something to change their life and that of their children."

Rosie's face brightened and her eyes shone. "That I like. Who are the two you suspect?"

Dela told her the names of the women she suspected.

Rosie nodded. "I've seen the change in them lately, too. I can see your concerns. I'll strike up a conversation with them the first chance I get." Rosie moved to the cash register as a customer walked up.

"See you later," Dela said, leaving the deli and heading for the door to the inner offices at the casino. She walked into the hallway leading to the various offices and walked all the way down the hall to the security office. Her second in command, Kenny Proudhorse, glanced up from where he'd been working on a report.

"Good to see you, boss," he said in his soft, lazy voice. His lopsided grin made her return a smile.

"Hey, Kenny. Ready for me to take over for the day?" Dela stopped beside the desk and glanced down at the report. "You know, you'd save yourself time if you just entered that into the computer instead of writing it out first." She glanced at the theft report.

"But when I get called away, I'm in the middle of writing up the report, and I have to start all over. This way, when I'm interrupted, it's sitting right here and I can continue. Then put it into the computer when I'm off duty and can't be interrupted." He smiled. "Which I'll do now that you're here." He took the earbud out of his ear, pulled the radio off his belt, and turned it off, before putting all of those and his taser in the drawer designated for him.

Dela opened her drawer and pulled out her earbud, radio, and taser. She shoved the earbud into her ear, turned the radio on, clipped the mic to her shirt, and hooked the taser to her belt. The security members had a class on using tasers last month. It was now mandatory for them to each wear one while on duty. They'd had a couple of drugged-out visitors who needed to be restrained to keep them from hurting the clientele or themselves.

Once she was "suited up," Dela nodded to Margie

at the security podium. Her job was to check employees coming in and out of work, log shipments for the restaurants and gift shop, and manage the phone and office. "I'm headed out to see if everyone is doing their job."

She loved her varying hours and being able to keep the security personnel on their toes. Her first stop was to talk to one of the security officers she'd seen standing in a corner, conversing with another security officer.

The man's eyes widened when he saw her coming, but he quickly smiled and nodded as she approached. "Didn't see you come in," Kurt said.

"I've been here a while. I attended the seminar on violence against women this morning." She inwardly smiled as he squirmed just a bit. "How's the floor been?"

"Quiet for a Thursday." He stared beyond her, scanning the people playing the slot machines.

Dela had learned to block out the sounds of the machines. If you didn't, it could drive you crazy. She nodded and asked, "Is that why you and Phil were in the corner visiting around eleven-forty-five?"

His gaze snapped back to her face. The tips of his ears were turning red.

"What was so important that it couldn't have waited until a break to talk about? When two security personnel are in a conversation while on duty, there are two sections of the casino not being monitored." She had learned the Umatilla way of shaming as punishment for a wrongdoing.

"I'd asked him if he'd seen the game last night. I know it was wrong, but it was so quiet I was bored."

His tone didn't sound like he was sorry or that was the reason for their conversation.

"Don't let it happen again," she said and walked straight over to Phil.

She could tell he'd seen her talking to Kurt.

"Phil, I'm checking in with everyone. How's the morning been?" she asked.

"Slow. Which is good," he quickly added.

"Not when you leave your section to talk to another security guard." She studied him.

He shrugged.

She didn't care for such a nonchalant attitude from her guards. "What was so important you left your post?"

"He asked me about the game last night." Phil didn't even flinch as he said the exact same thing as Kurt. But this time, she felt he wasn't lying so much as trying to make her believe him, by being forthright and stating it with confidence.

This led her to believe he was the one who had instigated the visit. Rather than force the issue, she'd get eyes on the two when they were at work. "Don't do it again. Your job is to stay in your area and keep an eye on things, not hide in a corner talking game scores."

She walked away and checked in with all the other security officers on the casino floor. When she'd finished, she tapped her entry card on the wall outside the surveillance room. A door not visible from the outside popped open, and she walked through.

Surveillance members sat at long tables with ten or more monitors in front of them. They were keeping an eye on the casino, inside and out. She walked over to stand behind Marie. She was keeping an eye on the monitors in the area where Phil and Kurt were stationed.

She leaned over the woman and pointed to the two security guards. "Did you notice them huddling in a corner about three hours ago?"

Marie didn't look up; she just nodded. "And again, after you finished talking to them."

Dela didn't like that the two had ignored her order to stay in their areas. "Have you seen them huddling before today?"

She nodded.

Blowing out a breath of disgust, she asked, "How often?"

"Once, sometimes twice a week. At least the days I'm working." Marie shrugged.

"How long have they been neglecting their duties?" She was starting to build up a temper about the two having neglected their duties for a while and no one told her.

"I'd say about six months, maybe."

"And you didn't tell me?" She knew it was wrong to take her anger at the two men out on the women filling her in, but there were times when her anger got the better of her. This was one of those times.

Marie spun in her chair. "I'm not in charge of taking care of security, you are." She smacked the gum she was chewing and spun back around.

Dela stomped into the surveillance office to ask a favor of Marty, the head of surveillance. She opened the door and found his second-in-command, Farley. His long hair was swinging like the fringe on a butterfly dancer's shawl as he bobbed his head in a rhythmic motion.

"Farley, I need…" When he didn't turn at the sound of her voice, she walked around in front of him and saw he had earbuds in. She tapped his shoulder and he jumped, shouting a string of curse words.

After gathering himself together, he said, "Don't go sneaking up on me like that again. I may only be twenty-three, but my heart could stop being scared like that."

Dela smiled and waved to the monitor in front of them. "I need some surveillance done on a couple of my guards."

He grinned. "You know I like it when you give me surveillance. Who and what are we looking for?"

She told him about Phil and Kurt meeting in a corner and the approximate time. "Marie said they have been meeting like that once a week for the last six months. Can you go back and see if you can find the first time they met and who instigated it?"

"Sure thing. But it might take a day or so. That's a lot of videos to watch."

"That's fine. I just need dates to try and figure out what is going on between them. They weren't talking about sports meeting regularly like they have been." She'd stopped other corruptions that had happened in the casino. If there was something illegal the two were caught up in, she didn't want them working for her or drawing the wrong kind of people to the casino.

She left the surveillance office and walked through the room full of monitors. Her phone buzzed. Checking the screen, she wasn't sure she wanted to talk to Heath, but they needed to get things straightened out before she delved deeper into Kaydee's circumstances.

"Dela," she answered as if she hadn't looked at the

screen.

"Hey, it's me. Do you have time tonight to have dinner with me?" His voice was upbeat, but they'd known each other since high school and she could tell he had something he wanted to say to her.

"Yeah, if you can come here. I don't want to leave until a couple of my employees are off duty."

There was a slight pause. "Something going on I need to know?" As a detective on the Umatilla Tribal Police force, Heath was usually the first person she called when something unlawful went down at the casino.

"Not yet. I'm not sure what's going on."

"What time do you want me to be there?" he asked.

"Seven." That would give her plenty of time to get the scheduling done and keep an eye on the two security guards right before they went off duty. A thought came to her. And have someone she trusted in the employee lounge when the two got off duty.

Dela sent Margie out to replace Nicki, a new security employee, and one who, like herself, was in the military and came back to the reservation after finishing her tour. Nicki was someone she could trust and who, being new, the other security personnel were used to her questions about protocol and things that happened at the casino.

When Nicki entered the office, her brow was wrinkled. "Did I do something wrong?" she asked, taking the chair Dela spun around from Kenny's desk.

"No. I need you to do a special assignment for me."

Nicki's eyes brightened and she straightened her slouched posture. "What do you need?"

"I want you to follow Phil and Kurt into the lounge when shift is over and just hang close enough that you can hear what they say. Don't look obvious. They already know I'm keeping tabs on them. I don't want them to know you are spying on them." Dela studied the woman about ten years younger than her thirty-nine years.

Nicki bobbed her head. A strand of dark hair fell forward, but the rest of her curly locks were in what could only be described as a messy bun.

"Just observe and listen. After they leave, come find me in the Pony. I'll be having dinner with Heath."

Nicki's cheeks flushed. "Okay."

"Now, try to go back to business as usual. Just pay attention to the two when it's about time to call it a day." Dela knew the woman could do this. She just didn't want her trying too hard.

"Got it." She left the office, and ten minutes later, Margie returned.

"I don't know what you said to Nicki, but she came back with a huge grin on her face."

Dela smiled. "I gave her something more interesting to do than watch people play slot machines all day."

Chapter Three

Dela sat in the Pony Bar and Grill waiting for Heath to arrive and realized Kaydee hadn't called her about going to the museum. She'd pulled her phone out to call when Nicki entered and walked over to the table.

"Have a seat. You want something to drink?"

She glanced at the bar and said, "It is after work."

Dela nodded, and when the waitress came over, Nicki ordered a beer.

Heath arrived just before the waitress brought over Nicki's drink. The young woman's face glowed a deeper bronze.

"Hey," Heath said to Nicki and then faced Dela.

She narrowed her eyes, reminding him she didn't like signs of affection at her workplace. Dela saw what was smoldering in his eyes and raised a hand to ward off a kiss. To her surprise, he leaned close as if whispering to her and kissed the side of her cheek before taking the seat next to her.

His actions had her gazing into his eyes. Why was

he being so kind and gentle? Had he done something he knew would get back to her?

Nicki cleared her throat.

That jerked Dela back to why the security guard was sitting at the table. "Nicki, what did you see or hear?" Her mind tumbled around to figure out why Heath had been so insistent to show her affection.

"Well, Phil left the casino floor first. I hung back pretending to carry on a conversation with an elderly woman." She smiled and then continued. "Kurt waited in a corner where he was kind of concealed for about five minutes and a woman walked by. I didn't think anything of it until Kurt squatted and came back up with something he tucked inside his shirt. It wasn't very big. When I walked by him, I couldn't tell he had anything under his shirt. When we both entered the lounge, Phil was gone." She sipped her beer and then continued.

"I tried to see if he took something out of his shirt before leaving, but then the old biddy from the laundry room saw me staring at him and started teasing me." Her face grew a deeper shade of bronze again.

Dela leaned forward. "Don't tell anyone I had you watching them, and don't tell anyone what you just told me."

Nicki nodded and finished off her beer. "See you tomorrow." She slid off the elevated chair and left the Pony.

"What was that all about?" Heath asked.

Dela told him about seeing the two guards visiting in a corner and asking the rookie who wanted to move up the ladder to spy on them.

"That was good thinking." Heath turned to the

waitress who came to get his order. "I'll have iced tea and the burger special."

"The same," Dela said. When the waitress walked away, she asked, "What was the kiss all about?"

"You know how you've been talking about Kaydee Wadass and how you were worried her husband was abusing her?" Heath had a hand on the back of her chair and leaned close, whispering.

"Yes?" She hoped this didn't mean something had happened to Kaydee.

"We picked up her brother-in-law today when we staked out a fentanyl deal."

Dela thought about what Marion had said about Quinn and Heath working together. "You and Quinn?"

Heath leaned back. "Yeah. How did you know?"

"I talked to Quinn's girlfriend today about Kaydee. She mentioned you two were working on stopping the fentanyl from coming onto the reservation. Why didn't you tell me about this?" They had been sharing all the details of their jobs since the day he moved into her house. His not telling her about working with Quinn and that fentanyl had entered the reservation hurt her more than she wanted to admit.

"I knew how much you were worrying about Kaydee, so I didn't say anything. Today was the first real evidence we had that it is coming in, even though there was a death on the rez from the drug last month." Heath sipped his drink and studied her. "I'm sorry I didn't keep you up to date on this. You've been kind of distant, and I've tried to give you space."

Dela's gaze flew from where she'd been watching a bead of water slide down her glass to Heath's eyes. "Have I?" She'd been having more nightmares lately about the IED explosion that took her lower leg in Iraq. Because of that, she'd been sleeping in the recliner rather than in their bed. Oh, she'd start in bed, but as her body began tensing and her stub aching, she'd slip from the bed and go to the recliner.

"I didn't want to bother you. I've been sleeping in the recliner because my nightmares have come back." She peered into his eyes and saw empathy. Not the pity that she had thought would be there. He hadn't been in the war, but he'd experienced a kind of war while working as a tribal policeman at the reservation in South Dakota.

"Why haven't you told me?" He reached over and touched her hand.

"It's not your battle. It's mine." She was the one who relived the day her patrol's Humvee blew up and she lost three people from her unit and her lower right leg. She had what her V.A. shrink said was survivor's guilt. She lived and they died. Heath knew she'd been seeing Darrin Shomer. But he thought it was to reconcile with losing her leg. She was okay with losing her leg. It was her punishment for not following her gut when she started to tell the unit to turn around but stayed with orders. She rarely did the opposite of what her gut said, now.

His thumb slowly caressed the back of her hand. "It *is* my battle. I want you to be happy and look forward to a life with me. Not dwell on something you couldn't control."

She moved her hand away from his, wanting to lean into him but not wanting to show weakness. Her strength had gotten her through school and sports, playing on teams with the Umatilla youth she grew up with. It also kept her from caving in during boot camp and being shipped to Iraq as military police. It was what kept her looking for a father no one would admit to.

Changing the subject, she asked, "Do you think Kaydee's husband is involved in the selling or using?"

Heath shook his head. "I don't know. But I don't want anyone, including you or Quinn's girlfriend, going out there alone." He peered into her eyes. "Did you hear me?"

Dela nodded. "I get the message. No going to see Kaydee at her home alone."

They finished their meal and Heath headed home. Dela watched Heath walk out of the casino before she texted Quinn. *What is Marion's phone number?*

Why? He texted back.

I need to ask her something about what she said today at the seminar.

He texted the number, and Dela texted Marion.

We need to go to Kaydee's tomorrow. What time do you want to meet at the casino?

She replied, *10 am.*

Dela gave her a thumbs up and went about her usual nightly duties.

Dela went home early because the casino had been so slow. She wanted to be well-rested and alert when she and Marion drove up to the Wadass home.

Heath questioned her about being home early. She told him she was tired and needed to be rested for the next night when the casino would be hopping. To further prove that she had listened to him at dinner, she spent the whole night in bed, snuggling with him when the dreams became too vivid for her to bear sleeping any longer.

The morning came as usual. She fed Mugshot and Jethro their breakfasts before swinging down the hall on her crutches to get dressed. She entered the bedroom as Heath buckled on his duty belt and holstered his firearm.

"What time are you going to work today?" he asked.

"Since it's Friday, probably around six and stay until two or three. You know I like to be at the casino during the busiest hours." She grabbed clothes out of the closet and sat on the bed.

"What are you doing until then?" Heath asked, leaning down and kissing the top of her head.

If she didn't know better, she'd think he was grilling her about her plans today. But he asked her the same question every day, since her schedule was so fluid. "I'm going to see if the plants in the backyard can be saved after Jethro decided to taste them. Then I may run over and see how Molly and Marty's house is coming along." Her best friend Molly married her friend Marty, who was head of surveillance at the casino. For years, Molly lived in a house connected to her veterinary clinic. But this year, her son, Travis, and his friends, began building her and Marty a house in Tutuilla. The same community on the reservation where Dela and Heath lived.

"That sounds like a good day. Let me know how the building is coming along. I'm sure Travis is doing a great job. He made this place perfect for you." Travis had remodeled Dela's house when she'd purchased it. It was set up for her needs as an amputee.

"I'll do that."

Heath kissed her on the lips. "See you tonight. I might drop by the casino after work just to say hi."

She nodded. "You know where to find me."

He grinned, then sobered, and said, "Stay out of trouble."

Shrugging, Dela asked, "Why would I get into trouble?"

"Because you are fixated on Kaydee Wadass. Let Family Violence take care of it." He grasped her chin and made her look up at him. "I don't want you getting mixed up with the Wadass family after we brought one of the family members in for drug trafficking. If they connect you to me, you could be in danger."

"I'll be fine. Go to work and don't worry. I'll see you tonight at the casino." She smiled and knew she shouldn't be hiding the fact that she was going to the Wadass house with Marion. However, she didn't want Heath to worry about what she was doing today. Because she would go, no matter how much he tried to convince her otherwise.

He left the room, and she heard him say goodbye to Mugshot before the front door closed.

She dressed in her regular attire of track pants, T-shirt, and athletic shoes. She checked on the plants in the yard with Mugshot and Jethro following her around, sticking their noses into what she was doing. After an hour of light-hearted time spent with her dog and donkey, she gave both a hug and left them locked in the pasture just outside the yard fence.

Twenty minutes later, she stood beside her car in the front parking area close to the entrance to the casino parking lot. As she waited beside her car, her phone buzzed. Farley.

"Farley, what did you find?" she asked, answering the call.

"Your two guards seem to meet in that corner regularly every Thursday. But it appears, going back six months, that Kurt is the one who invited Phil into the corner the first time."

"Did you get anything on the lady who dropped something that Kurt picked up?" She was worried her guards were part of the fentanyl coming onto the reservation.

"She's a regular. Comes in about three to four times a week. Usually, she plays the same slot machine in Kurt's section. And she does do a sort of drop every Thursday." His voice grew shrill as he recited his discovery.

"Slow down. We don't know if this is anything other than Kurt possibly fooling around with the woman. Can you send a photo of her to me, and I'll see if I can figure out who she is." Dela waved as Marion pulled into the parking lot in a blue Rav4.

"I can send you a still. Anything else you want me to do?"

"Keep an eye on Kurt and Phil. See if they talk to anyone or hand something over to anyone." She walked toward Marion's vehicle still talking on the phone.

"You think they are dealing?" Farley's shrill voice dropped to an ominous tone.

"I don't know what they are doing, but we need to find out. I have to go. I'll be in about six, but only tell that to Marty and Kenny."

"Gotcha, Boss Lady." The humor in his voice made her smile as she ended the call and slipped into the passenger seat.

"Good morning. You're in a good mood," Marion said, backing the car out of the slot she'd pulled into.

"Just glad I work with some fun and trustworthy people." Most of her security crew were trustworthy, but the ones in the higher-up positions were the most trustworthy. She was glad to have them on her team.

Marion pulled onto the road in front of the casino, heading north.

"Do you know where Kaydee lives?" Dela asked. She'd looked it up before heading to the casino to meet with Marion.

"Yes. *Xislipispa*. She and her husband have a place on the road just past the community." Marion took a right onto Mission.

"I don't think I've heard of that. When I looked up the address it said Homly."

"That's it. *Xislipispa* was a wonderful berry-picking place before the treaty. Afterward, it was called Homly after a Walla Walla head chief. Growing up, Mom taught me all the place names in our original language. She was sad that so many don't know the names of places given to them by our people. She wanted to make sure that they weren't lost." Marion shrugged and continued on Mission, making a slight right and then going straight.

"How long were you away from here?" Dela asked.

"Too long. Nearly twenty years. I didn't realize how much I missed it until Gabriel brought me back." Marion sighed and rolled down the window, slowing her speed. "There is nowhere else that smells like this."

Dela agreed but didn't say anything. Only she and Heath believed she had Umatilla blood in her veins.

They turned left and then made a right and drove

through the small community of Cayuse before crossing the Umatilla River and continuing east.

"That should be the driveway up ahead," Marion said, slowing down to make the turn into the driveway.

"How did you know the location so precisely?" Dela asked, again feeling as if this woman would make a good detective.

Marion shot her a smile and said, "Quinn showed it to me on his phone when I told him we were coming out to check on Kaydee."

The thought Marion would share more with Quinn than she shared with Heath made her nauseous. Once Heath found out where she was and that she'd not even had the courage to stand up to him and argue her case, it would make him think she was shutting him out of everything, not just her dreams.

The car stopped beside a gray early 2000s pickup. The little red car that Kaydee drove to the basket weaving lessons sat on the other side of the pickup. "That's Kaydee's car," Dela said, opening her door.

Marion followed her up the dirt path to the door of the single-story house. The paint was fading and the windows could have used a good scrubbing.

Dela knocked on the door, and a small child shrieked.

"Quiet!" a male voice shouted above the shrieking.

The door opened and Sonny Wadass stood behind the screen door, holding a less than two-year-old, with a shrieking three or four-year-old clinging to his leg.

"What do you want?" he shouted above the shrieking, shoving a long strand of dark hair that had become loose from his braids out of his face.

"We're here to talk to Kaydee," Dela said.

The man's eyes widened before his eyes narrowed. The glare he bestowed on them would have made a timid person back away from the door. "Why are you here to talk to Kaydee?"

"We'd like to come in if you don't mind," Marion said, reaching to grab the screen door handle.

"I don't want some outsiders coming into my house." He backed up with a hand reaching toward the door.

"It looks like you could use a hand with those girls," Marion said. "If I can get the one on your leg settled down, will you talk with us?"

A smirk curled the man's lips, and he shoved the screen door open, nearly hitting them in the face. "Good luck."

Dela held the door as Marion walked in. She knelt beside the child and talked to her in a soothing voice. The child stopped shrieking and then reached out her arms for Marion to take her.

Dela was surprised at how adeptly the woman took the child into her arms and stood, smiling at the father.

"Shall we have that talk?" Marion asked, walking into the living room and taking a seat on the couch.

Dela followed, sitting on the end of the couch.

Sonny sat with his youngest daughter on his lap in the only chair.

Marion nodded to Dela, which she took to mean, you ask the questions.

"Sonny, I've been taking basket weaving lessons from Kaydee. She missed a lot of the lessons, and I discovered it was because she was so bruised. Can you tell me what happened to her?" Dela decided it was best not to ask him why he did it. When Marion nodded slightly, she knew she'd gone about it the correct way.

"She just falls down a lot," Sonny said, not looking her in the eye.

"Should she be checked by a doctor to see if something is wrong with her?" Dela asked. "Maybe there is a medical issue that is causing her to fall so much."

"She's just clumsy," Sonny said, still avoiding eye contact.

"She wasn't clumsy before. She was one of the basketball starters who took Nixyáawii to the state playoffs her senior year. If she's clumsy now, it has to be a medical issue." Dela glanced around the house. "Where is she? Her car is out front."

"One of her friends came and picked her up. I told her I didn't have to work today. She said she was going to enjoy some time away from the girls and let me be a dad for a change." He patted the head of the child on his lap and stared at the one still sitting contentedly on Marion's lap.

"Which friend did she go with?" Dela asked.

He shrugged. "I don't know. I was in the shower when whoever it was pulled up, and she left."

Marion stood, placed the child she'd been holding on the couch, and reached into her purse, handing Sonny her card. "Give this to Kaydee when you see her. I'd like to talk to her about getting free childcare for her a couple times a week. It helps young mothers cope better."

Dela took that as her cue to stand and head for the door.

"This card says you're from the Family Violence Department. I don't beat my wife." He glared at her and tossed the card on the couch.

"We also offer free childcare to help young families, like yourselves. It takes some stress out of your life if she can shop without children or the two of you want to have a night out, like a date." Marion pulled a flyer out of her purse. "As you can see, we are more than dealing with abusive spouses. We try to help keep conflict from happening. Yesterday, I gave a seminar at the casino on how to notice when someone might be being abused. We want to prevent it from happening."

Sonny's gaze shot to Dela. "That's where I've seen you. You're the head of security at the casino. I suppose you sat in on that seminar and immediately thought I beat up my wife."

"Kaydee was one of several women who came to mind when I sat in on the seminar. If you aren't hitting her, then who is?" Dela had listened to this man talk. While he had a temper, he seemed more caring than she'd expected. His tone when he talked about Kaydee wasn't placating or vicious. The photos around the room all showed two people who cared for one another. Always smiling and touching. There wasn't fear in her eyes or malice in his. A thought came to her. "Does your brother come around a lot when you're gone?"

Sonny's eyes widened and his mouth clamped shut, before he asked, "What are you trying to say?"

"I'm just wondering if your wife's bruises happened the same day your brother might have come around." Dela reached for the door.

"Your boyfriend can't get my brother on drug charges, so he sent you out here to get him on woman-beating charges?" The man laughed. "That's pathetic."

Dela studied him. He didn't look so confident. "Just think about the visits and how your wife acted that night." She pulled open the door and said, "And by the way, my boyfriend doesn't even know I'm here. He has his business, and I have my own agenda." She walked out of the house, knowing that Marion would be right behind her.

When they were both in the car and Marion had it headed back toward Mission, she asked, "Is that true? Heath doesn't know you came out here today?"

Chapter Four

Dela's gut started burning, and she answered, "Yeah. I didn't tell him about our little trip."

Marion gave a soft whistle and said, "From what Quinn has said, you two are like Velcro, always knowing where the other one is and what they're doing. Are you having doubts about Heath?"

Dela shook her head and stared out the window. "I have doubts about myself and whether I'm really what Heath wants. I'm damaged, I'm headstrong, and I can never give him children." She hadn't voiced that to anyone, not even her mom. Not only had there been damage to her leg, requiring it to be amputated, she'd taken shrapnel to the abdomen that left her sterile.

She felt the car swerve and stop. Dela sat staring down at the Umatilla River.

"Look at me," Marion said, in the same soothing voice she'd used on the child.

Dela hadn't planned to blab what she had to this person of all people. She'd been in love with Quinn in

Afghanistan and if he'd said one word or flicked a glance toward a cot, she'd have jumped in without regrets. Until he'd let a rapist go free for information. Then she couldn't believe she'd fallen for such a lowlife person.

"Dela, I am the perfect person to talk to about this." Marion's voice cracked with emotion.

Twisting her neck, Dela glanced over at the other woman. From the tears glistening in her eyes to the sad droop of her lips, Dela realized they may have more in common than Quinn Pierce.

She shifted in her seat and stared at Marion. But didn't say anything. She'd let the other woman start the conversation.

"I know what it's like to find love and wonder if the other person will think of you the same once they find out you can't give them children. When I was doing mission work in South America during a college break, I contracted mumps. I'm not sure why. I'd been vaccinated for it, but there I was in a foreign country and an isolated region. The fever raged and it wasn't until I returned to the States and saw my gynecologist that I learned I would never have children. The disease had gone into my endocrine glands." She sighed, peered out the side window then returned her gaze to Dela. "When I fell in love with Adrian, I was so worried he'd reject me because of my inability to have children. He said that would allow us to focus fully on one another. I think I fell even harder for him the evening he told me that. After I'd finally gotten up enough courage to tell him." She smiled and stared forward. "If he hadn't been murdered, we would have had a wonderful life together." Marion shook herself and studied Dela. "If

Heath loves you, he won't care."

Dela wrung her hands in her lap and choked out the thoughts that had been spinning. "He was kind and gentle about my having lost a leg. He's seen the scars on my body from the shrapnel but has never asked about them. He's been good at letting me tell him when I'm ready, but this…" She held her breath and then blurted out, "It's something that I should have told him before we moved in together and started talking about marriage." Blowing out a breath, she continued, "He is not one to quit something if he's started it. I don't want him to grow to hate me when we remain childless and it's my fault because I didn't tell him from the beginning."

"You and Heath need to sit down and discuss this. It's important. It was the first thing I told Quinn when we started dating. If you stick around, you won't be able to produce children with me." She chuckled. "He thought it was some kind of joke at first. But once he realized I was serious, we had a good talk. He'd wanted children in his first marriage, and she hadn't. Now he said, it didn't matter. After more years doing what he does, he knew his life was hectic and not one that would make him a good father."

Dela thought about that. Both she and Heath had dangerous jobs. Especially when she kept being caught up in murders. It might be for the best that they didn't have children. Though she'd wanted to practice all her mother had taught her on a child. She smiled at Marion. "Thank you for this talk. I haven't been able to say anything to anyone. Not even my mom. I've felt like I had to prove myself in my job because that would be all I'd have for people to judge me by."

Marion's eyes softened, and she said, "The only ones you need to worry about judging you are yourself and the Creator."

♠ ♣ ♥ ♦

Dela was putting on her slacks and polo shirt for work when Mugshot started barking. Before she could finish dressing, she heard his happy talk and the front door closing. Heath was home. She glanced at the clock on the bedside table and saw she had time to sit down and talk to him.

"How was your day?" he asked, walking into the bedroom and taking off his duty belt.

"Good. The more I hang around with Marion Shumack, the more I like her." Dela pulled her shirt over her head and faced him.

"You and Marion went to the Wadass home, didn't you?" He put his gun in the drawer of his bedside table.

"We did. You said I or she shouldn't go alone, so we went together. Kaydee wasn't there. Sonny was taking care of the girls, but he didn't know where his wife was. It was kind of weird."

She'd been turning over Sonny's words and actions ever since she'd come home.

"Weird how?" Heath asked.

"Well, he was adamant he didn't hit Kaydee. I kind of believe him. When I threw out that maybe his brother did, he acted scared. I think his brother beat up Kaydee to keep Sonny in line." This had been the assumption she'd come to from the conversation.

"I could see Duke doing that. He's been a bully and in trouble with the law since he was old enough to drive." Heath had removed his uniform while Dela talked. Now he stood in his boxers and socks, scratching his arms. Dela grinned at the sight. She loved that they could be themselves around each other and they knew all the other person's secrets. A dark cloud crossed her thoughts. He didn't know all of hers.

She grasped his hands and sat on the bed, pulling him down beside her.

A grin spread across his face. "You feeling frisky?"

Her lips tipped slightly into a grin as she shook her head. Her sorrow must have shone in her eyes, because Heath pulled her into his arms.

"What's wrong? It's more than not seeing Kaydee or your nightmares, isn't it?" He held her tight.

She wanted to stay wrapped in his arms and ignore Marion's insistence that she tell him the truth. But if they were to have a life together, she had to tell Heath.

She pulled out of his arms and rubbed her hands together. "It turns out that Marion and I have something in common." She figured this was the best way to work into telling him.

"What's that?" He rubbed a hand up and down her right arm.

She peered into his eyes and said, "Neither of us can have children."

He blinked and swallowed, then pulled her into his arms. "I'm sorry to hear that. But it doesn't make me love you any less." He held her away from him.

She saw the truth in his eyes. He was sad they wouldn't have children, but the love she always saw in his eyes still shone bright.

Dela threw her arms around his neck and clung to him. She'd feared his love of carrying on the family name and traditions would have outweighed anything he felt for her. To know he was with her, no matter what, lifted a heavy burden she'd been carrying.

"Did you think so little of my love for you that I'd abandon you just because you couldn't give me a child?" Heath asked, prying her arms from his neck and holding her head in his hands. His eyes peering into hers.

"I know how much you cherish family and carrying on traditions. I didn't want to be the one who kept you from being able to teach your children." Tears burned behind her eyelids and trickled down her cheeks.

"I have nieces and nephews who are family. We can teach them and they will teach their children." He kissed her. When she opened her eyes, he said. "I'm glad you told me this. It makes me understand why you have been holding back and keeping things to yourself. From here on, we don't hide any secrets from one another."

Dela's heart raced with happiness and the feeling that they had just become stronger as a couple. "I agree. No secrets." She wiggled out of his grasp and stood. "I have just enough time to eat a quick meal with you before I go to work."

"I'll get dressed and be right out." He smiled and rose from the bed. He pulled her into his arms and kissed her again, before releasing her.

She steadied herself, smiled, and walked down the hall to the kitchen.

Mugshot stood at the sliding door, wanting out. She opened the door and left it open. The fresh spring air carried the scent of the lilac bush in the corner of the yard into the house.

Dela set out the salad she'd prepared and pulled the

chicken that had been baking in the oven out. She'd planned to leave a plate heating in the oven for Heath. Now they could enjoy the meal together. As they would for the rest of their lives. She'd planned not to marry until they'd discovered all they could about Dory Thunder, but while she still wanted to find him or find out what happened to him, she wanted to start her life with Heath more.

Heath sauntered down the hallway toward her, a grin on his face. He carried something in his hands.

"Why do you look like the cat who caught the bird?" she asked.

"Because I've caught the prettiest, most intelligent bird." He motioned for her to sit at the table.

"This is silly, why do I need to—" Her words dried up and her jaw dropped as he opened a ring box and lowered to one knee.

"From what I gather from television shows, this is how a man asks a woman to marry him." Heath plucked the wide band with one purple stone embedded in the silver metal. "I knew if I gave you a fancy ring, you wouldn't wear it. But a band that symbolizes the strength of our bond and a stone that is a sacred color, I figured you'd wear."

Dela's heart beat so hard it felt like it would come out of her chest. "It's beautiful! Are you sure you want to make this a binding thing?" She raised her gaze from the ring to his face and knew she'd just asked a foolish question. Love shone in his dark brown eyes and crinkled the lines at the corners of his eyes. His lips were tipped into a loving, indulgent smile.

"I wouldn't ask if I didn't mean it."

She threw her arms around his neck and kissed

him. Drawing out of the kiss, she said, "Yes, I'll marry you. We can pick a date after this weekend."

Heath's eyes shone with happiness as he placed the ring on her finger. "You're really ready to set a date? I thought you wanted to wait until we found Dory."

"I want to find him, but it shouldn't keep us from moving forward in our lives." She said the words that had been haunting her for a while. She needed to stop using excuses to keep from moving her life forward.

Mugshot stood outside the open sliding door and woofed. Jethro stood beside him, his lips curled up in his donkey smile that showed off his green and yellow teeth.

"I think those two are happy about it," Dela said, sitting in her chair and picking up a fork.

Heath settled onto the chair opposite her and stared.

"What?" she asked, with a forkful of chicken headed to her mouth.

"Aren't you going to call your mom or Molly?" He seemed hurt that she wasn't spreading the word already.

"I need to eat to get to work. I'll call them on my way there."

When he raised an eyebrow, she said, "I promise."

Chapter Five

On the way to the casino, Dela first called her mom.

"I always knew you and Heath were the perfect match. Have you set a date?" Mom asked, her voice sounding choked up as if she were crying.

"We'll discuss it after this weekend when work slows down for both of us." Dela looked at the ring and smiled. After years as high school sweethearts and then meeting back up again decades later, she and Heath were finally doing what they'd talked about as seventeen-year-olds.

"Let me know as soon as you pick the date. I can't wait to help plan it."

"I will let you know as soon as we make the decision. I have to go, I'm at work." Dela turned into the main Casino parking lot and continued to the back of the building and the employee parking area. She parked and dialed her best friend. She didn't want Molly to hear about her engagement from someone else.

The phone rang several times before her friend answered, "Hi, this is Molly."

"Hi, it's Dela." A smile tugged at the corners of her mouth as she thought about what she had to say.

"What's up? You have a happy lilt to your voice." There was a pause, and before Dela could say anything, Molly squealed, "He did it. Heath asked you to marry him, didn't he?"

"Yes, and I accepted." They chatted for about five minutes. "I just pulled into work. I need to get inside so Kenny can go home."

"Okay, I'm so happy for you and Heath. Let me know what I can do to help when you decide on the date," Molly said.

"I will. Bye."

Dela entered through the employee entrance, waved to Tammie, who was tending the security office tonight, and headed to her desk to put her purse away and pull out her taser, radio, mic, and earbuds.

Tammie showed up beside her and grasped her hand. "Is that a ring I see?" She held Dela's hand up, inspecting the piece of jewelry. "It's not very blingy."

"It's not supposed to be," Dela said, extracting her hand from the woman.

"I guess it fits your personality. Where did you find it? You don't usually wear jewelry."

Tammie was walking back to her station when Dela said, "It's an engagement ring from Heath."

The woman spun around and ran back, giving Dela a hug that pressed all the air out of her lungs. "That's wonderful. It's about time you two made everything official."

"Hold it down. I don't want a bunch of people giggling around me and asking questions." She stared at Tammie until the woman nodded. "Thank you. Now I'll check in with Kenny and send him home."

As she left the office, she spoke into the mic, asking Kenny for his location.

"Deli," he responded.

"Copy." She walked through the office door and onto the casino floor. She stood a moment, taking in the noise of the machines and voices, the heat and odor of many bodies, and the distant sound of piped music along with the various scents from the restaurants. This was what she loved about the casino. It elevated all the senses. Sometimes to the point of overload.

Pivoting to the right, she headed toward the deli. Dela was glad that Rosie wasn't working tonight. She wanted to tell her friend about the engagement, but not here.

Kenny sat with his back against the far corner and his eyes on the casino. Dela sat down beside him to also have an eye on things and asked, "How did the day go?"

"Nothing unusual. Though Kurt complained that Nicki seemed to be hanging out more in his area than her own." Kenny studied her. "Any reason for that?"

Dela's instincts said Kenny had more to say. "Do you have a theory?"

He grinned, took a sip of his drink, and began, "He and Phil have been hanging out in a suspicious manner a few times a week, and there's a woman who is consistently playing machines in Kurt's area. According to Alfred, she's the girlfriend of someone the law has been looking into." He smiled and said, "I think you have Nicki keeping an eye on Kurt."

Dela returned his smile and said, "You could have told me about Kurt and Phil's suspicious behavior and the woman. I had to find out about it yesterday when I was here for the Violence Against Women seminar." She cocked an eyebrow and studied him. He didn't even feign an apology.

He shrugged. "I've been watching Kurt and Phil and didn't see a reason to go to you until I had some kind of evidence against them. And the woman was brought to my attention by Alfred."

"I see. Well, I'm here for the rest of the night. Go home and get some rest. I'll see you on Monday." Dela rose as did Kenny. He pushed his chair in and ambled out of the deli.

Dela also walked out of the deli, but she went straight into the noise and bodies to check in with her security members who were on duty. Halfway through checking in, her earbud scared her.

"Dela! I have something!" Farley practically screamed.

"Holy Shit!" she blurted, yanking the earbud out of her ear.

Ross, the guard in front of her, said, "What?"

"Not you. Farley's yelling in my ear. I'll catch up with you later." She grabbed the mic and said, "I'm headed your way. Don't break anyone else's eardrums."

She entered the surveillance room through the hidden door and walked straight back to the room where Farley and Marty worked. She didn't knock, knowing Farley was waiting for her.

As soon as she stepped into the room, he spun his chair and jumped up as if someone had jabbed him in the ass with a spear.

"Dela! I know what they've been doing!" He swung his arms as if that gave his statement more impact.

"What have they been doing?" she asked, taking a seat at the desk and resting her prosthesis on the box underneath. Marty had placed the box there when she first began working at the casino.

"I watched all the exchanges from the first one six months ago. I think the lady is dropping off pills. I enlarged all the still shots I could get of the little packets she drops, and that's what they look like. Pills."

Dela sighed. She'd been afraid of that. She didn't want any of this to get out. The casino didn't need to have it publicized that drug dealers were exchanging merchandise in the casino. "Do they do the drops at the same time every Thursday?"

"No. None have been at the same time. The only constant is the day. What are we going to do?" Farley plopped down in the chair in front of the computer keyboard.

"Put all the still photos and the video that is incriminating together. I'll give it to Heath. He and the FBI have been working to find out how fentanyl is coming onto the reservation."

"I heard a kid died from it. Damn shame. When will they figure out there is more to life than drugs and alcohol?" Farley said.

She stared at him. He was only in his twenties, yet he sounded like someone twice his age. "Some people don't see a way off the reservation or can't seem to find a way to participate in the traditions, so they try to dull their despair with drugs and alcohol." She'd witnessed classmates who ended up killed or disabled from drinking and driving, or drugs and doing stupid things. Many felt they were destined to be treated as non-citizens and would never be able to gain traction as viable citizens. While others learned how to navigate the White world and came back to make the reservation a better place for the tribal members who wished to make something of themselves and the tribe.

Farley shook his head. "All I know is the people who sell drugs are the lowest scum of humanity."

"I agree. Put that together and I'll take it to Heath when I go home." She stood and then thought of something else. "Make sure I get a good photo of the woman who does the drop. Since Alfred thinks he knows who she is, I'm going to talk to him."

"I can do that." He turned to the keyboard and as she put her hand on the doorknob, he said, "We're going to stop them."

Dela spun around and saw the look of determination on his face. "Yes, we are."

She stepped onto the casino floor, did a scan to make sure everything was running normally, and walked to the front entrance.

Alfred was an elderly Umatilla man past retirement age. He liked to valet at the casino on weekends for extra money, and since his wife passed, he worked there during the week when he felt lonely. His mind was sharper than a computer. He remembered people, their arrivals and departures, who they were, and what they drove. Dela had utilized his knowledge to get herself out of murder charges and assist in finding killers.

"Dela, my girl. It's always good to see you."

Alfred smiled, showing dark holes where three teeth should be. His gray hair hung in long braids down the front of his western-cut, long-sleeved shirt.

"Hi, Alfred. How are things tonight?" She pulled up the other tall stool used by the valets and sat beside the elder, facing the casino floor.

"It's pretty quiet for a Friday night. Not too many been wanting a valet." He patted his breast pocket.

"I'm sorry to hear that. I have a question to ask you about this woman." Dela brought up the photo of the drop woman that Farley had sent her.

Alfred's head slowly nodded as he studied the grainy image. "She comes in twice a week. Tuesdays and Thursdays. Well, I guess she comes in every Tuesday and Thursday. At least when I'm here those days I see her. She goes into section five on Tuesdays and section nine on Thursdays. She plays the machines about an hour and then leaves."

Dela didn't like the fact the woman was spending time in two different areas of the slot machines every week. She'd have to pull up the work schedule and see who worked in section five on Tuesdays. Off the top of her head, she thought it was Phil. Her first instinct was to change Kurt and Phil's schedule to give them Tuesdays and Thursdays off or put them on the night shift, but that would make it easier for them to do a drop during the busiest part of the day.

"Do you ever notice her dropping something?" Dela asked.

Alfred studied her. "No, but I don't watch her constantly. Should I the next time she comes in?"

"I just want you to call me the next time you see her enter."

"Is she using the casino for illegal business?" His eyes narrowed as he asked.

"I'm not sure. But I want to get to the bottom of it quickly."

Her back was to the doorway. Someone grabbed her by the arm and yanked her off the stool. Her prosthesis landed wrong, causing her to topple sideways.

Alfred stepped beside her, giving her a chance to catch her balance. She swung around and stared into the wild eyes of Sonny Wadass.

Chapter Six

"What the hell, Sonny?" Dela said, yanking her arm from his grasp.

Two security guards arrived at her side before she could straighten her polo shirt.

"We need to talk." He waved a hand between the two guards. "Alone."

"That's not a good idea," Alfred said, standing beside her.

"What's this about?" Dela asked, taking in his disheveled appearance and the panic in his eyes.

"What we talked about earlier today." His gaze flashed back and forth from her to the guards.

"Thanks, guys. I think Sonny will behave now." Dela waved her guards away and started walking into the casino. She glanced over her shoulder, expecting to find Sonny following her. He stood at the door, shifting his weight back and forth on his feet. She walked back toward him. "We can go somewhere private and talk."

He shook his head. "I shouldn't have made a scene.

I should have let your guys haul me into your office. I don't want anyone to know I'm talking to you."

He said this so quietly that she was sure Alfred hadn't heard anything.

"Okay, we'll walk away from each other, and you can pick a fight with one of my guards." She glanced around to see who was closest. She barely tipped her head toward Mick and walked away. Holding the button on her mic, she said, "Mick, guy coming toward you wants a word with me without others knowing. He's going to pick a fight with you. Don't hurt him."

She'd walked to the door of the office when she heard shouting and turned to see Mick holding Sonny by the back of his shirt collar, heading her way. Dela slipped into the hallway and waited outside the security office door.

Sonny was walking on his own, with Mick herding him down the hall.

"Thanks, Mick," she said, opening the door to the office. After Sonny stepped into the room, Dela said, "Tammie, go take a fifteen-minute break. And if anyone asks, I'm in the office by myself doing paperwork."

"Got it, boss." Tammie picked up her purse, hung it on her shoulder, and walked out the door.

"There, we're alone. Why did you nearly topple me to the floor out there?" Dela shoved a desk chair toward Sonny and sat in her chair.

The man sat and ran a hand over his head. "This morning, I thought Kaydee had gone shopping with a friend. She'd mentioned it last night. When I came out of the shower this morning and she was gone and the girls were at the table eating cereal, I thought she'd been picked up."

Dela's attention was riveted on Sonny. "What do you mean you thought? Did you call all of her friends?"

He nodded. "When she wasn't home by dinner, I started calling everyone I could think of. No one has seen her. Then I thought about what you said. You know, about the bruises and if they were when my brother had been at our house. And they were. All of them." He scrubbed his hands over his face and then peered at her. "He knew that Kaydee didn't like what he did. That boy who died a while back? He was the brother of one of her friends. Every time she'd see my brother, she'd start in with how he was the problem that kept our people from rising to their full potential. She begged me to turn him in, but he's family, and I know his anger. He can be a mean son-of-a-bitch. That's what made me realize he had to be the one who was hurting Kaydee. He had to be pressuring her to keep her mouth shut."

"Okay, but he's in jail. He couldn't have taken Kaydee." Dela's mind was reeling, trying to figure out who he could have contacted to show Kaydee and his family that he wouldn't take kindly to anyone ratting him out. "Do you know who he worked for or who worked for him?"

Sonny shook his head. "He knew I didn't want to know anything about how he got his money. He never talked about what he did around us. But I think Kaydee heard other people talking and figured it out."

Dela leaned back in her chair. "Why didn't you go to the police?"

He reached into his pocket and pulled out a piece

of paper. "This is the grocery list Kaydee was working on last night." He turned it over. Scrawled across the back was: *Keep quiet or she dies*. "I found it under my windshield wiper when I got in my truck after a tow job this evening."

"Where are the girls?" Dela hoped they hadn't become hostages like their mother.

"With Kaydee's sister."

"Does she know Kaydee is missing?" Dela wondered if everyone had believed Sonny that his wife was out shopping.

"She was the one who made me start thinking. When I dropped the kids off with her, she said Kaydee hadn't texted or called all day. Those two talk several times a day. I told her I thought she went shopping. She started asking me with who and when I couldn't say, she looked scared and said she'd call around while I was working." He stared into her eyes. "Am I going to get her back alive?"

Dela's throat constricted, making it hard to swallow. She finally said, "I'm going to try to find her before anything bad happens. Where was your truck parked when this was put on the windshield?"

He told her, and she wrote it down on a piece of paper. "Go about life the best you can. Since your sister-in-law is wary of where Kaydee might be, let the girls stay with her. She'll keep an eye on them. In the meantime, you need to see if you can find out who your brother's friends and associates are to help me look for Kaydee."

His eyes widened. "If I start asking about his associates, I could be the next person missing. Then what will the girls do?"

Dela glared at him. "Do you want your wife back?"

"Yes."

"Then you need to help. Can you think of anyone he spends a lot of time with?" She held a pen over the paper where she'd written the address.

"I've seen him with a White guy a couple of times. They were walking into Hamley once, and then they met in the parking lot here at the casino. I was helping someone jump a car."

This was good news. She could have Farley look at outside video footage for Duke Wadass and ask the manager at Hamley for their video, since the tribe owned the steakhouse and saloon in Pendleton. "Do you know when you saw them together?"

His face screwed up in thought and he shook his head. "I don't know for sure."

"Just approximately. Was it this month? Earlier in the year, last fall?" Dela didn't want Farley, or herself, having to go through a year's worth of video, but she would if it helped find Kaydee.

"I can look in my logbook for the car jump. Though there were a few during the winter."

"That's okay, it will narrow down our search. And what about at Hamley?"

"They were wearing coats. I recognized Duke because he had on his Pendleton coat and the other guy had on a fancy long coat." Sonny peered over her head. "I think it was between Christmas and New Year's. Yeah, I remember I was taking the kids to Walmart to spend their Christmas money." He smiled.

Dela returned his smile. "Good. That helps a lot. Now, go straight to your truck and go home. Then tomorrow, I want you to report Kaydee missing to the tribal police."

He shot out of his chair. "That note, they'll kill her for sure."

"I'm keeping the note, and you are going to pretend you never received it. If you don't report her missing and she doesn't show up where she's supposed to, people will think you did something to her. Trust me. The police will take it seriously because of your brother's arrest. And I'll tell Detective Seaver about this. He'll know you are only trying to find your wife."

Worry creased the skin around his eyes. "You're sure this is the best way to handle this?"

"No. But it's the one that makes the most sense. With you saying she's missing, when I start asking questions, it won't look so suspicious."

He thought about that and nodded. "Yeah, if you just started asking questions, they would know I told you, and they'd know I received the note, which could get her killed. Okay, I get it."

The door opened, and Tammie walked in. "Oh, sorry, the fifteen minutes are up."

"Are we good?" Dela asked Sonny.

He nodded.

"Tammie, will you let him out the employee door, please?" Dela watched as Sonny followed Tammie to the door. He glanced back once and then disappeared.

When Tammie walked back to her desk, Dela said, "You didn't see him in here."

She nodded.

Dela picked up the note and the pad she'd written on and headed back to the casino floor and the hidden door to the surveillance room.

When she entered the surveillance office, Marty wrapped her in a big bear hug.

"Congratulations! I heard about your engagement." His infectious smile made her grin.

"Thank you. I'm not shouting it from the rooftops, so you can tone it down." She glanced around the room. "Where's Farley?"

"He took the night off to go to a family thing. You have me for whatever you need. He told me about looking through the surveillance video to catch a couple of bad guards." Marty sat back down at the console in front of four monitors.

"A woman is missing, who I believe was taken to keep her from being a witness against Duke Wadass, who was arrested for trafficking fentanyl on the reservation."

Marty gave a low whistle. "I heard about that arrest. You think he had her kidnapped and possibly killed?"

"I hope not the latter. Her husband, Duke's brother, said he saw Duke with a White man on two occasions. From how he described the man's clothing, I'd say he has money and could be who Duke is working for. But we need a photo. Sonny is going to send the dates he was at the casino parking lot, jumping cars. We need to check the video for his brother and the guy talking in the parking lot. He also said he saw the two going into Hamley Steakhouse between Christmas and New Years."

Marty grinned. "We need video from the steakhouse. I'll call Jessup and ask if I can access the video. Since I installed it, I have all the access codes. But I want it to be on the up and up."

"I agree. When we find the two together, I'll pass it over to Heath. I'm sure he and the FBI can figure out if the man is caught up in drug activity."

As if he'd heard his name, Mick's voice in her ear said, "Heath is here looking for you."

"I'll be right out," she replied. That's when she remembered he'd planned to stop by this evening so they could spend a little time together. She glanced at Marty, who was on the phone with Jessup. She gave him a brief wave and headed out to the casino floor to find Heath.

Chapter Seven

Heath stood at the entrance, talking to Alfred. Dela cringed inside, knowing that Alfred had told Heath about the man who accosted her. She had planned to wait until tomorrow to tell him about Kaydee being missing and the note. It looked like that wasn't going to happen.

She smiled and walked up to Heath. "I forgot you were coming by."

"Alfred was just telling me about the excitement you had tonight." He said it lightheartedly, but his gaze was probing.

"Yeah, about that. We need to find a quiet place to visit." She tipped her head, and he followed her around the edge of the casino floor and down the dark hallway to the convention center. Using her all-access card, she opened the door of one of the conference rooms and stepped inside, grasping Heath's hand, pulling him in behind her. When the door clicked shut, she groped along the wall and found the light switch. Flicking on only one of the switches, the back of the room was lit in dim lighting.

Still holding his hand, she led him to a row of chairs along the back wall. She sat and he lowered onto the chair next to her.

"What's this all about?" he asked.

"Sonny Wadass was the man who pulled me off the stool."

"Did he threaten you?" Heath's voice quivered with anger.

"No. He was distraught. He wanted to talk to me but didn't want anyone to know. So, he faked a fight with a security guard and was brought to the office." She went on to explain what he'd told her and what she'd told him. "I planned to tell you all of this tomorrow, but since you found out about his visit, I felt you should know now."

"I'm glad he wasn't here to hurt you. But you can't take on finding Kaydee by yourself." Heath still held her hand. He gave it a slight squeeze.

"That's why I told him to go to the police and act like he didn't get the note." She pulled the note she'd put in a plastic bag out of her pocket and handed it to Heath. "It's not a proper evidence bag, but it's all I could find without Tammie seeing what I was doing."

Heath took the baggy and read the message. "Where did he find this?"

Dela told him where the truck was parked.

Heath grinned. "The store across the street has video cameras. They've been broken into twice in the last year. I'll check on that tomorrow."

"It's Saturday, you won't be working," Dela said.

"As long as Kaydee is missing, I'll be working

every day. Especially since it ties into the drug case against Duke."

Dela loved that about Heath. He always put the good of others before himself. She went on to tell him about the man Sonny had seen his brother with twice. She told him about Marty going through the parking lot video and that he'd contacted Hamley's manager for access to their surveillance cameras.

"It sounds like you've taken all the right steps." He leaned forward and kissed her. "What did your mom say about the ring?"

"She was happy, of course. Said it was about time." Her mom had been telling her to marry Heath ever since he returned to the reservation. But Dela had to make sure she wouldn't be a burden on anyone, including Heath.

He laughed. "She's been pushing us together since we were teenagers."

"Yeah. Molly even commented that she knew from when we were teens that we would be together." Dela settled back in the chair. "They both said they were ready to help with whatever we need when we set the date."

"About that. Are you sure you're ready to marry before we find out what happened to Dory?" He peered into her eyes. She saw his concern for her swimming in their brown depths.

Nodding, she said, "You were right back when you said I shaped myself into who I am and discovering he was a serial rapist won't change who I am, only my ideas I had about him." She held onto his hand. "You have always been here for me. In good and bad. You are the person I want to live up to, not my mother or my father.”

He pulled her into his arms and kissed her like she remembered from their early days of dating.

“I found it!” rang in her ear, and she pulled back from Heath, cursing.

He released her and stared. “What did I do?”

“Nothing. Marty just shouted in my earbud. I think he's found the video of Duke meeting the other guy.” Her face flushed thinking about how they'd been making out in the empty conference room. She hoped none of the employees saw them enter.

“Let's go see,” Heath said, taking her hand and helping her to her feet.

“I'd rather we didn't walk out of here together.” She straightened her shirt, all of a sudden aware that Heath's hand had been under her shirt as he kissed her. She shot a glance at the surveillance camera in the corner. It shouldn't be on since there wasn't supposed to be anyone in the room.

“We're engaged,” he said, kissing the back of her hand.

“But I'm at work, and I would be reaming any employee I found making out with their spouse or significant other while on duty.” She tightened her ponytail and motioned for Heath to go first. “I'll meet you outside the surveillance door.”

He shrugged and walked out of the room. She waited a long, silent five minutes before she turned on the flashlight on her phone, flicked off the light switch on the wall, and walked over to the door, opening it and then making sure it locked behind her.

When she caught sight of the wall with the surveillance door, she saw Heath talking to someone.

The man's back was toward her, but he shifted slightly, and she knew who it was. How the heck had Quinn learned about Kaydee being kidnapped when she'd just told Heath?

"Quinn," she said, approaching the two men. "What brings you here?"

"Our sources said you were running facial recognition on a person of interest in our drug case." Quinn nodded to Heath.

"That's interesting. I guess you can join us. We were just going up to see who Duke had been hanging around with in the casino parking lot." She tapped her key card on the surveillance door, causing the door to swing open.

The three of them walked in. A few heads turned, but most of the surveillance personnel kept their gaze on their monitors. Dela did a quick scan of the monitors to make sure none of them were on in the conference room. It didn't appear so. Lionel had the hallway to the conference area up on one of his monitors. He would have seen her and Heath walk down the hall together and come out alone.

She didn't make eye contact with the oldest surveillance person. Instead, she strode up to the office door, knocked once, and walked in.

"Dela, I think I found—" Marty stopped when he spun around and spotted Heath and Quinn.

"It's okay. Heath knows all of it, and Quinn is here because Farley wasn't careful hacking into the facial recognition." Dela took her seat at the table. "What did you find? We'll get Quinn up to date after I see who we're looking for."

The top middle monitor came to life after Marty

tapped some keys on the console. The inside of Hamley Steakhouse came into view. It appeared to be a busy day for the restaurant.

"There in the back corner. It's Duke and a guy dressed in a fancy long coat, like you described." Marty pointed to the back corner of the establishment.

"Do they ever get out in more light so you can see his face?" Dela asked.

"What are we looking at?" Quinn asked. "Besides a busy afternoon at Hamley."

Dela told Quinn about Sonny, that his wife was missing, and that he'd seen his brother with this man twice. Once in the parking lot at the casino and once walking into Hamley Steakhouse.

"This could be who Duke works for," Heath said, leaning over Dela.

She glanced up and saw him squinting at the screen. "Can you make it larger while we watch?" she asked Marty.

The video enlarged but became grainier. "I can't do anything about clarity with the dark atmosphere."

The two finally rose to leave. Duke walked in front of the camera and paid the bill. The other man left the establishment without them getting a good look at his face.

"Damn! I thought for sure we'd get a good look at him," Marty said, falling back in his chair and staring at the screen as Duke walked out the door.

"We'll have to rely on Sonny getting the dates he jumped cars at the casino to try and get a look at him or the license plate of his car," Dela said.

"Is Sonny reliable? He is the brother of our suspect," Quinn said.

"He loves his wife and is scared of his brother. He'll help us if he thinks he'll get his wife back and his brother in jail," Dela said.

"Marion told me about you two going to see his wife and she wasn't there." Quinn pulled out a chair and sat. "Do you think when he told you she was shopping, he didn't already know she was missing?"

"He didn't look shook up. He was harried taking care of the two little girls, but he didn't seem to think much about his wife being gone. But when he showed up here tonight, he was frightened." She nodded to Heath. "Show him the note."

Heath pulled the note she'd given him out of his pocket and handed it to Quinn. "That's why he came to Dela instead of the police."

"What did you tell him?" Quinn asked.

"To pretend he didn't get that note and go to the police saying his wife was missing. With Heath knowing the truth, he could get officers looking for her, and you can bring in a couple of extra Feds to help in the search. I'll also get Mimi Shumack to round up her MMIW people to help look. If we put enough pressure out there looking for her, hopefully we can find her alive and connect her kidnapping with Duke."

Quinn stared at her. "You're playing roulette with her life by having him go to the police."

"No, I'm getting more bodies out there looking for her. Which will give her a better chance of being found." Dela glared at Quinn. She would not have told Sonny to go to the police if she thought it would end up with Kaydee killed.

"I hope you're right. Does Sonny know why they took her?" Heath asked.

"He thought because she had been vocal about knowing that Duke was bringing fentanyl into the reservation. The boy who died was the brother of one of her friends." Dela knew that made it sound like they probably had already killed Kaydee.

Quinn shook his head. "I don't buy it. Why would they leave a note telling Sonny they had his wife and to be quiet? It sounds more like he knows more, and they wanted leverage to keep him quiet."

"That's what I thought, too," Heath said.

Both men stared at her. Dela peered into Heath's eyes and then glanced at Quinn. "He told me he knew little about where his brother got his money or who he hung out with."

Marty spun in his chair and faced them. "It sounds to me like he is in over his head and knows Dela will dig to find his wife, whom he doesn't want harmed because of his actions."

Chapter Eight

Dela herded Heath and Quinn to a back corner booth of the coffee shop. It was nearing midnight, and fewer and fewer people were using the shop for dessert or meals. They were discussing what each of them would do to hopefully further the investigation of both the drug charge and the missing woman.

Her phone dinged. Dela didn't know the number, but when she saw the text, she immediately forwarded it to Marty. "Sonny just sent me the dates he jumped people's cars in the casino parking lot. That narrows Marty's search down a lot."

"If we get that man's name, we may be closer to finding Kaydee," Dela added with more hope in her voice than she felt.

"I'm still not convinced that Sonny doesn't know anything about his brother's involvement in the drug trafficking," Quinn said.

"I think he knew Duke was doing something

illegal. He just didn't know what." Dela stood her ground with Quinn. She wasn't going to let him sway her about anything. He'd managed to do that once before and a rapist went loose and a woman took her own life.

Heath stood. "I think we've talked this to death. I'm going home to get some sleep." He faced Dela. "I'll get to the police station first thing in the morning and try to be the one who takes Sonny's statement about his missing wife."

She nodded. "Thank you."

"What if he doesn't show?" Quinn asked.

"If he doesn't show by noon, Heath will come get me and we'll go see what's going on," Dela said, rising to her feet.

"That's more of a plan than I have. Be sure to send any photo you get of the guy with Duke to me." Quinn also stood.

That reminded Dela. "Since you said you came here because we were hacking facial recognition and it was someone you are interested in, who is it?"

Quinn glanced at Heath before he said, "Farley was trying to find out about the girlfriend of the head of a known drug cartel."

Dela's gaze shot to Quinn's face. "Farley was checking out a woman who has been dropping something in the casino. One of my security guards has been picking it up." Anger whooshed in her ears as she thought of how many lives could be in jeopardy because of her employee's greed. She'd sit him down and— That wouldn't happen until Monday. Unless she called him in to work because someone was sick.

"No," Heath said with force. "I see your wheels

spinning. You will tell me and Quinn who this security guard is, and we will question him."

She shook her head. "I want in on the questioning. He is part of the casino, and I'm the head of security. He jeopardized the other employees and all the patrons of this casino with his actions. I won't just hand him over and walk away."

Quinn and Heath exchanged a look, and Quinn finally nodded. "Tell me who he is and we'll pull him into the FBI Office after Heath has talked to Sonny."

Dela narrowed her eyes. "I'll give you his name after I've heard from Heath tomorrow." She pivoted on her good foot and walked out of the coffee shop. She knew that if she gave Quinn the name now, he'd roust Kurt out of bed and question him without her present.

"That wasn't a good idea, not giving Quinn the name," Heath said from slightly behind her.

She stopped and spun to study his face. "You know as well as I do that if I gave him the name, I'd never be allowed into the conversation between him and my guard."

"But by keeping it from Quinn, he's going to dig to find out who it is."

Dela smiled. "There are only two other people besides myself who know who it is. And they are both off duty until Monday." She raised a hand as he started to speak. "And I haven't written anything up on it yet. I wanted all the facts before I started the report." She smiled smugly. "Call me when you hear from Sonny. I'll try to be quiet when I come to bed."

He watched her long enough that she wondered what was going through his head. He finally nodded and headed toward the casino entrance.

Without another thought of her visit with Heath and Quinn, she pulled out her phone and called Marty.

"Yo."

"Anything yet?" she asked.

"I'm watching the oldest date first. So far on this one, I haven't found Duke."

"Ok. Let me know as soon as you do."

"Copy."

She ended the call and made the rounds of the casino. Two more hours before she could go home and sleep until Heath left for work.

♠ ♣ ♥ ♦

Dela unclipped her radio and mic and reached for her taser when her cell phone buzzed. Marty. She answered, "Did you find a good photo?"

"Yeah. And I followed the guy around the casino. He appears to be a regular by the way all the staff treated him."

Dela groaned. "Great. That means our guy has worked his way in with, we don't know how many, employees at the casino. We need to find out if he is part of the drugs coming onto the reservation."

"I've already found his name. Dillon Travers. As far as I can tell, he's an investor with a clean record." Marty's voice rang with apology.

Dela had an idea. "Take a peek at the woman who Farley was checking out and see if she ever meets up with this Travers person."

"Can I do that tomorrow? Molly's waiting for me."

"Sure. Just call me as soon as you find anything. I'm heading out the door now." She ended the call, said good night to the guard at the podium, and walked out to her car. Tomorrow, well, today, was going to be busy.

Staying awake on the ten-minute drive home was easy. She had the windows down, letting the cool spring air flow through the car. Marion had been right. There was nothing like the smell of this area in the spring.

She arrived at her house around 2:30. The porch light was on for her to see. Heath was thoughtful like that. More so than she was. Nights when she was home and he came in late, she didn't always have the porch light on for him. Not that she wasn't thoughtful, but many of those nights, she'd fallen asleep in the recliner while it was still light out. That would be where Heath would find her when he came home.

Her work hours were all over the place, and she caught sleep when she could. Just like she'd had to do in Afghanistan.

She unlocked the door and was met by Mugshot, who put the top of his head against her good leg, waiting for an ear scratch. "You didn't have to wait up for me," she whispered to the dog as she scratched his ears and sniffed the air. The aroma of freshly-baked cookies made her mouth water. She hung her purse and jacket on the coat rack by the door and walked into the kitchen.

Heath had been baking. The dishes were in the sink. Cooling racks on the counter were covered with cookies. She plucked one from the rack and bit into it. There was nothing like warm chocolate chip cookies to make her feel loved.

"I didn't think you'd make it home this early," Heath said, entering the kitchen and turning on the dimmest light.

"Did I wake you?" she asked, walking to the refrigerator to get milk.

"Not really. Everything you found out today has been playing in my head. That's why I made cookies, hoping it would relax me." He grabbed two glasses from the cupboard and placed them on the counter.

She filled his glass and then hers. Heath grabbed a handful of cookies, and they both sat at the table. "Marty found the guy Duke was talking to in the parking lot. Said he seems to be a regular at the casino. Visits with a lot of the employees." She studied him as she said it.

Heath's attention shot from the cookie he was dunking to her. "He could just be a high roller who likes to be nice to the employees."

"Or he could be talking to them to see who needs money and is willing to deal drugs for him." Dela drank some milk and said, "Marty's going to see who all he talks to and find other visits he's made to the casino."

"Did you send the photo to Quinn?" Heath asked.

"No. Marty called me as I was leaving. I forgot to tell him to send me a photo. I'll ask him to send one to me and one to Quinn in the morning. He put in as many hours today as I did."

She yawned and walked to the sink, adding her cup to the cookie-making dishes. "I'll take care of this in the morning when I get up."

Heath added his cup, and they walked down the hall together with Mugshot walk/hopping behind them. She knew some might think it wrong, but she loved the way his missing leg gave him a unique gait when he walked, trotted, and ran. Just like her prosthesis made her movements not as fluid as they once were.

She grabbed her pajama shirt and shorts while Heath brushed his teeth. When he left the bathroom, she walked in, carrying her bedclothes and her crutches. She'd need them to get to the bed after her shower.

"Don't take too long," Heath called out.

Dela woke the following morning around ten and found several messages on her phone. One from Marion, one from Quinn, and one from Heath.

She listened to Marion's first. "Kaydee's husband came to Mom last night asking her to start a search for Kaydee. After talking to Quinn, I think he decided not to involve the police. Mom is gathering the usual people who help when a tribal member is missing. She's already put out a missing person post on the MMIW social media sites. The meeting is scheduled for noon at Mom's house if you want to come."

Dela texted Marion and said she'd be there.

Quinn's message wanted to know if they'd found the person Duke had met up with in the parking lot, and when she would wake up and tell him the name of the employee. She smiled, knowing he was asking because no one at the casino knew anything or would tell him without asking her first. She texted Marty to send Quinn and herself a photo of the man.

She listened to Heath's message. "Word is that Sonny went to the MMIW for help finding his wife. I'm heading out to his house to talk to him." She glanced at the time of the message, 45 minutes earlier. She texted him. *There will be a gathering at Mimi Shumack's at noon. He should be there. Marion asked me to come. See you there.*

Heath sent her a thumbs-up.

She grabbed a granola bar and a couple of cookies, eating them as she washed the dishes in the sink. Mugshot thumped on the French door. She dried her hands and let him in. Jethro stood on the patio as if waiting for an invitation to enter. "Sorry, you have to stay outside. I'll bring you a carrot as soon as I get these dishes done." She closed the door and went back to cleaning up the kitchen. When that was finished, as promised, she walked out into the yard and gave Jethro a carrot. When he'd finished his treat, she walked to the gate that led from the backyard to the small pasture behind. He walked through, followed by Mugshot.

"You two stay out of trouble while I'm gone. I'll be back before I go to work, I promise." She wouldn't have time to go for a jog today. The exercise was good for both her and Mugshot.

In the house, she gathered her phone and purse before heading out the front door.

Molly pulled in behind her car. Her friend exited her vehicle and asked, "Where are you going? I thought we could talk about wedding plans."

Dela shook her head. "Kaydee is missing. Sonny went to Mimi, and she's organized a meeting to get a search going."

"Did he also go to the police?"

"No. That's what I advised him when he came to me last night." Dela was mad that he hadn't followed what she'd told him.

Molly narrowed her eyes. "You knew she was missing last night and didn't tell me?"

"I told the people who needed to know. Heath and Quinn. Sonny thinks it has to do with his brother being arrested."

"No. That means Kaydee could already…"

Molly didn't need to finish her sentence. That had been playing around in Dela's head as well. It was as if Sonny didn't want anyone to find his wife the way he was going about spreading the word of her disappearance. "We have to hope for the best. Do you want to come to the meeting at Mimi's?"

"I wish I could. I have an appointment at one." She thought for a moment. "But I could come for half an hour."

"Then we'll take separate cars. I'll follow you there."

Chapter Nine

There were a dozen cars already at Mimi's house when Dela drove up. The woman was known for getting results when someone from the reservation went missing. With so many Indigenous women, children, and men going missing each year, in numbers that were much higher than those of other cultures, the tribes had banded together with the Missing and Murdered Indigenous Women, Children, and Two Spirits. The National movement had finally brought light to the atrocities that had been happening for centuries.

Dela thought of her friend Robin, who was murdered and tossed alongside the Interstate like garbage. Her gut twisted and her heart ached. They'd been best friends all through school. Until that day when they'd gone to Pendleton to shop. Dela had to get back for basketball practice. Robin told her she wanted to stay longer and would catch a ride back with someone she knew was in town.

That was the last she'd seen of her friend. It wasn't until the next day when Robin's mom called and asked if Robin had spent the night with her that she realized something was wrong. And at the time, they couldn't get the Tribal Police, the Sheriff, the City Police, or even the State Police to do anything until it was too late and her body was found.

Now, with the MMIW movement, there was action taken right away with the tribes, and recently, due to the Savanna's Act, surrounding law enforcement agencies were called in to help.

Dela didn't see Sonny's pickup. She couldn't stop the anger that began in the pit of her stomach and burned up her throat. If he didn't show up for this, he was guilty in her eyes.

"Dela! Come in!" called Marion as she ushered tribal members into Mimi's house.

Waving a hand to show she'd heard Marion, Dela texted Heath. *Sonny isn't here yet*. She walked up to the open door and into the packed house.

The elders sat in the chairs while the younger women and a few men stood behind them.

Mimi rose from a chair at the far side of the room. "I think we should have had this meeting at the Longhouse. Thank you all for coming."

Murmuring ebbed as they gave their attention to Mimi.

"I have printed out photos of Kaydee. We need to glue them to poster boards as well as a page with her description and information about who to call if she's been seen."

Three of the older women raised their hands.

"We can't do the legwork, but we can do that," Mrs. Wolf said.

"If you three would go into the kitchen, everything is sitting on the table." Mimi scanned the room.

"Jackson and Rudy, would you please carry their chairs into the kitchen?"

Two of the men in their thirties grabbed the three elderly women's chairs and packed them into the kitchen. When they returned, Mimi thanked them and continued.

"Kaydee has been missing since yesterday morning. Sonny thought…where is that man? He was supposed to be here to tell us how he realized she was missing." Mimi's gaze landed on Dela.

She shrugged and texted Heath. *Do you have eyes on Sonny?*

Her phone buzzed. Heath. Moving through the people, she walked out into the yard and answered, "Where is he?"

"When you said he should be at the meeting and I didn't pass him on the road, I continued to his place because the video from the business across from the towing yard didn't show anyone going near his truck last night." There was a long pause, and Heath let out a whoosh of air. "I found him beside his truck. Someone came up behind him and slit his throat."

Dela gasped. Her mind shot back to her conversation with the man and what she'd told him. "Do you think his coming to me got him killed?"

"We aren't going to know anything until we investigate."

"I'm at the MMIW meeting. Do you want me to tell them so they know they need to get busy looking for Kaydee or do you want to do it?" Dela's mind raced with horrible things that could have happened to Kaydee. The innocent in all of this.

"I have to stay here and investigate the homicide.

I've called in Quinn and a forensic team. But I agree, they need to know that finding Kaydee is of the utmost importance. So, it's up to you to get that across. Sorry." Heath's tone said he wished she didn't have to do it, but he was needed at the crime scene to investigate.

"I'll do it. Keep me updated, please."

"I will. Good luck."

"Yeah, you too." She ended the call, drew in a deep breath, and returned to the house. Instead of staying in the back of the room, she made her way through everyone to the front. Mimi and Marion questioned her with their eyes. Dela debated whether she should tell the two women before everyone else, but knew that would take up more time. And time was what they had little of if they wanted to get Kaydee back alive.

"Most of you know me, I'm Dela Alvaro. I'm head of security at the casino. I was just on the phone with Tribal Police Detective Heath Seaver." She swallowed and scanned the faces. They were all waiting for her to continue as if she were a storyteller. "The news he told me only makes the need to find Kaydee more important. Detective Seaver went to the Wadass home to speak with Sonny and found him murdered."

The room became a frenzy of talk and mournful cries as part of the people present were from Kaydee's family and the Wadass family.

Mimi stepped forward, raising her arms and quieting the group. "Dela is right. We need to find Kaydee. All those precious girls will have now is their mother. Those of you who are willing to drive the roads of the reservation, go to Marion; she will give you the areas of the reservation to search. The rest of you, who are going to go door to door, talk to people, and put up the posters, come to me." She turned to Dela. "I think you are best used in the way you know best. I can tell you have an idea of where to find her."

Dela nodded. "When you have them canvassing the reservation, have them also ask about vehicles parked in unusual places, and if they talk to someone who might be a drug user, ask some questions about that as well. Nothing that will make them a target. Just subtle questions of observances. We believe this is part of the fentanyl that has been coming onto the reservation."

Mimi's lips pressed into a tight line before she said, "We'll learn as much as we can."

"Thank you." Dela headed to the door when a hand grabbed her arm. She spun and found a woman about her mom's age. "Yes?"

"I'm Sonny's mother. Do you think his death has anything to do with my other boy being in jail?" The woman's eyes swam in tears.

"I believe Kaydee was used as a pawn to get Sonny to do something. When he came to me and then to Mimi, they felt they couldn't trust him and killed him. Do I think it has to do with Duke? Yes. I just hope we can find Kaydee before something happens to her. I need to go." Dela knew the woman was grieving for her dead son, her son in jail, and possibly her daughter-in-law, but as Mimi said, she could help the most by using her resources at the casino.

Even though she wasn't dressed for work, Dela headed to the casino.

Parking in the front parking lot since she wouldn't be going in to work, she turned off the engine as her phone dinged. The photo she'd asked Marty to send. Studying the man, she realized she had seen him several times in the casino when she did her rounds.

Thanks. She replied to the photo. *Are you in the casino now?*

Nope. Took the day off. What do you need?

Sonny is dead. I wanted to watch the video of this man. She hoped by watching his activity, she could figure out who, besides Kurt, might have information about Kaydee.

Call Farley. He's always up for overtime.

Copy.

She scrolled through her contacts and found Farley's number. She tapped it and waited while it rang.

"Hey, Boss Lady, what's up?" Farley answered.

She smiled despite the crappy day. Farley reminded her of Barney the big purple dinosaur she watched as a kid. "Marty said you like overtime. Can you come into the casino and set me up watching videos?"

"Sure. Give me about an hour. If I don't get the wash in the dryer before I leave, Mom won't let me do my laundry at her house anymore."

"That's fine. I have some people to talk to while I wait." She ended the call, wondering where Farley lived that he had to do his laundry at his mom's.

Stepping inside the front entrance, she scanned the water feature, a pool of water with two warriors mounted on Appaloosas. Usually, the running water and quiet swagger of the men on the horses comforted her. Today, the urgency to find Kaydee vibrated through her body. From there, her gaze did a full scan of the restaurants and gaming floor that she could see. It was Saturday afternoon. The slot machines were ringing, dinging, and chattering to the multitude of people pouring money into them.

She'd wanted to visit with Alfred, but he wouldn't be in to valet cars until the evening. She spotted one of her security guards who had been doing the job the longest. He was in his sixties and liked the busy days.

Dela walked over to Benji. He was fit for his age and didn't act as if he would be retiring any time soon. As she walked up, he smiled and motioned to her street clothes.

"I'm not on duty yet," she said.

"What are you doing in here when you should be out enjoying the lovely spring weather?" he asked, still scanning the area around him, even though she'd noted it was mostly older couples playing the machines around him.

"I have some questions about this man." She held up her phone and scrolled to the photo Marty had sent her. "Do you recognize him?"

He shook his head. "No, he doesn't look the type to play quarter slot machines." He continued studying the photo and then snapped his fingers. "He was playing roulette a couple of weeks ago when I was working the gaming floor. It was Wednesday. That night, the Bingo fanatics were in high spirits. Several of them thought they'd try roulette for the first time. This guy," he pointed at the photo, "was giving them pointers."

"Who was running the table?" Dela asked.

"It was Roger, but that new girl, Celia, the one who does breaks for everyone, came over, and the guy started flirting with her. She seemed pleased to have caught his attention."

Dela smiled. "Thanks, Benji. This is all good information."

She headed to the office area and walked into the personnel office.

"Can I help you?" a woman behind the front desk asked.

"I'm Dela Alvaro, head of security for the casino." She pulled her ID from her purse.

The woman studied it. "Why are you in here if you're head of security? Shouldn't you be in that office?"

Dela didn't like the woman's attitude, but held her tongue. "I'd like the address and phone numbers of Roger, who is a roulette table dealer, and Celia, who gives the games' dealers a break."

"Last names?"

"I don't know their last names. You should be able to look them up under the casino directory." Dela smiled even though she wanted to shove the woman out of the way and look herself.

The woman glared at her and started typing. After what seemed like half an hour but was only five minutes, the printer whirred to life, and the woman stood. She walked over, plucking a piece of paper from the machine. "This is the list of all the dealers. You'll have to find the ones you want."

"Thank you." Dela took the paper, left the office, and walked down the hall to the security office.

Nadine looked up from the book she was reading and smiled. "You're early."

"I'm not here to work yet. But something came up and I needed information." Dela sat at her desk and read through the list. Finding Roger, she picked up a highlighter and highlighted his information. Scanning the list, she didn't find a Celia.

Dela picked up the phone and called the personnel office.

"Spotted Pony Casino Personnel Office, Maisie speaking," answered the woman.

"This is Dela Alvaro. I was just in your office."

"Yes."

"There wasn't a Celia on the list. Could you go back a couple weeks and see if she was on the list then?" Dela knew the woman wouldn't like doing more work for her.

A rush of air blew into the phone, and Maisie said, "You can put in a request, and we'll look into it on Monday."

"I need the information today. It pertains to a woman who is missing." She decided to appeal to the woman's sisterhood.

"I'm sorry, there is protocol to follow." The line went dead.

Dela didn't like going over people's heads, but this information could be vital to finding Kaydee, especially since it seemed the Celia person didn't work at the casino anymore. She scrolled through her contacts and called Barbara, the head of personnel. After a brief conversation with her, Dela walked back to the personnel office.

Maisie glared at her and handed a paper over. "You didn't have to go to my boss."

"There is a woman's life at stake. I had no choice. The sooner we find her, the more likely we'll find her alive. You weren't going to help me, so I went to someone who I knew would care."

Dela scanned the paper and found the name. Celia Storm. Sounded like the name of a dancer.

Chapter Ten

By the time Dela had called Roger and talked to him about the man, Dillon Travers, Farley texted, saying he was in the surveillance office. She took the information for Celia Storm with her.

One of the employees turned from her monitor and asked, "What are you doing here in civilian clothes?"

Dela read the woman's name tag and said, "Paula, I'm trying to help find a missing woman."

"Is there anything we can do to help?" Kay asked.

Dela smiled at Kay. "Thank you for asking." She held out her phone and walked along where the surveillance team sat at monitors, flipping back and forth between the photo of Travers, the drug dealer's girlfriend, and Celia. "If you see any of these people in the casino during your shift, contact me on my phone."

"Isn't that one a dealer?" Kay asked.

"Yes, but she no longer works here. Just let me know if you see any of them. Thanks." Dela walked to the surveillance door and knocked before opening the door and walking through.

"What are we looking for?" Farley asked.

"I want to see the video Marty found last night of Duke Wadass and the man in the parking lot. His name is Dillon Travers. Then we need to find footage for the gaming floor, specifically the roulette table from a Wednesday two to three weeks ago. Travers is playing at the table. I want to watch his interaction with a woman who was working here as the break relief for the dealers."

"Okay, the first request is easy. Marty left it in the memory. Which monitor do you want?" Farley asked as he tapped on the keyboard.

Dela took the seat to the right of Farley and propped her prosthetic foot on the box under the table. "This one."

The monitor came to life, showing the front parking lot after dark. Johnson Towing's smaller truck pulled into the parking lot and over to a car. A sleek, expensive car swung into the parking lot, driving past the tow truck. It parked under a light and sat there for ten minutes before someone walked up and knocked on the window.

The video zoomed in on the two. Dela had never seen Duke, but she deduced he was the one who knocked on the window. The door opened, and Travers stepped out of the car. It was too dark and grainy to see if he was smiling. But he held out a hand, and Duke took it. After the handshake, they conversed for fifteen minutes. Duke shook hands again and walked away. Travers headed for the casino.

It didn't look like two friends meeting up. It

appeared to be a business meeting. Dela rewound the video and watched it again. She sat back, knowing there was little she could use from this to get either man to talk.

"I found the night you wanted," Farley said, making her monitor go black and then flash on with the gaming tables and the people playing roulette for her to view. Farley leaned and pointed. "That looks like the guy you want."

"Yeah. That's him." Dela watched him as he smiled, joked with the other players, and talked with anyone open to visiting. Roger had said the man seemed to have a limitless amount of money and didn't get upset when he lost. Several times when he won, he slid the money toward one of the other players, saying it might give them luck. Travers was a smooth operator.

Celia arrived to relieve Roger for his break. She took her time getting everything just the way she liked it and then smiled at everyone and flicked the marble around the ball track. While the ball was spinning and everyone else was watching it, Celia and Travers stared at each other. The ball dropped, Celia said something, and then called out the number.

The winners clapped their hands and grabbed their winnings while the losers watched their chips being pulled away. Once she had cleared the board, Celia waved her hand to stop any more betting and then flicked the ball in the ball track. Once again, she and Travers watched only each other as the ball spun around the track and fell.

Their behavior was the same until Roger returned. Celia stood, thanked everyone for playing, and gathered up the chips handed to her as a tip. She moved slowly past Travers. He held out a hand and dropped something into hers. But it happened so fast and with the dexterity of a magician that Dela barely spotted the exchange.

What had he given her? Why was she no longer working at the casino?

"Did that video help?" Farley asked.

"Yes and no. It just makes things more confusing." She had a thought. "Can you bring up video of the other tables that Celia relieved for breaks, please? And while I'm watching that, could you follow her when she finished giving breaks and see who she talks to and what she does, please?" Dela knew she was asking a lot of Farley, especially calling him in on his day off.

"Sure. Why are you so interested in this person?" Farley asked as he tapped away on the keyboard.

"She had an interesting exchange with Travers and no longer works here. I want to know everything about her." Dela's screen flickered and it picked up Celia moving over to the first blackjack table to relieve that dealer.

"What does this have to do with Kurt and the other lady?" Farley had a video up on his monitor, but he paused it. "Popcorn?"

"Sounds good, I missed lunch." She heard him open a cupboard and then the door of a microwave open and shut. The whir in the background was comforting as she watched Celia deal cards and talk with the people seated at her table. Dela wondered what the woman was saying.

The microwave dinged, and the door sounds interrupted Dela's thoughts.

"Here you go. I only have one bowl. I gave that to

you." Farley placed the bowl in reach of Dela's right hand before he sat in his chair and started the video on his monitor.

"Thanks." She grabbed a handful and watched Celia for fifteen minutes, and then she moved away from the table. "How do I follow her? She just left table eight."

"That's where I picked her up. That was the last table in her rotation." Farley shoved a handful of popcorn in his mouth and tapped the keyboard. "That's what I'm watching. She didn't talk to anyone up to this point."

Dela nodded, munched on popcorn, and watched as, instead of going to the employees' break room, Celia entered the elevator to the guest rooms. "Can you see what floor she's going to?"

"No. But I caught the time and can go through all the floors and see who comes out of the elevators at that time." Farley started typing.

"I think I have a faster way." Dela pulled out her phone and called the registration desk. "What is the date of this video?"

Farley told her as she waited for someone to pick up.

"Spotted Pony Casino Registration Desk, this is Shana. How may I help you?"

"Shana, it's Dela."

"Dela! I heard the news. Congratulations. We all knew you and Heath would marry when he came back." Her friend from high school was the perfect person for a registration desk. She was always cheerful and thought the best of everyone.

"Thanks, but I need you to look up and see what

room Dillon Travers was in on April ninth."

"Okay. Must be security business. Otherwise, why are you here when I've seen Kenny wandering around?"

Dela would have told Shana to focus if she hadn't heard the clicking of the keyboard.

"Here it is. Seven-ten."

"How long did he stay, and is he considered a high roller?" Dela decided to get as much information as she could. Placing her hand over the phone, she said, "Seventh floor," to Farley.

"He stayed four nights. Which is his normal routine. He usually comes in on Wednesday, the second or third week of the month, and stays until Sunday. And yes, he puts a lot of money into the casino. And he wins a lot of money." Shana paused and asked, "Why are you asking all of these questions?"

"I saw one of our employees being 'friendly' with him. I just wanted to check him out. Thanks." Dela ended the call as Celia stepped out of the elevator on the seventh floor on her monitor. She walked down the hall to room 710 and let herself in with a keycard. That was what Travers had handed her.

"This is all very interesting. As well as what I found out about the man who paid for that room. Thanks Farley. You can go home and enjoy the rest of your Saturday." Dela rose from the chair and wondered how Heath was getting along at the crime scene and if the MMIW volunteers had learned anything.

Her stomach growled. The popcorn hadn't filled the emptiness. She needed to tell Rosie about her engagement, now that Shana knew and was sure to call everyone they both knew. She walked out of the surveillance room and onto the gaming floor with her phone in her hand. She scrolled through her contacts and called Rosie.

"Hey, Dela. I was just thinking about you."

Dela could tell by her friend's tone she already knew about the engagement. "Rosie, I was just calling to tell you Heath and I are engaged."

"I know. Your mom called my mom last night." Rosie wasn't one to be petty, but she sounded so disappointed that it made Dela feel horrible.

"I'm sorry I didn't call you sooner. Things have been going so fast, I haven't had time. Did you hear about Kaydee?"

"Yes! I planned to go to Mimi's meeting, but Mom tripped, and I had to take her to the Emergency room. Did you go?"

"Yes. But I have a lot to tell you. Can we meet for lunch at the market?" The market was only a couple miles up the road from the casino and about three miles from where Rosie was renting.

"Give me about twenty minutes. I'm at Mom's."

"I'll be waiting." Dela walked out to her car and headed to the market at the corner of Mission and Highway 331. It was a small market that had three small tables where a person could sit while eating Microwaved pizza, hotdogs, fried chicken, fries, and nachos. The usual not good for you food that filled up and comforted.

She pulled in, parked, and texted Heath. *How's it going?*

Not finding much in the way of evidence. Hope the pathologist finds something to work with. You?

A relief dealer was fooling around with Dillon

Travers, the person Duke met up with in the parking lot.

That is one of the people of interest in the fentanyl case Quinn and I are working. Don't talk to him by yourself.

Dela rolled her eyes and replied, *I don't plan on talking to him at all. I'm interested in the woman and finding Kaydee. I'm leaving the drug thing to you and Quinn.*

Good. Gotta go. Talk to you when I see you.

She sent a thumbs up and then scrolled to Marion and hit the text icon. *Have you heard anything yet?* Her stomach growled again, and she slid out of her car and walked into the market, heading to the right and the fast-food area.

When she didn't get a reply from Marion, Dela stepped up to the counter and ordered nachos to stave off her hunger until Rosie arrived.

Sitting at one of the tables, her phone dinged.

Everyone is canvassing as fast as they can, but also talking to everyone. The feds and tribals have been out talking to the few neighbors around the Wadass house. No one has seen anything.

Dela texted, *Can you get a list of Kaydee's close friends? I want to show them a photo of someone and talk to her sister. I'll do that later this afternoon.*

I'll get that list to you.

Thanks.

Dela had half the nachos eaten when Rosie parked in her bright yellow Volkswagen. The color and car fit Rosie's personality.

"What? You didn't wait for me before you started eating?" she joked, inching into the bench across from Dela.

"I was starving. These are just my appetizer. What do you want?" Dela stood to walk to the counter to order.

"The chicken box, please. And a large soda."

Dela ordered the same but with iced tea for herself and sat back down.

"Let me see the ring." Rosie stretched her arm across the table to grab Dela's hand. "Nice, definitely you. Understated but sturdy."

Dela laughed. "I love how you tell it like it is."

Rosie smiled and added, "That ring, that's how well Heath knows you. That's why you are the perfect couple."

A grin tugged at Dela's lips. Yes, they were definitely meant to be together. It just took her a long time to get it through her thick brain. "As much as I'd love to start planning the wedding, I can't until we find Kaydee." The mention of their basket-weaving teacher sobered them both.

"Did Sonny kill her?" Rosie half whispered.

Their order was called out, and Dela retrieved it. Once they were both picking through their food, Dela told Rosie about Sonny coming to her, not following her instructions, and going to Mimi. Dela lowered her voice and said, "And now he's dead. Heath found him this morning when he went out to question him about Kaydee's disappearance."

Rosie gasped and leaned back in her seat. Her eyes widened as her round face showed the horror she was feeling. When she gathered herself, she asked, "What does this mean about Kaydee?"

"I don't know. I don't think he killed her. After I suggested that maybe his brother was the one knocking her around, he confessed that she didn't like Duke and accused him of killing the boy who died from the fentanyl. He was the son of one of her friends. I wonder if Sonny did know what his brother was doing, and to keep him from testifying or saying anything, they took Kaydee. Then when he came to me and then went to Mimi, they decided he was better dead than being blackmailed."

"But what about Kaydee? Do you think she's still alive?" Rosie set down the chicken she'd been nibbling on and peered at Dela.

"I've been praying that she is and that we will find her. I have a lead on someone who I believe is higher up the drug chain than Duke. And I've tied him to two employees at the casino."

Rosie picked the chicken back up. "There's scandal at the casino again? You'll get to the bottom of it."

"I hope so. I know the drug dealer wouldn't have come into the deli. He looks the type to only eat in the fanciest of places. But have you ever had a conversation with Kurt, one of my guards, or Celia, a relief dealer?"

"Kurt likes to come in and use our cups to pour his drink from his thermos into. He never buys anything, and the couple of times I tried to strike up a conversation, he just smirked at me. I don't like the guy." Rosie shrugged. "Now, Celia, she's been in the deli a couple of times when I've worked the late shift. She was chatty but asked more questions than I did. Mostly about the casino. I can't really help you with either of them."

"That's okay. I plan to talk to Celia today if she's still around. She left the casino after visiting the drug guy's room at the casino." Dela wondered if she had been working for him as a person on the inside gathering information. Kurt would have talked to Celia, she was pretty, built like a model, and young. Kurt only tolerated Dela because she was his boss. He only had eyes for shapely women who wore lots of makeup. Rosie was pretty, but in a natural way. Glowing skin, large brown eyes, a happy personality, and an infectious laugh. But her body type was apple, not one most men even looked at. "And the FBI and I plan to have a chat with Kurt tomorrow."

They had finished their food. Dela stood, scooping up the paper boats, napkins, and plastic utensils and tossing them in the trash. Her phone dinged. It was a message from Marion.

Patsy Leantree, Megan Phillips, Sunshine Allen, and Echo James are her closest friends.

Thanks.

Dela showed the names to Rosie. "Do you know any of these women? They're Kaydee's close friends. I want to talk to them, see if I can find out more about her frame of mind and who she's been seeing."

"I know Sunshine."

"Can you text her and ask her to gather the other three and meet us somewhere of their choosing?"

Rosie nodded her head.

"They may be out helping look for her, but tell them I need to talk to them this afternoon." Dela left her phone sitting on the table while Rosie wrote the text and sent it. The phone vibrated and she answered the call from Marion.

"Dela, one of the people canvassing said the neighbor about half a mile down the road from Kaydee's place saw a gray van, like the type people camp in, sitting alongside the road early on the morning that Kaydee went missing. They figured the people were either lost or had stopped to make breakfast. It wasn't until people started coming around asking questions that he thought about it."

"Did they notice anything besides a gray camper van? Any logos or stickers on it? I'm sure they didn't think to look at the license plate." This was a clue, but it could also be just what the person thought it was.

"No, they didn't mention that, but the neighbor is Horace Running Bear if you want to question him yourself."

"Thanks, I'll do that. I want to see exactly where the van was parked. Keep information like this coming." Dela was grateful that Marion respected her investigative skills.

"Want to go for a ride while we wait to hear back from Sunshine?" Dela asked.

"If it has something to do with finding Kaydee, yes." Rosie inched off the bench and stood.

"It does. One of her neighbors saw a suspicious vehicle down the road on the day she went missing. Let's go talk to him and see the spot where the van was parked."

Chapter Eleven

Halfway to Horace Running Bear's, Rosie received a call from Sunshine. She and the other friends would meet them in an hour at the longhouse.

Dela pressed down on the accelerator to give them more time to investigate before they would need to be back at the longhouse. She pulled into Horace's driveway and found an elderly man bent over, pulling weeds from a small flower bed that had daffodils and tulips growing.

They exited the vehicle and walked over to the man. Dela introduced herself, and Rosie won him over with her bubbly personality.

"We heard that you mentioned seeing a van parked out on the road the day Kaydee Wadass went missing. Could you show us where and tell us what you remember about it?" Dela asked.

"Sure, sure. It was a new-looking thing. One of those that people camp in. You know, tall enough to stand up in and windows with curtains." Horace set down his trowel and started walking down his driveway.

"Did you notice if it had any rental stickers or see anyone?" Dela asked.

"No stickers. It was shiny and slick like a new one. In fact, it only had a dealer name where the license plate should be."

Dela exchanged a glance with Rosie and asked, "Do you remember what the dealer name was?"

"Yeah, that one that has dealerships all over the northwest."

Dela named off the two she knew.

"Yeah, that one. The second one."

Rosie pulled out her phone and started typing.

About fifty yards past his driveway on the side of the road that led to the Wadass driveway, the man stopped. "It was parked along here. I walked about halfway to it and decided they had too much money for me to get in a pissing match with them. I don't like these people in campers thinking they can just stop and spend the night wherever they feel. That's what RV parks are for."

"Do you find campers parked along this road often?" Dela asked.

"At least once a month since last fall. Not sure why anyone would want to camp during the winter. Makes no sense to me."

They may have just discovered how the fentanyl was getting onto the reservation. "What other families live on this road?"

Horace started naming them. Three of the families were Wadass, one of them being Duke.

"Thank you for all your help. Do you mind if I have a tribal policeman come ask you questions about seeing the vans here on a monthly basis?" Dela could see him thinking and possibly coming up with the conclusion she had.

"I don't want them drug people thinking I ratted them out." Fear widened his eyes and tightened his jaw. "I live all alone here."

"How about I give you the number of a tribal officer to call, and you can meet him in Mission, and he'll come out of uniform?" Dela dug in her purse for a piece of paper and wrote Heath's number on it. "I'll let him know you'll be calling, and he will make sure no one knows the information came from you."

Horace took the paper. "Do you think this van has something to do with drugs and Kaydee being missing?"

She wouldn't lie to him. Both things could be harmful to him if he blabbed any of this meeting to anyone. "Yes, I believe it does."

He nodded. "I heard about that boy who died a while back. Bad thing. I want drugs off the reservation, too." He held up the piece of paper and walked back to his house.

Rosie spoke, "Do you really think this van could be tied into both the drugs and Kaydee?"

Dela nodded. "It's too much of a coincidence. Let me take a look around. You get your phone on camera. If I find something, we'll need photos." She crouched by the tire prints in the dirt. "Take some photos of these tracks. I'm sure most new vans will all have the same tread, but it doesn't hurt to be thorough."

While Rosie snapped photos, Dela inched her way along the ground, searching for anything that might be out of place. It was something she'd learned from Hawke, Marion's brother.

She found boot tracks about where the driver's door would be. "Take photos of these tracks, too."

Rosie moved up behind her and clicked her phone.

Dela moved around to the passenger side, where the sliding door would be. Smaller athletic-looking tread pocked the dirt by the passenger door. At the point where the sliding side door would be, she noticed the dirt was scuffed and dug into, like from the toe of a shoe. There were also twisted indentations as if a struggle had happened. "These definitely need to be photographed before wind comes along and wipes it away."

Once Rosie started photographing the scuffle marks, Dela began a wider search, moving away from the van and into the bar pit. She found a tissue that appeared to have been used by a woman to wipe after peeing. "I need a photo of this. Stay here and make sure it doesn't blow away. I'm going to run up to Horace's and see if he has any plastic bags I can bring back to bag things."

"How do I keep it from blowing away?" Rosie asked.

"Find a stick you can hold it in place with. I'll hurry. Don't worry unless the wind picks up." Dela took off at a jog back to Horace's driveway. It was an awkward jog since she wasn't wearing her running prosthesis. As she jogged, she glanced up at the darkening sky. They were going to get a spring shower any minute. They had to get the evidence she could find documented before the weather wiped it away.

"What are you doing back here?" Horace asked, looking up from where he sat on a small box as he worked up the dirt in a different flower bed.

"I need a small or large plastic bag. A clean one that hasn't been used for anything."

He studied her. "Like to put evidence in? You didn't say you were a cop."

"I'm not officially one now. I'm head of security for the casino, but I was in the military police before I came home." Dela wasn't going to tell him any more than that.

"In the kitchen, top drawer to the left of the stove, you should find a box of sandwich bags. Are those big enough?"

"They'll work for what I've already found. Do you mind if I take the box?" Dela didn't know if she'd find more or not, but she didn't want to have to jog back here. Her stub was already letting her know that she shouldn't run in this prosthesis.

"Go ahead, I can get more. I hope it helps you find Kaydee."

"Me, too." Dela climbed the three steps to a rickety porch and opened the screen door. It appeared the man had been living alone for a while. There were photos of him and a pleasant-looking woman. He'd been married, it appeared, and had lost his wife.

She walked into the kitchen, found the drawer he'd mentioned, and returned to the porch. Horace was still digging in the flower bed as a few raindrops fell from the sky. Dela started jogging as soon as she stepped onto the dirt path to the driveway.

Rosie was standing with her legs spread on either side of the paper, looking nervous. "I didn't want it to get wet," she said.

"Good thinking." Dela handed the box to Rosie.

Dela pulled the one she kept over her hand with the

outside against her skin. Then she reached down and picked up the tissue, turning the bag right side out, and zipping it shut. She glanced at her watch. 2:36. When they were in the car, she'd write the time, date, and location on the bag.

"We need to get going if we're going to meet up with Kaydee's friends," Rosie said.

"Yeah. I wish time and the weather were with us, but they aren't. Come take a photo of my foot next to the prints. That might help forensics figure out what size they are."

"I have a tape measure in my pocket." Rosie pulled out a small plastic cat and pulled on the cat's tail. A quarter-inch wide tape measure appeared.

"Why do you have that in your pocket?" Dela asked.

"You know I like to craft. If I come across something that I think might work on a project, and I know the size I need, I can measure and make sure it fits." She shrugged and leaned down, measuring the print. She recited the numbers to Dela, who put them in her phone.

"Let's go. This will have to be enough for Heath to give to forensics." Dela walked back to the car. Her stub was throbbing from all the jogging. Her walking prosthesis didn't have all the impact-reducing features of her running one.

"You're limping. Did you pull a muscle while jogging back and forth?" Rosie asked, stopping at the passenger door and peering at her.

"Yeah. I should have stretched a little first." She slid into the car, and they headed to the Mission Longhouse.

Chapter Twelve

Dela pulled into the Longhouse parking area and stopped beside two cars. One car was empty, and the other held four women Kaydee's age.

"Can we go into the Longhouse?" Dela asked.

"Only if it's unlocked." Rosie stepped out of the car, and one of the back doors on the car full of women opened.

"Hi, Sunshine. This is my friend Dela. She's the one who has questions for you about Kaydee." Rosie walked around to the other car and Dela followed.

The other three women walked toward the Longhouse, with Rosie and Sunshine trailing behind. Dela stayed a few steps back, observing them closely. They walked close enough to touch if they wanted to, revealing they trusted one another. She hoped they understood that they needed to share everything they knew about Kaydee to help find her.

One of the women pulled a hand out of her pocket and slid a key into the door. "My grandfather takes care of the longhouse," she said as if needing to apologize for having the key.

Once they were inside, the women placed six chairs in a circle and sat, indicating that Dela and Rosie should sit.

Once she was settled, Dela let her gaze slide from woman to woman as she explained who she was and why she wanted to talk to them.

Then they each introduced themselves and waited for her to ask a question.

"When did you last see or talk to Kaydee?" Dela asked.

Patsy's brow furrowed. "Are you going to ask us the same questions the police did already?"

Dela smiled at each of them. "Some of them may be the same, but it's your answers that will help me formulate new questions."

"Dela knows what she's doing. Do you remember when Sherry Dale went missing?" The women all nodded. "Dela was one of the people who helped find her."

The women all stared at Dela with less wariness. "When did you last speak to or see Kaydee?" she asked again.

"I saw her on Tuesday at the market. She had the kids with her and was in a hurry to get home and make dinner for Sonny," Patsy said.

"I talked to her on the phone Tuesday night," Sunshine said.

"What did you talk about?" Dela asked. She had other questions but didn't want to put ideas in the woman's head.

"Her next basketweaving class. We were deciding

where to go to collect more tule reeds. But she kept pausing as if she wanted to say something."

"Did you ask her if anything was wrong?" Dela wondered if Kaydee had confided in one of these women about the bruises.

Sunshine glanced at the other women and said, "I asked her if Sonny hit her again."

Dela studied the women. "Sonny beat her?"

They each nodded their heads.

"Since my brother died of an overdose, he's been beating on her to keep her quiet," Echo said.

Dela focused on Echo. "It was your brother who died from the fentanyl?"

"Yes. And I'm sure it was Sonny who gave it to him. When I told Kaydee, she didn't deny it, only said that Sonny had been more uptight lately and had more money, which should have put him in a better mood. Then, she started showing up with bruises. First, she told us she fell or the baby kicked her, but when I saw the mark of the ring Sonny wore all the time embedded in a bruise, I told her to stop covering for him and if she wasn't careful, she'd be the next person he killed."

The others nodded.

"This is interesting. When I asked Sonny about the bruises on his wife, he made me think his brother beat her up." Dela scanned the faces. They all held the same expression: disgust. "Did you know that Duke was dealing?"

"Kaydee didn't come out and say it, but she told me that she thought Sonny was working on the side for Duke." Megan glanced at her friends and continued, "And we all knew Duke has always been one to find a way to make lots of money with the least amount of effort."

Dela nodded. "Has Kaydee mentioned anyone she'd been hanging out with lately?"

"A guy?" Sunshine asked, sounding as if that was the most absurd thing she'd heard. "Kaydee would never cheat on Sonny. Even if he beat on her."

Dela shook her head. "No, I'm thinking a woman. Where would she have come in contact with a woman who would have struck up a conversation with her?"

They all exchanged glances and shook their heads. "We always went places together. I'm not sure where she would have met up with anyone," Patsy said. "Do you think someone took her? We've been afraid we were looking for Kaydee's body since Sonny beat her."

Dela knew she had nothing to lose by sharing her thoughts with these women. "I think someone took Kaydee to keep Sonny from saying something." She told them about her trip to the house and how Sonny found her at the casino and asked for help. "He did the opposite of what I suggested and contacted Mimi instead of the police. I think he wanted us to find his wife, so we didn't think he killed her, and because he was scared that whoever had her would kill her and he'd have to take care of the kids by himself."

"I can see him thinking that," Echo said.

"But his going to either me or the MMIW backfired, and they just shut him up. I think now that they don't need Kaydee for leverage, they will either kill her—" everyone gasped, "—or traffic her. Drug cartels are usually involved in both illegal activities. That's why I think a woman might have approached her somewhere and used the bruises on Kaydee to get into her confidence. That woman was waiting for the right moment to pick her up and haul her off." An idea hit that she hadn't thought to ask Sonny, and it was too late now. "Did Kaydee like to run or jog in the morning?"

"Yeah. Sometimes, the two of us would meet up at the school track and run some laps. But she also liked to go for a run in the morning before Sonny headed off to work." This was the most animated Megan had been. It appeared she and Kaydee had running in common.

"She must have been out for a run when she was abducted. That would explain the van," Rosie said.

"What van?" the other women asked in unison.

Dela held up a hand and studied Rosie. "But why did that scumbag Sonny tell Marion and I she'd gone shopping with a friend if she'd left the house to run?"

"He knew she was being picked up!" Rosie said, her face glowing with anger.

"He staged it all as a ruse. I'm glad the bastard's dead," Dela said.

"What? Sonny's dead? What will happen to the kids?" Sunshine asked.

"Excuse me." Dela stood and walked outside. She pulled out her phone and scrolled through the names for Heath.

"Dela, it's not a—"

"Listen," she interrupted. "There was a gray camper van parked about a half mile from Sonny Wadass's place the morning Kaydee went missing. Rosie and I took photos of the footprints and scuffle marks. And I picked up a tissue that may have been used by the woman who helped grab Kaydee."

"How did you find out about this van? We talked to the neighbors."

"When the MMIW folks went around asking

questions, the old guy who lives about sixty yards from where the van was parked told them about it. And it isn't the first time there has been a camper van parked there. He said once a month he sees one there. I told him to call you and tell you, but he's a bit scared the people bringing drugs onto the reservation will find out. He's old and lives alone."

"What's his name?" Heath asked.

"Horace Running Bear. I'll have Rosie send you the photos we took. This rain is going to wash everything away. We had to leave or I would have looked around more."

"What are you doing?" His tone wasn't curious. It was a warning.

"Rosie and I are talking to four of Kaydee's friends. Getting a picture of what her life was like. That bastard Sonny was the one who beat her. I believe she went out for a jog as usual in the morning, and someone was waiting for her. I also think Sonny knew it was going to happen. All his wanting help to find his wife was a ruse, or he was scared of whoever did it and figured he would be safe by sending people looking for her."

"You keep looking for Kaydee, but stay away from the drug dealers. Leave that to me and Quinn." His tone was an order. He quickly tacked on, "Please. Look for Kaydee, but stay out of Sonny's death."

"I am talking to Kaydee's friends. I will keep looking for her. She is my priority, but if I run into the drug cartel while doing it, I can't help it. This brings me to my other thought. They wouldn't kill someone as young and pretty as Kaydee."

"You're thinking they took her somewhere that

they hold women to traffic?" Heath interrupted.

"Yeah. Could you find out if Quinn knows those locations? You know he's not going to tell me." Dela had helped Quinn and Hawke find a woman who had gone missing several years earlier. The trafficking gang had been working out of the casino. This time, she was sure they weren't working from the casino, but they had to be working in the Pendleton area.

"I'll see what I can find out. He's waiting for you to give him the name of your guard. You might be able to use that to get the information you want. I have to go, the forensic guys think they found something."

The call ended, and she smiled. He didn't want her near the drug dealers, but he gave her a way to find the traffickers.

The door opened, and Rosie stuck her head out. "Are you coming back in? You ran out like your feet were on fire."

"Yeah, I had to call Heath and tell him about the van. I told him you'd send him the photos." Dela shoved her phone in her pocket. She'd call Quinn when she finished with the friends.

"Did they tell you any more while I was gone?" Dela asked, placing a hand on Rosie's arm to stop her inside the door.

"Nothing that I think will help you. They just talked about how they all grew up together and had been friends for years."

Dela nodded, and they returned to the circle of friends. "Sorry about that. I thought of something that I needed to tell the police investigating Kaydee's disappearance." She smiled and asked, "Did Kaydee ever go to the casino with you or alone?"

The women exchanged glances, and Patsy said, "We, all five of us, have gone to the casino a few times to either a symposium or a show. As for whether Kaydee went on her own, I don't know. She never said anything if she did."

The others nodded.

"We know it isn't safe to go alone to the casino, the Pendleton Roundup, or anywhere there are a lot of outside people," Megan said.

Dela knew what she meant. Because of the violence against Indigenous women, they had learned not to go alone to events where they could be lured away.

"Okay. I can't think of anything else to ask, but if you think of something that might be helpful, you can text me." She recited her phone number and thanked them for meeting with her.

"Are you going to be able to find her?" Echo asked.

"I'm going to do everything I can to find Kaydee and bring her back." Dela meant it. She didn't like it when the bad guys won. She would bring Kaydee back even if it went against Heath's wishes.

Chapter Thirteen

Dela drove Rosie back to her car at the market and headed to Mimi's to see if anything else had been learned and to talk to Marion. She needed to call Quinn and see if he'd swap information, but first, she wanted to find out what he might have told his girlfriend.

Five cars that didn't belong to Mimi or Marion were parked in front of the house. Dela eased out of her car and walked up to the front door. She could hear people talking before she knocked.

The voices lowered and Mimi appeared at the door.

"Come in. We were wondering where you've been." Mimi opened the door and motioned for her to enter.

Dela saw it was the elders who had been at the meeting earlier who were talking and making signs. "Is Marion around?"

"She's in the kitchen handling calls from the people canvassing the reservation." Mimi sat down and picked up a paintbrush.

Dela wandered into the kitchen. Marion sat at the table with a map of the reservation spread out in front of her. She glanced up and shook her head.

Taking a seat next to her, Dela said in a quiet voice, "I don't think you're going to find her on the reservation. I went to the place where the neighbor saw the van. It looks like she was taken. I've given all the information to Heath, but I need to speak to Quinn. I think she's going to be trafficked. Drug cartels usually sell both drugs and women."

Marion leaned back, her eyes wide and her lips pressed together. She studied Dela for several seconds and asked in the same quiet voice, "How do you think Quinn can help?"

"If they have been after this cartel, they would have all the information on all their businesses. I need to know the closest place they would have to take her." Dela added, "We need to move quickly because they could send her overseas to get rid of any connection to them."

Marion picked her phone up from the table and tapped it twice.

Quinn's voice sounded loud as he asked, "Have you had any luck?"

"No. I have you on speaker phone. Dela thinks she knows something and needs your help." Marion nodded to Dela.

"What has—"

"Listen. I found marks where a neighbor saw a van parked." Dela went on to tell him about the marks they photographed and the tissue she had. "I think she's been taken somewhere to ship out of the country. Can you give me any information you have on holding places this cartel uses?"

"Dela, you aren't equipped to go after traffickers," Quinn said in his pompous way.

"I'm not going after them. I'm only going to confirm they have Kaydee, which would help your case against Duke and those he works for."

Quinn sputtered and said, "I told you not to get involved with the drug dealers."

"Meet me, and I'll tell you everything I know in return for information about where they could be holding Kaydee." She glanced at Marion.

The woman gave her a triumphant smile.

Quinn tried to say they didn't need her help, but they did. They didn't know which of her guards were on the take.

"Never mind. I'll do your work for you." She reached over and hit the end icon on Marion's phone.

"That's only going to make him mad," Marion said.

"He'll either come around, or he'll ignore me. Either way, I'm good. I have some people to talk to. Thank you for trying to help. I'll keep you informed with what I find."

She stood, and Marion grabbed her arm. "You aren't going to do anything dangerous, are you?"

"Not for me." Dela smiled and walked into the other room. She leaned down and said quietly to Mimi. "We need information about non-tribal vehicles being seen on the reservation. If your people can get the where and when, it will help."

Her watery eyes peered into Dela's. "You think she was taken?"

Dela nodded. "From what I've found so far, that's

what I think. We need to know more about the vehicles traveling in and out of the reservation. The information needs to go to Heath. It could stop the drugs coming in."

Mimi nodded. "I'll change the search and let Heath know what we find out. What are you going to do?"

"Find Kaydee."

Dela left the Shumack home with a fire of determination in her gut. She couldn't save her friend Robin, but she was going to make sure Kaydee came back to her children.

♠ ♣ ♥ ♦

Dela went home, put on her polo shirt, slacks, and work shoes. She fed Jethro and Mugshot, leaving them in the backyard, and headed to the casino.

When she arrived, Joyce, the office guard on Saturday nights, studied her. "You're here early."

"I need you to call…" Dela walked over to her desk and wrote down Kurt and Phil's names. "These two. Tell them they are needed here to cover for guards who are sick. Don't tell them I'm here or that I requested them. Say their names came up on the revolving list to cover." Dela handed the names to Joyce.

The woman read the names and looked up. "You sure they'll come in?"

"If they balk, tell them it's time and a half." Dela sat down at her desk and listened as Joyce called each guard. It sounded like Kurt was trying to talk his way out of it, but he gave in when she told him time and a half.

Dela picked up the casino phone and dialed the number she had for Celia. The phone was no longer

112

available. She tapped her pen on the paper with the number. Why would her phone no longer be available? Unless she had been put here to gather information for Travers. Once he had what he needed, he sent her somewhere else. Her phone would have been stopped to avoid anyone from the casino contacting her.

"Glad you could come in," Joyce said.

Dela glanced up and saw Phil clocking in.

His eyes widened when he spotted her. "Surprised you didn't make the call," he said, walking up to Dela. "Where do you need me?"

She nodded to the small room off the office where they kept people waiting to be picked up by the tribal police and where she interviewed people. "In there. I would like to talk with you first."

He studied her as his skin paled. But he slowly walked over to the room and went inside.

Dela walked over to Joyce. "When Kurt gets here, tell him to wait until the person in charge tonight shows up to tell him where he's needed."

Joyce stared at her as if she'd been asked to capture a dragon.

Dela picked up her phone, walked into the interview room, and closed the door.

Phil shifted back and forth in the chair. "Did you really need someone to fill in?"

"No. I want to know what you and Kurt really talk about when you meet in the corner hidden by slot machines every Thursday and some Tuesdays." Dela opened the photos on her phone and showed him one of the videos they had of the two men.

Phil rubbed a hand over his face and squirmed more in the chair. "It wasn't my idea. In fact, I'm barely an accomplice."

"How do you figure that?" Dela asked.

"Kurt tells me what time I'm supposed to be looking the other way or doing something that I don't see the person who does the drop. For being blind, he pays me a hundred dollars every time." He held up his hands. "But I don't know what he's picking up or who the drop person is."

"That's on Thursday. Tuesdays, it is dropped in your area. You pick it up. That's more than an accomplice." Dela peered at him.

Phil crossed his arms. "I didn't know what was in the envelope I picked up. I'd hand it over to Kurt."

"In my book, you are an accomplice and will lose your job right along with Kurt. No one uses this casino to bring drugs onto the reservation. And by not telling me what was going on, you jeopardized this casino and everyone who works here." She glared at him. Happy he was squirming and scared. "I'm giving both your names to the FBI. Bringing fentanyl onto the reservation is a Federal Offense."

"Hey, I didn't bring it or do anything with it. Shit, I don't even know where he's getting it or what he's doing with it."

"You can tell that to the Feds and see if they believe you." Her phone dinged. Joyce sent her a message that Kurt had arrived.

Dela tipped her head toward the door. "Kurt's out there. When you go out, don't speak to him or make eye contact. Just walk to the exit and leave. Don't come to work on Tuesday. We'll mail your last check to you. Don't run; the Feds will find you."

Dela stood, walked to the door, and motioned for

him to exit. She followed behind to see Kurt's face. As expected, he tried to talk to Phil. But the man did as she said and walked out the back without looking at Kurt or saying anything.

"Come on in."

Kurt glared at her and walked toward the room. "What's this about?"

"You'll find out soon enough." When he walked through the door, she closed and locked it. Pulling her phone out of her pocket, she texted Quinn. *If you want to talk to the guard selling drugs, get to the casino security office. I'm about to interview him.*

Her phone pinged. *Wait for me.*

She smiled and asked Joyce, "Who is the relief guard tonight?"

"Wesley."

"Call and ask him to come to the office, please. Then, go through the list of people who have applied to be security guards. I marked the applications if they were good prospects. We'll need to hire a couple more."

While she waited for Wesley, Dela made a list of the things she knew about Kurt and his part in the drug exchange. She hoped to pressure him to find out where the cartel kept the women they were trafficking. He probably didn't know. He was low in their chain, but if she could get the information about the woman who did the drop, then she might have more to go on.

Wesley walked into the office and greeted her. "Wondered when you'd check in tonight."

She smiled. "I had some things to deal with before I could come in." She tipped her head toward the interview room. "Special Agent Quinn and I will be interviewing someone in that room. I'd like you to stick around and make sure he doesn't try to get away."

"I can do that."

"And we'll need you to take on a daytime position starting Tuesday. Can you do that?"

His smile broadened. "My wife has been asking when I'd get to go to days."

"I'm glad we could accommodate her."

Quinn shoved through the door into the office, glaring. "Why didn't you tell your employees I was coming to see you? I was detained when I tried to come into the office area."

Dela hid the smile tickling her lips. "Sorry, I've been busy and didn't think about the Saturday night shift not knowing who you are."

She walked toward the interview room. "Let's go."

"Aren't you going to fill me in?" Quinn asked.

"You'll learn what you need to know as I question him." She unlocked the door and it was yanked from her hand.

Kurt slammed her into the door, thumping her head. She slumped to the floor as Quinn and Wesley wrestled Kurt to the ground.

Dela blinked, clearing her sight and mind. Kurt was handcuffed, sitting in a chair. Wesley stood behind the chair.

Quinn crouched next to her. "Are you okay? I know you have a hard head, but the contact with the door was loud."

She waved him away and tried to push to her good foot and couldn't.

Joyce came into her sight. "I called for the EMTs."

Dela waved her hand. "No. I'm not leaving. I'm

sitting in on this conversation."

"We'll wait until they can look at you," Quinn said, sliding his hands in her armpits and raising her to her feet. He maneuvered her out to her desk chair.

"What's the name of the guard in there?" he asked Joyce.

"Wesley."

"Watch her, and I'll go talk to him."

Dela wanted to glare at Quinn, but he had said she'd be in on the questioning. "Make sure he doesn't start talking to Kurt without me," she said to Joyce.

The woman was wringing her hands. "I'm not sure I could stop him."

"Just listen, and if it sounds like he's trying to question Kurt—" She stopped when Quinn walked out of the room.

"While we're waiting for the EMTs to check out your thick head, tell me what you know about this guy." Quinn pulled a chair over in front of Dela.

She made a face and wished she hadn't. Having had a concussion before, she knew this wasn't one, but her head was throbbing where it had hit the door. She glanced at Joyce. "You can go back to your post."

The woman nodded and wandered back to the podium.

"His name is Kurt Wilson. I saw him and another guard, who just left here, meeting in the corner between their two areas." She went on to tell him about having Farley watch them on video, learned about the Tuesday and Thursday drops and the woman, who Quinn had said was the girlfriend of the man he was after.

"So you plan to get him to roll on the woman and hope that gets us to the highest person?" Quinn asked.

The door opened and two Tribal EMTs walked in. "Someone reported a person with a head injury?"

Quinn stood and pointed at Dela.

She groaned. One of the EMTs was Heath's friend.

"Dela, what on earth did you do to get a head injury?" Aaron asked.

"I was thrown against a door. Just look at my eyes and leave me be." She knew she was being rude, but she wanted the EMTs to go away so she could get in the room with Kurt and ask him who the lady was that dropped off the drugs he had picked up.

"Hmmm, feeling bitchy?" Aaron asked as he felt her pulse and stared into her eyes. A grin spread across his face.

Quinn put a hand over his mouth as he laughed.

The other EMT just grinned.

She narrowed her eyes and started to say something when Heath walked up behind Aaron.

"Heard the call and I thought, that can't be my fiancée needing medical care. She told me she was talking to four young women and staying out of my homicide. But my gut said, you better go see." He knelt on the opposite side as Aaron and stared at her. "What happened?"

"She brought in the person I've been wanting to talk to," Quinn said.

"I contacted you and invited you to interview him with me." She flinched when Aaron touched the back of her head where it met the door. "And you were with me when he slammed me against the door, so don't act like this is all my fault."

Heath spun and stood at the same time. "You were with her when this happened?" He took a step toward the FBI agent.

Aaron stood. "She'll be fine. I don't see any signs of a concussion. The back of her head will be tender for a few days. I'll write this up as the patient refused to be transported." He gave Dela a wink and strode toward the door.

"See, nothing to be worried about. Let's go talk to Kurt." She pushed to her feet and swayed slightly but straightened when Heath reached out to help her. "I'm not walking in there hanging onto anyone. I don't want him to have the satisfaction of thinking he took me down."

Chapter Fourteen

Dela glanced at Heath and Quinn, sitting on each side of her, and then across the table at Kurt.

Quinn set his phone in the middle of the table and hit record. "This is an interview at seven- forty-three pm on April twenty-sixth with Tribal Detective Heath Seaver, Head of the Spotted Pony Casino Security, Dela Alvaro, and myself, Special Agent Quinn Pierce, interviewing Kurt Wilson, a security guard with the casino."

Dela was pleased to see Kurt's eyes widen when they were each mentioned. He'd thought he was going to try and outsmart her, but now he had to lie to two law enforcement officers. She cleared her throat. "This conversation is about the product that a woman has been dropping in this casino, and you have been picking up regularly on Thursdays and retrieving from another guard who does the pickup on Tuesdays." She held up her phone. "And we have it all on video."

Kurt slammed his body back against the chair and

glared.

"What is the product you pick up?" Heath asked.

Kurt continued to glare, his lips pressed tightly together.

"I know what it is. Julia Rivera, the woman dropping the product, has been sleeping with the head of a drug cartel. They specialize in producing and transporting fentanyl." Quinn leaned toward Kurt. "Which means, we have you accepting and selling a lethal drug on Indigenous land. That also means not only the FBI will be prosecuting you for a federal offense, but the DEA will be interested in charging you as well."

"Kurt, other than picking up and distributing drugs, you have been a good security guard." Dela did her best to look sympathetic when all she wanted to do was reach across the table and slam his face into it. "If you help us, the FBI could give you a deal. And keep the charge to selling drugs on the reservation and not add on murder and human trafficking."

He leaned forward, staring at her as if she'd gone crazy. "What are you talking about? I didn't kill anyone, and what the hell would I know about human trafficking?"

Dela shrugged. "One of the other people who was selling fentanyl on the reservation was found murdered this morning. And he was higher up the line than you are. I think they had you kill him, or they are starting to one by one get rid of the people who could connect the cartel to the sale of fentanyl here."

"I didn't kill anyone. And I'm nothing. I don't know anything." He was getting scared. His voice had raised a register, and his face was blotchy.

"What's the name of the woman who dropped the drugs?" Heath asked.

Kurt's head jerked, and he studied Heath. "You know. He said she was the girlfriend of the cartel leader." Kurt shifted his gaze to Quinn.

"But do you know her name?" Heath insisted.

Kurt pointed to Quinn. "He just said it. Julia Rivera."

Dela studied him and asked, "Did you know it before Special Agent Pierce said it?"

Kurt shook his head. "She told me her name was June and that she had a way for me to make enough money to retire early."

"Where did you meet her?" Dela asked.

"Here. She was playing the slot machines in my area about eight months ago. I was just walking around, and she stopped me and started flirting. It was a slow day, so I talked to her for a few minutes and then moved on. She came back every day for a week and flirted some more. She told me all I had to do was pick up what she dropped on the floor and leave it in a mailbox on my way home. I'd find money in my mailbox the next morning." He swallowed and continued. "I couldn't believe my eyes that first morning after I did the pickup and drop when I found a thousand dollars in my mailbox. I didn't know what was in the little packages. Then I got curious and opened one before I put it in the mailbox." His face contorted in anger. "The next time she came, she didn't drop a package. She dropped photos of me putting the packages in the mailbox. A note said, *If you tell anyone, you are going to jail for distributing drugs.*"

"They didn't just drop you then?" Quinn asked.

Kurt shook his head. "The next time she came, she asked me if I wanted to continue. They would still pay but if I tried to screw them over, the photos would be sent to the cops." He shrugged. "I decided to keep working for them to show I wasn't going to go to the cops."

"And to make yourself rich while people died from what you were helping them distribute." Dela had to let out the frustration she felt. "What do you know about their human trafficking?"

He stared at her. "Nothing. All I did was pick up the package and put it in a mailbox."

"What mailbox?" Heath asked.

"It was a different one every time. The packages would have the address on them."

"Always on the reservation?" Heath asked.

"Yeah. They were always rural places on dirt roads. Mostly to the east."

Dela glanced at Heath. He had to be thinking that was the direction of the Wadass brothers' homes. They could easily drive to one of the mailboxes and no one would think anything of them driving around the roads.

Quinn reached over and hit the button to turn off the recording. "Sit tight. I have some friends coming to pick you up." He motioned to Heath and Dela to follow him out of the room.

Once they were in the office, Quinn said, "I have a couple of agents coming to get him. What he said about the location of the mailboxes, you both looked like it meant something to you."

"The rural area to the east would be near the Wadass brothers. No one would have been suspicious of them driving around out there," Heath said.

"But if the drugs were being delivered to them by Kurt, why would people have been seeing camper vans in that area once a month?" Dela asked.

"What's this?" Quinn asked.

She told him that the same person who told her about the van the morning Kaydee went missing had been seeing them once a month on the same road.

"That is interesting," Quinn said.

"I gave you Kurt, where are the places the cartel could be keeping women?" Dela asked.

"I don't think it's a good idea you go poking around where a drug cartel is trafficking women," Heath said.

"This morning, you told me if I would concentrate on Kaydee and let you take care of the homicide, you would be happy. Now you're saying you don't want me finding Kaydee?" She put her hands on her hips and glared at Heath.

"That's not exactly what I said." Heath grasped her shoulders.

"It is EXACTLY what you said. Don't try to deny it now." She pulled out of his grasp and turned to Quinn. "If you don't help me, I'll find it another way. Which," she looked over her shoulder at Heath, "will be more dangerous."

"I'll send you the list tomorrow. I have too much to do—" he was interrupted as two FBI agents entered the office.

When the FBI agents went into the interview room, Heath stood in front of her and said, "I want you safe. Why don't you understand that?"

"I do. But I promised Kaydee's friends I'd find her, and I promised myself I'd find her for Robin." She peered into his concerned eyes and said, "I have to do this for myself and Robin. I didn't save her. I can save Kaydee. Her children deserve not to live without her."

Heath pulled her into his arms. She stayed in his embrace as the FBI took Kurt away. When there was only her, Heath, and Joyce left in the office, she finally pushed out of his arms. It was close to time for her to go home. It was rare she left the casino before 3 am on a Saturday night, but she was wrung out from all that she'd accomplished, or not accomplished today.

"I'm going home. I need some sleep." She picked up her purse and walked out the back door with Heath. He walked her to her car and kissed her.

"I'll be home in about twenty minutes."

"I'll see you there." Dela slid into her car, started it up, and waved to Heath before driving out of the parking lot. If Quinn didn't come through with the information she needed, she was going to see if Farley could do some digging for her.

At the house, she let herself in, listening to the braying and barking. Jethro and Mugshot were happy she was home. They both liked to be snuggled up for the night. Jethro in the backyard and Mugshot in the house on one of his large dog beds.

"Come on in," she told Mugshot, opening the French doors that led out to the patio and backyard. She held a carrot out for Jethro. He curled his lips in a thank you and took the carrot in his yellowy-green teeth.

She was hungry but wanted to get the prosthesis off her aching stub. Once she had her slacks off and the prosthesis off, she decided a soak in the tub would make it feel better. She started the hot water running in the tub and added Epsom salts.

Using her crutches, she swung down the hall and made sure the front door was locked as well as the French doors. Then she put a handful of cookies into a sandwich bag and poured milk into a travel cup and swung her way down the hall, back to the bathroom.

Once she was settled in the tub with the cookies and the milk on the edge within reach, she closed her eyes and thought about what she knew and what she needed to learn.

♠ ♣ ♥ ♦

Mugshot barking startled Dela awake. She slipped down in the tub and, reaching to gain purchase, knocked the travel cup to the floor and the bag of cookies into the tub.

"Are you okay?" Heath asked, standing in the bathroom doorway. He started laughing. "Is that a new bath fragrance, chocolate chip cookie?"

Dela wanted to be mad, but she was still trying to wake up. "I fell asleep in the tub. Mugshot barking startled me."

Heath knelt by the tub and picked up the travel cup. "This didn't spill." He placed the cup on the counter and stood. He reached down. "Let me help you out."

She took his hand, and he had her standing on her foot on the bath mat much quicker than she could get out using the handrails. Dela put her arms around his neck and said, "I'm sorry I can't always stay safe for you. I have to find Kaydee."

He wrapped his arms around her wet body and hugged her. "I know you need to find Kaydee. I just wish there was a way that you weren't charging headfirst into trouble."

"Me too. But I don't know any other way to get the

information and find her before it's too late."

"Put your pajamas on, and I'll scoop some ice cream." He carried her into the bedroom, setting her down next to where she'd laid out her sleep shorts and shirt. He glanced at her stub. "Why is your stub so red?"

"I jogged from where the van was sitting to Horace's house and back to get the bag I put the tissue in." She shrugged. "It will be fine tomorrow. That's why I was soaking."

"Sorry I surprised you."

"You didn't. Mugshot did. I soaked enough. And I'm hungry."

He took the hint and left the room.

Dela was dressed and sitting up in bed when Heath brought in two bowls of chocolate, chocolate chip ice cream.

Heath handed her a bowl and sat on top of the covers next to her.

Heath grinned. "This is one of my favorite things."

"Eating ice cream in bed?" Dela asked, spooning another bite into her mouth.

"No, just hanging out with you when we aren't talking shop or arguing over you staying safe." He gave her a sideways glance.

"I don't try to find trouble. I just want to find Kaydee."

"I understand. You want to help the people of Nixyaawii just like I do." Heath turned his head and studied her. "But I've trained to deal with people like the drug cartel."

"I may not have trained to deal with the cartel, but I trained to deal with terrorists. It's kind of the same, isn't it?" She didn't wait for his answer. "All I want to do is step up to help our people." Since they discovered that Dory Thunder might be her father, she'd embraced the idea that she could be part Umatilla.

Heath put a hand on hers. "If we get time to dig deeper into Dory and where he could be, then we can show people you belong among us." He frowned. "If you could get your mother to clarify what we know, that would help."

Dela nodded. "But Grandfather Thunder told me not to bring up Dory to her. That it would hurt her." She thought about that. "They have both been keeping the information about my real father from me. Why? Because they believe he raped all those college girls? That he brought shame to the family?" She thought about the journal she'd found in the Thunder family cabin in the Blue Mountains. "From what I've read in the journal, I don't think he raped those women, or if he did it was because he was mentally unstable after coming back from Vietnam." She remembered the part about him saying the monster was back. What had he meant? The monster within him, or someone else?

"We'll deal with that after we find Kaydee and find Sonny's killer," Heath said, rising to put the dishes in the kitchen.

Heath returned and went in to take a shower. As soon as she heard the water running, Dela picked up her phone and dialed Farley.

"Yo, Boss what's up?" Farley answered. "You need me to come to the casino?"

"Not tonight. But I need you to do some research for me tomorrow. Not at the Spotted Pony. It's not casino business. Where can we meet?"

"Oooo, this sounds like fun. You can either come to my house or I can meet you at the Cayuse conference room."

Dela was intrigued. "Why the Cayuse conference room?"

"My cousin works there and can get us in. They also have the strongest internet with the best blocking software. If we're going to be digging into something secret, it would keep someone from knowing we are looking around."

"Like the Feds coming around when you were trying to find the name of the woman in the casino?"

"Yeah. I can keep other hackers from seeing what I'm doing."

"How about eleven?" Dela asked as Heath walked out of the bathroom.

"I'll be there."

Dela ended the call.

"What are you doing at eleven?" Heath asked, sliding into bed.

"Meeting with Farley to do some digging into Kaydee's social media to see if we can figure out who she would have trusted enough to go near the van." Dela set her phone on the bedside table and slid down into the bed. "You know, there had to be someone she knew in that van for her to have not just run past it. Every female on this reservation knows that when you're alone, you don't go near vans or men you don't know. Even if the vehicle is on the reservation."

Heath nodded. "Her friends didn't have any idea who it could have been?"

"None. Makes me wonder if she was meeting with someone in hopes of getting away from Sonny with the least amount of hassle." Dela had been thinking this ever since visiting with Kaydee's friends. The woman could have been trying to get away without anyone on the reservation knowing. If one person had found out, it would have spread like a wildfire through the reservation, and Sonny would have learned about it.

"Let's get some sleep. Maybe we'll have answers when we have clear heads in the morning." Heath clicked the light off.

Dela listened to Mugshot's loud breathing and hoped she did have a clear head in the morning and that she and Farley would find something useful tomorrow.

Chapter Fifteen

Dela was surprised to find the doors to the Cayuse Building open on a Sunday. Farley was waiting for her in the reception area.

"I'm set up in the conference room. My cousin said we can use it until three. They have a meeting at four, and she needs to get it ready."

"I hope we find what we need long before that." Dela followed him down a hallway to a door with a plaque that read: Conference Room.

Farley opened the door. She was impressed by a large map of the reservation on one side and a floor-to-ceiling glass wall on the other side. The pane-glass wall faced the Blue Mountains.

"Wow." She stood, staring at the April sunshine glinting off small patches of snow still on the highest spots and the blue-green of the trees on the slopes. "This is impressive."

"Yeah, the first time I was in here, I couldn't stop staring out the window." Farley sat down at a laptop and peered up at her. "What am I looking for?"

Dela dragged her gaze away from the mountains and sat beside him. She pulled out the notepad she'd used to put down the information she wanted to know. "First, I need to tell you, we will be digging into a drug cartel. If Special Agent Pierce had sent me what I wanted to know this morning, I would have cancelled our meeting."

"I understand this is dangerous. They aren't going to know we're looking into them. I've already set up a fake identity and routed it around the world. You should have what you need and I'll be off this computer before anyone can trace anything we do."

That made her feel better. She didn't want the drug cartel coming after Farley because she asked a favor. "Ok. First, I want to dig into Kaydee Wadass's social media. See if she has any photos or mentions meeting or talking to a woman other than her friends."

They started with Facebook and Instagram. Nothing unusual there. Then Farley looked in Tiktok and Twitter. She had a Tiktok account but again, nothing.

Dela tapped her pen. Sonny would have had access to the same social media. It made sense that she wouldn't post anything there. "Try Pinterest. Most guys don't go on there."

He found an account for her. The things she pinned had to do with dealing with an abusive spouse.

Dela nodded. "This is where she might have met up with someone."

"It looks like she started up a conversation with this person." He copied and pasted the username in the search bar. A photo popped up. "Hey, it's the lady you had me looking for that brought the feds."

Dela's chest ached. The drug cartel did have Kaydee. There was no telling what had happened to her so far. "Okay, we know she is the one who abducted Kaydee. Now we need to find out where they keep women to transport." She stared into Farley's eyes. "This is where we'll be digging into things that could get risky."

"If it brings back one of our women, I'm all about the risk."

This was the most serious she'd ever seen Farley.

"Ok. The name of the leader is Dillon Travers. He drives this model car with this license. Dig up all the information you can on him. When you have that, we'll dig into his financial records to see what kind of buildings he might own or rent that they could store women in."

It was two-thirty when Farley finished printing out the property owned by Travers.

"Shut down everything and go on about your life as if you didn't help me," Dela said, taking the papers from Farley and shoving them into her purse. She would take them home and go through the possibilities.

"Sure you don't need help with anything else?" Farley asked, turning off his computer and putting everything in his backpack. "I could do an online search and see if he is using the buildings or if they are standing empty."

"I'm good. I can do that easily enough. Once I determine where she's being held, I'll get Heath and Quinn in on the retrieval."

"Be careful investigating." Farley held the door for her as they walked out into the hall.

"I will." At the front of the building, they parted. Farley walked to his car, and she walked to hers. She wanted lunch and to go through all the information they'd dug up. If she were lucky, a few phone calls and surveillance would determine which buildings were the most likely to be used by the drug cartel.

♠ ♣ ♥ ♦

After a peanut butter sandwich and chips, Dela found maps of Oregon, Washington, and Idaho. Those were the states with the closest businesses owned by Travers that had a building where abducted women could be housed and used shipping overseas to move their products.

One was in Spokane and one in the tri-cities in Washington. There were two businesses in Idaho. One in Coeur d'Alene and one in Boise. The closest one in Oregon was a warehouse in the McNary Industrial Park in Umatilla. That was less than an hour away.

It would make sense to use the closest facility to hold and transport from there.

Her phone dinged. She glanced down at the screen.

Heath texted. *We have a match on the tissue you found.*

Julia Rivera. She texted back.

How did you know? What have you been doing?

Farley and I went through Kaydee's social media. Julia chatted her up on Pinterest. Kaydee had posts about spousal abuse.

Her phone buzzed. She answered and said, "Julia didn't use her name, but she did use a photo. It was the photo that gave her away. She had to have been the person in the van that Kaydee wouldn't be afraid of."

"And now what are you doing?" Heath asked.

"I'm going to have my security pick her up if she sets foot in the casino." Dela had stopped by the casino on the way home and sent the photo she had of Julia to all the security guards, telling them to apprehend her when they saw her.

"That's a good idea. If they know that Kurt has been arrested, she probably won't show up there. They will have to move on to another place to drop the merchandise."

"What have you discovered about Sonny's death?" Dela asked, so he didn't ask her what else she was doing about it.

"Very little. The pathologist said how the neck was slit it looked like the killer was skilled. We do know he was left-handed by the motion of the cut. Forensics picked up everything within a twenty-foot radius of the crime. None of it appeared to be evidence in the case."

"I would think the cartel would have someone in their organization who was good at killing people," Dela said, spreading peanut butter on another slice of bread.

"You want to go out to eat tonight?" Heath asked.

"Huh?" She'd been contemplating how to make a trip to Umatilla when Heath asked a question.

"What are you doing that you aren't paying attention?"

"I'm making a sandwich."

"If you're that distracted while making a sandwich, I'm definitely taking you out to dinner. Be ready to go at seven. I'll buzz home, take a quick shower, and we'll go to Hamleys."

She smiled. "That sounds nice. I'll be ready."

He ended the call, and she ate the sandwich,

smiling. That gave her two hours to figure out when to go to Umatilla and who to take with her.

♠ ♣ ♥ ♦

Heath arrived home earlier than he'd said. Dela shoved the pages she'd been reading into her purse when she heard the front door lock click. She'd dressed for dinner right after he'd called. She didn't want him coming home and finding her not ready and asking why.

"I'll just be fifteen minutes," he said, hurrying through the living room and down the hall.

Dela rose out of the recliner and ushered Mugshot out the French doors. She crossed the yard and let Jethro in from the field. She liked having the two close during the night. They had raised the alarm twice when someone tried to break into the house. They were better than the surveillance cameras Heath had talked her into installing. She gave Jethro a carrot and Mugshot a dog biscuit.

By the time she'd locked the French door and checked to make sure she'd cleaned up her mess from making a sandwich, Heath strode down the hall. He wore a Native American print shirt, his best pair of slacks, and the moccasins his mom had made him. His hair was still wet, but he had it brushed out straight and not braided.

She'd dressed in work slacks, a flowy shirt with flowers on it, and had her hair pulled back in a ponytail.

"You look great!" he said, kissing her.

She pulled out of the kiss and said, "You look good yourself. Why are we going out to dinner?"

"Because we didn't get a chance to celebrate our engagement. I thought with everything going on, we needed a night out." He opened the door, and she walked out onto the porch.

"We'll take your car, I'm sure it's cleaner than my pickup." Heath walked to the passenger side and held the door open for her.

"My, are you going to use your best manners all night?" she joked.

"Just like our senior prom," he said, and they both laughed.

He'd picked her up for the senior prom, held her door, closed her door, and when they arrived at the prom, the back hem of her prom dress was black and nasty from dragging all the way from her house to the school.

Heath's mom had been there as a chaperone. She took Dela into the girls' restroom and cut the dress to make it knee-length. Because of the type of material, she used a lighter to singe the ends where the dress should have been hemmed. Only a few students and a couple of adults who were at the entrance when they arrived knew about the change in her dress.

After recounting that evening, they arrived at the steakhouse in Pendleton. The drive took about twenty minutes.

"I called and reserved a table in the corner where we can sit and watch everyone." Heath grinned.

Dela loved sitting in the corner booth, watching the locals and the out-of-town people. "You know how to make me happy, don't you?"

"I try."

"This could be our lucky night." Dela knew she was smiling more than normal. Her cheeks hurt, but she didn't care. This was what life with Heath would be like. He would always do his best to please her. She would always be grateful that he still loved her one leg and all.

They entered through the main entrance and walked up to the counter where the hostess stood.

"Two for Seaver in the corner booth," Heath said, holding Dela's hand.

"I'm sorry, it has been reserved for a larger party. You'll have to settle for the booth over there." She pointed to a booth that wouldn't give them a good view of anything except the wall and one other booth.

"Is the booth next to the corner one reserved?" Heath asked.

The woman looked at the screen on the desk. "No, but it is at eight."

Dela glanced at her watch. "That gives us an hour and a half to eat. We shouldn't have a problem being out of there by then."

The hostess nodded and led them to the booth beside the one they had wanted. When the hostess gave them the name of their waiter and left, Dela said, "I wonder who the larger party is?"

"We'll find out when they arrive." Heath opened the menu and started reading.

Dela did a quick scan of the people in the restaurant and the bar. Since there wasn't anything hiding the saloon from the steakhouse, she could see all the way through to the large door that opened onto the street.

Their waiter arrived, took their drink and food order, and left.

Dela glanced up and grabbed Heath's arm. "Does Dillon Travers know you?" she asked.

Chapter Sixteen

"Not that I know of, why?"

Dela pointed to the saloon door.

Heath's gaze slid to the saloon where Travers, Julia, and two men stood. "This is interesting."

Dela faced Heath, since they had sat on the same side of the booth, and used him to block her from the approaching group. "We probably shouldn't let them see us."

Heath sat on the outside of the bench seat with his back to the door. "Keep an eye on them, but don't be obvious," he whispered.

Dela watched the hostess lead the group to the corner booth. She shifted on the bench to face the table and not Heath. He also faced the table. She felt someone slide and inch their way to the back of the corner booth.

How lucky was it that they would be able to hear everything that was said at the table next door? Her body vibrated with nerves and excitement. This could be what they needed to find Kaydee and apprehend her kidnappers.

The conversation from the corner booth was hushed. Dela didn't want to look obvious by leaning back against the seat to hear better.

Drinks were brought over to the table by a man in a suit. It was the first time Dela had ever seen a waiter in a suit in this establishment. The waiters wore white shirts and slacks but no tie or jacket.

He said, "Mr. Travers, the meals you ordered will be up in about ten minutes. Is there anything else we can get for you?"

"I asked that no one be seated in the booths on either side of us." Travers' voice held authority as it could clearly be heard in their booth.

Dela glanced at Heath. He shrugged. She took that to mean, let's see how this plays out.

"Excuse me, sir, would you mind moving to another table?" the person, Dela now presumed to be the manager, asked Heath.

Heath nodded. "Yes, I do mind. My fiancée and I came here tonight to celebrate our engagement. We had reserved that booth," he tipped his head to where Travers and his crew sat. "When we arrived, we were told we couldn't have it. Since this is as close as we can get to our favorite booth, we aren't moving."

Dela jumped when a man appeared beside the manager. He was one of the men who had walked in with Travers.

"It would be in your best interest to move," the man said.

Heath started to slide toward the end of the booth.

Dela grasped his arm. "We don't need to make a scene." She didn't want anyone in Travers' employ to see her. She had plans of staking out the warehouse in Umatilla tomorrow.

The manager's face was white. "There's no need to get ugly," he said to the man before turning to the corner booth. "I could move your group down to the Cattle Baron room. You would have it all to yourselves."

"That's an excellent idea. The next time I make reservations, that's where I want to be," Travers said.

There was the usual sound of people getting out of the booth. Dela slid with her back against the wall to watch them walk away. She twisted her head when Julia looked back over her shoulder.

"Now we can't hear what they were talking about," Dela said.

"But I didn't have to pull out my badge to keep the peace." Heath picked up her hand as the hostess came over.

"I'll get the corner table set up, and you can move into it."

Dela smiled. They'd get their view of the whole restaurant and lounge after all.

Before their food arrived, they were seated in the corner booth, talking about what they would miss since Travers and his group moved to the secluded Cattle Baron's room.

"Maybe it's best we aren't eavesdropping," Heath said. "This way we can concentrate on our conversation."

Dela studied him. "What conversation is that?"

"When and where do you want to get married?"

She opened her mouth to say, 'Did they really have to decide that now?' when she saw the determined set of his jaw. He wasn't going to let her push this off since she'd accepted his ring. "I'd like to have the wedding in Mom and Lance's backyard unless you would rather have it on the reservation." That should make him happy.

"If you want it in the backyard, then we need to make sure the weather is nice and not too hot." Heath leaned back as their food arrived.

They spent a few minutes cutting meat and moving food around on their plates before he asked, "So that means either May or September."

Dela jerked her head up to study him. "May is next month. There is no way everything can be done before then."

"Then I guess it will be September." He raised an eyebrow as if challenging her to say it wouldn't work.

Dela repeated the month in her head and stumbled over it a couple of times. But she'd told Heath nothing was holding her back from marrying him. She didn't need to look her father in the eyes to determine if she would turn out crazy like him. She really didn't. *Yeah, keep telling yourself that.* She smiled, but it must not have been convincing.

Heath set his utensils down and put an arm around her shoulders as they sat side by side in the crook of the booth. "When you told me some months ago you were ready to marry and we talked about your father, you said it didn't matter if we found him. And again, when I proposed, you said it didn't matter." He grasped her chin and made her look at him. "Were you telling the truth or just saying what you thought I wanted to hear?"

Staring into his concerned brown eyes, she couldn't lie. "I don't want you marrying me and then we discover my father is crazy. You would be legally bound to me. I love you and don't want to strap you to me if I'm going to be a boulder around your neck."

"You won't be. Haven't we always fought challenges together?" He smiled. "You are the only person I want to grow old with. Any time I'm with you, there is never a dull moment or a second that I regret knowing you."

Dela wrapped her arm around his neck and kissed him. She leaned back. "Then September it is. I'll let Mom and Molly know when we get home."

Heath smiled, kissed her, and then released her. "Let's eat. I can't wait to tell my mom. She's going to be very happy."

Dela was happy, but she didn't enjoy being fussed over, and she didn't like making decisions about what kind of dress she'd wear or what flavor of cake. But then that was what her friends were for.

When they finished eating, the group that had moved to the Cattle Baron's room hadn't left yet.

"Let's use the restrooms and then wait in the bar and see when they leave," Dela said when the waitress handed Heath the bill.

"You go first. I'll pay this and follow."

Dela didn't wait for him to say anything else. She walked to the hallway that led to the restrooms. Along the hall was a door with a plaque. It was the Cattle Baron's room. She heard loud voices coming from inside. She glanced down the hall and didn't see anyone coming or looking her way. She pressed an ear against the crack in the door and listened.

They were arguing about getting a ship to pick up the cargo. Julia wanted to get the cargo moving, and Travis wanted to gather more before shipping.

Dela stepped back. If they were talking about women, then she would have a little more time to find where Kaydee was being kept, if she was still alive. That was her fear. To get caught watching for kidnapped women and have Kaydee's body discovered elsewhere.

"What are you doing here?" a voice behind her asked, shaking her from her thoughts.

Chapter Seventeen

Dela spun around and grimaced. It was one of the men who had arrived with Travers. He'd come from the restrooms. "I'm waiting for my fiancé." She glanced down the hall and spotted Heath. "Here he comes. We were going to check out the wine cellar."

The man glared at her as Heath walked up and grasped her hand.

"Ready?" he asked.

"Yes, I'm excited to see the wine cellar."

To his credit, Heath didn't raise an eyebrow. He led her down the hallway to the stone stairway, and they started down. Dela glanced down the hall just as she took the step that hid her from the hallway. The man was watching them.

"What was that about?" Heath whispered as they kept walking down the stone steps.

"He came out of the restroom as I was standing outside the door to the Cattle Baron's room. I'm lucky he didn't catch me with my ear to the door."

They stepped into the cellar and strolled hand in hand to the far end, just in case the man came to see what they were doing.

Heath pulled her into his arms and whispered, "Did you hear anything?"

"Julia is anxious to get the cargo on a ship. Travers said they needed a full load." She leaned back to look into his eyes. "I think they're talking about kidnapped women."

"Could be. Are you finished touring the wine cellar?" Heath released her but grasped her hand.

"Yes. I don't think we need to hang out in the bar. Let's go home." Dela made up her mind to contact Quinn about what she'd heard and what she believed about the warehouse at the McNary Industrial Park.

They climbed the stairs hand in hand. At the top, she tugged on his hand, seeing the back of Julia going into the women's restroom.

"I didn't get a chance to use the restroom." She slipped her hand from his and walked to the door, pushing it open and stepping inside.

The woman stood in front of the mirror, fixing her makeup.

Dela smiled and walked into a stall. She did her business and walked out to wash her hands. The woman was still there, primping.

"That's a nice shade of lipstick. What's it called?" Dela asked, unable to think of anything else to comment on.

"It's Pink Flamingo." She made a kissing motion with her lips. "I like that it makes me look younger." She speared Dela with a look that said, 'Don't say anything different.'

"It is a vibrant, youthful color. And it makes your cheeks flush." Dela knew nothing about makeup or what it could do for a woman, but she'd overheard a group of women at the casino one night talking about makeup while their escorts were gambling at the blackjack table.

Julia smiled and said, "You know, for someone who doesn't wear any makeup, you seem to know something about it."

"My friend is obsessed with makeup magazines. I prefer the natural look, as does my fiancé."

Julia waggled her plucked and colored eyebrows. "He is a looker. Good catch. When's the wedding?"

"September. We were discussing the arrangements tonight." Dela was finding it hard to keep her tone excited and what she thought of as girly. She had never been a girly girl. She loved sports and hunting and despised shopping and dressing up.

"Nice. It was obvious he's Native American. Are you?" She studied Dela long enough that it made her feel like a commodity rather than a person.

"I'm half."

The door opened slightly. "Dela? You okay?" Heath called into the restroom.

"Yeah. Coming." She smiled at Julia. "Gotta go." She hurried from the room and ran into Heath.

"Whoa, what was going on in there?" he asked, steadying her with his hands on her arms.

"Let's go." She turned, and he followed behind. She didn't stop walking until they were at her car.

He opened the passenger door for her but didn't move to shut the door when she was seated. "What went on in the restroom?"

"I saw Julia enter when we came up the stairs. I was talking to her." Dela was still trying to make sense of the woman. "I think she was in there messing with her makeup because she was told to get lost for a while. I tried to talk makeup with her—"

Heath chuckled and said, "I bet that went well."

She punched him. "It went better than you think. Anyway, she asked me if we'd set a date, I said September, and then she said you were good looking…"

He grinned. "And what did you reply?"

"I said yes, you were. And then it was odd, she said it was obvious you were Native American, was I." Dela stared at Heath.

"What did you say?"

"That I was half. Then she just stared at me in an uncomfortable way. You called to me, which broke her stare, and I got the heck out of there." Then it hit her. If Julia was kidnapping the women, and she was looking to fill the ship… "I wonder if she was trying to decide if I'd make a good woman to kidnap."

Heath shook his head. "She won't go for you. You are about to be married, which means you have a suitor who would be knocking down doors to find you. She picked Kaydee because her husband wouldn't care what happened to her, and they were making a point to Sonny that didn't work." He kissed her cheek and closed the door.

As Heath walked around the front of the car, she pulled out her phone and texted Quinn, telling him to call her in the morning.

Heath slid into the car and said, "Since we're in Pendleton, want to drive out to your mom's and have her help us pick a date in September that will work for her?"

"We might as well. It will make her night. But I'll text her and let her know we're coming so we don't catch them in their pajamas." Dela texted her mom. *Heath and I are coming to see you. Should be there in fifteen minutes.*

Good news? She texted back.

Yes. Dela replied.

Heath drove through town, and they headed out a county road to the property Lance owned and farmed. Dela had been surprised when her mom told her she was getting married. Her mom hadn't dated at all while she lived at home. Only Grandfather Thunder, who lived next door, babysat her when Mom attended meetings or classes to enhance her teaching certificate. Once Dela came home as a disabled veteran, finished her rehab for her leg, and moved into her own house, Mom announced she was getting married. The man happened to be a wealthy farmer who, it seemed, had been after her mom for many years. Deborah had turned Lance down until she knew her daughter was an adult. Now they were both blissfully happy and that made Dela happy.

At the driveway to the farm, Heath continued past it.

"Where are you going?" Dela asked.

"There's been a car following us. I didn't want to lead it to your mom." Heath pulled into the driveway of the farm a mile beyond Lance's farm. He slowly drove down the lane, watching the car in the mirror. "It went on by and picked up speed. It could have been a local coming from town, but it didn't go around me when it had the opportunity."

He drove up to the parking area in front of the house and turned around as three dogs ran at the car, barking. He drove slowly down the road, and Dela stared in the direction the car that had been behind them went. She didn't see headlights coming back toward them.

At the correct driveway, they turned in, and Dela grinned. Her mom had all the outside lights on. The large living room windows were bright with light from within. "I think she knows what this visit is about."

Heath turned off the engine and peered at her. "You did call her after I proposed."

Dela nodded. "True, and I told her when we picked a date, she'd be the first to know. Okay, now I'm prepared to be hugged and squeezed."

"She loves you." Heath gazed into her eyes, and she understood what he was saying. If her father had raped her mom, she wouldn't show as much love and affection as she did. That knowledge made her heart skip a beat and her grin grow.

Heath came around and opened her door, and they walked up to the open front door, framing her mom, backlit by the interior lights, with her arms wide open.

After hugging them together and then separately, Mom allowed them to enter the house. Lance stood by an end table that held a bottle of champagne in a bucket and four glasses already filled with the bubbling liquid.

"I'm so happy for you two," Mom said, giving Dela another hug. "Lance, hand us each a glass, and let's toast to Heath and Dela and a long life together." Tears trickled down Mom's cheeks as she sipped her drink.

"We came here tonight because we've decided on having the wedding in September. Will that work for you? Because Dela would like to have the wedding in your backyard." Heath put his arm around Dela's shoulders.

Mom put the glass down and clapped her hands together. "Oh, that is perfect, isn't it, Lance?"

"As long as it's early in September. The grain harvesting will start in mid-September. That will make a lot of dust with all the machinery running around on the farm." Lance put a hand on Dela's shoulder. "It would make me proud to have your wedding here."

Mom rushed back into the room with a calendar. "The first Saturday of September is the sixth. Is that what you want?"

Dela knew there was no turning back now as she peered into Heath's eyes. "Yes, that's fine."

"I can sit down this week with Virginia and see how many relatives to invite. You two can give us the names of the friends you want to invite. After we have that total, we can look at invitations." Mom was glowing. "This is going to be so much fun!"

"You'll have to keep my mom from inviting people she calls relatives, but they aren't," Heath said.

Mom nodded and asked, "Who will be your bridesmaids and maid of honor?"

Dela stared at her. "I-I guess Molly for maid of honor and Rosie for the bridesmaid." She shrugged. There wasn't a need to have a whole string of people involved in the wedding.

"That's it? What about your other friends?" Mom asked.

"I only want the two to stand up with me at the

wedding. And I want the wedding to be small." Dela felt her chest constricting and her breathing becoming labored. She pushed out from under Heath's arm and hurried out the front door. She stood on the porch, breathing in the cool evening air, willing her body to relax.

Heath arrived at her side. "What's up?"

"I want to marry you, I do. But I don't want a circus."

"Your mom is just excited that we are finally getting married. You can't blame her for that."

Dela shifted her gaze from the stars that had popped out to his face. "I don't blame her. I just wish she would understand I don't want to parade around in front of a bunch of people to show off I'm getting married. I want a small, simple service with only our friends and family. I don't want a bridal shower or a girls' night out. I just want to marry you and then spend the rest of my life with you."

"Then you need to tell your mom that you and Molly will take care of the plans and all she has to do is give you a list of her close friends and family she wants to invite." Heath kissed her. "Come in and tell her now. Then turn it all over to Molly and Rosie. They know you, and they know what you will like."

"You don't care that I want a small wedding?"

"No. I only want what you want. If you said let's go to the justice of the peace, I'd take you down there tomorrow, and this would be all over with." He studied her.

She could tell he would do that if that was what she asked for. "As lovely as that sounds, I can't deprive Mom of at least a wedding. Even if it will be small and not elaborate."

Heath grinned. "Let's go tell her and go home."

Dela entwined her arm with his, and they walked back into the house. She told her mom exactly what Heath had suggested. To Dela's surprise, Mom smiled and said, "That sounds like an excellent idea. I'll make sure the backyard is beautiful, so they don't have to worry about ordering any flowers other than the bridal bouquet."

On the drive home, Dela was thankful for the thousandth time that Heath had fallen in love with her and understood her.

Chapter Eighteen

The next morning, Dela woke and found Heath had already left for work. She scrubbed her eyes with her fists, listening to Mugshot's tail beat against the bed. "Why didn't you wake me up sooner?" she asked, scratching behind his ear and stretching before she swung her leg over the side of the bed and fit her crutches in her armpits.

She swung down the hall to the kitchen and found a pot of coffee warming. She filled a mug and sat down at the table. Turning over her phone, she saw that Quinn had tried to call. It was 9:00, and he'd tried calling at 8:00. She tapped the call icon and sipped her coffee, waiting for him to answer.

The phone beeped and his voice said, "Special Agent Pierce, leave a message."

"Quinn, it's Dela. I have information about where Kaydee and other women may be hidden. Give me a call."

She hit the off icon, sipped her coffee, and became

agitated that she and Quinn were playing phone tag. The longer it took to get eyes on what could be trafficking, the less likely they would have the chance to intercept before the women were shipped to who knew where.

Standing and putting bread in the toaster, she decided to go with plan B. She dialed Kenny first.

"Dela, do you need me to come in early?" he asked.

"No, but I need you to cover for me tonight. I'm taking a short trip to look at something, and I don't think I'll make it back in time before you would normally go home. Call in Nadine to take your shift today, and you take my night shift. I'll be back tomorrow for sure."

"Okay. This have anything to do with you getting married?"

She heard the smile in his voice. It was weird how everyone was so happy she was getting married. Had they all felt she was becoming a grumpy spinster? "No. Just going to check something out. Thanks." She ended the call before he could ask anything else.

Now that her shift was covered, she had to figure out who to take with her. It needed to be someone who could listen and move with dexterity. She thought of Travis, Molly's son, but she was pretty sure if Molly found out, she'd be unhappy with Dela for taking her boy where it could be dangerous.

Farley was smart and could think on his feet, but he wasn't physically capable of getting away if someone was running after him. If she was going to pull in someone from the tribal police, she should ask Heath, but he was working on the homicide with the FBI. She knew who to call and who would be as interested in catching the kidnappers and finding Kaydee as she was.

She scrolled and tapped the icon for Tribal Officer Jacob Red Bear. Robin's younger brother. Dela and Jacob had bonded over the death of his sister.

"Hey, Dela, heard you and Heath are finally making your shacking up legal." He laughed and she smiled.

"Yeah, we are. Are you working today?" She decided to cut right to the reason for her call.

"Not until tonight. Why?"

She told him about Kaydee. He knew she was missing and had been helping the MMIW group in their search for her or information about her. "I think she might be at a warehouse in the McNary Industrial Park in Umatilla."

He asked, "Did you tell Heath?"

"No, I've been trying to contact Quinn and keep missing him. If we wait much longer, it could be too late to do anything. Would you go with me to see if we can tell if there are women being held in the warehouse?" She held her breath, waiting for him to decide.

"Yeah, I'll go with you. Give me twenty, and I'll pick you up. But you have to call Heath and tell him what we're doing."

She knew she did, and he would be less likely to get mad since she'd picked a police officer to go with her. "Okay. I'll call him as soon as we hang up."

"See you in twenty."

She ended the call, found Heath's name, and tapped the number.

"You've reached Tribal Detective Heath Seaver.

Leave a message, and I'll contact you as soon as possible."

Dela's heart raced. This was better. She didn't have to actually speak to him. "Hi, Heath. It's Dela. Just wanted to let you know that Jacob and I are heading to Umatilla to check out a warehouse owned by Travers. I think it might be where Kaydee is being held. I'll call you when we get back." She tapped end and let out the air that had been making her chest ache.

She hurried to the bedroom to put on her prosthesis and get dressed. She'd have to do it at record speed because she'd wasted time calling Heath.

Dela stood on the porch, her hand resting on the Sig M11 in her fanny pack. She usually kept the weapon in her bedside table. But she wasn't walking into a drug cartel's trafficking ring without a weapon. Jacob pulled up in his Jeep Wrangler. She walked down the steps and jogged to the Jeep.

Once inside, she fastened her seatbelt and glanced at Jacob. "Thanks for doing this with me. I couldn't think of anyone else that I could trust other than Heath and Quinn, and they're tied up with the homicide and drugs."

"No problem. I'm glad you called and didn't go by yourself." He backed out of her driveway and headed toward the interstate. "Tell me how you came to the conclusion that there could be a trafficking ring in Umatilla."

Dela told him about Travers being head of the drug cartel, Julia's visits to the casino, and what they'd learned about her contact with Kaydee. "Then I had someone help me get hold of a list of properties that

Travers owns and discovered the warehouse in Umatilla. It has access to containers that go by barge to Portland, and from there can go all around the world. It makes sense that he'd take women he's kidnapped there and ship them out."

Jacob nodded as he accelerated onto the Interstate headed west. "But why the rush to check it out?"

"Last night, I eavesdropped on a conversation at Hamley. Julia was pushing to move the 'cargo,' and Travers said he wanted to add more to the shipment." She glanced at Jacob. "That sounded to me like Julia wants to get the women out of here quickly, and Travers wants to make more money by adding more women."

"I agree, it does sound like that. Okay. I think your information is solid enough to warrant our snooping around."

Dela sat back and let Jacob navigate the traffic as they headed toward Umatilla.

Within forty minutes of hopping on the Interstate, they were taking the offramp to Umatilla. Dela gave him directions with her GPS to the warehouse. It sat all by itself with only stacked containers on one side of the building.

They drove by, checking out where there might be cameras or guards. The building looked as if no one cared if someone came snooping.

Jacob parked in the lot of a construction company office building. "What's the plan?"

"We need to find a spot to watch who comes and goes and see if we can get into the building. We also should try to see if there is anyone in the containers." That would be a feat since they were stacked three high.

"Let's walk over and use the containers to hide between while we check them out and watch the building." Jacob reached into the back seat and pulled out a small backpack. "Did you bring water and a weapon?" he asked.

She put her hand on her fanny pack. "A weapon. I didn't think about water."

"I have two bottles in my pack. Let's go." He slipped out of the driver's side.

As soon as she closed her door, the vehicle beeped, meaning it was locked. She followed Jacob over a block and down to where they could get close to the building by walking between the stacked containers.

"Good news," Jacob whispered. "These are close enough together that I can climb up between them using my hands and feet." He nodded to the front of the containers. "Get as close to the opening as you can to see the whole building, but stay hidden in the shadow. Keep an eye on the building while I start knocking on containers."

Dela gave him a thumbs up and walked between the containers. When she could see all of the warehouse, she stopped and looked back at Jacob moving up the second level of containers. She heard his three short raps and listened for a reply. When nothing happened, he continued spread-eagled, using his hands and feet on each side to press against the containers and move upward. When he could reach the top containers, he rapped, waited, and then started down.

Dela watched his progress in between keeping an eye on the doors she could see from this position and the vehicles in the area.

The main door with a sign that said 'office'

opened, and two men, built like the two that had been at the steakhouse with Travers, walked out and climbed into a tan SUV. She took a photo of the men, the vehicle, and zoomed in on the license plate.

Jacob dropped to the ground, pulled out a water bottle, drank, and then pointed to the right. He walked to the back of the containers and disappeared.

Staring at the building, she barely heard the taps as he tried first the bottom containers and then the second and third on both sides. If they didn't come up with evidence, she wouldn't be able to convince Quinn that this place needed to be raided.

Her phone buzzed. Quinn. "Were your ears burning?" she answered the call.

"Why? Where are you?" Quinn was never one for small talk. Which was why she liked him.

"I'm sitting between containers at a warehouse in the McNary Industrial Park in Umatilla. Travers owns the warehouse. Jacob Red Bear and I are staking it out to see if this is where he has Kaydee."

"Shit, Dela. You're supposed to leave that up to us. I can have a team there in two hours."

"That's it. I don't know for sure if there are women here. If Jacob and I can be certain, I'll give you a call. Right now, he's knocking on the containers to see if anyone responds. I'm keeping an eye on the warehouse. I'll send you the photos I took of a couple of guys who left the warehouse. They didn't look like workers." She texted the photos to Quinn. "Do they look familiar?"

"Yeah, they're two of Travers' bodyguards."

"Does that mean he's in the warehouse?" Dela asked, keeping her gaze on the building.

"He has several bodyguards. They could have been

there checking on something for him or he is there and sent them on an errand." Quinn let out a long breath. "I don't like what you're doing. I'll send two agents to take over surveillance on the building. When they arrive, you and Jacob clear out."

"Okay. Tell them we're in between the containers." Dela's phone vibrated in her hand. She glanced at the caller. Heath. She pushed the end on Quinn's call and answered Heath's.

"Hey, everything is good. Just talked to Quinn. He's sending two agents to relieve Jacob and me."

"That's good to hear. Why didn't you tell me you planned to do this?"

She heard concern in his voice and a bit of irritation. "Because I hadn't planned to do it myself until Quinn didn't get back to me. I have a gut feeling this is where we'll find Kaydee. But we won't find her if we don't look before they ship her overseas."

"At least you had the good sense to contact Jacob. Can I talk to him?"

"Not at this minute. He's been climbing up the containers and rapping on them to see if anyone responds. I'm between containers keeping an eye—" A utility van pulled up close to the side of the building. "I'll call you back."

"Don't—"

Dela ended the call, ran to the back of the container, down to the last two, and back to the front. She had a better view of what the van was doing.

"I see," Jacob said from above her.

She watched as two men carried what looked like a woman out of the warehouse and put her in the back of the van. "We have to follow that!"

"You see which way they go. I'll get the Jeep." Jacob disappeared.

Dela kept her eyes on the van. A woman walked out of the warehouse. By the way she walked, poked her finger in one man's chest, and then flung her hair, Dela knew who she was—Julia.

The woman walked back into the warehouse, and the two men climbed into the front of the van.

She watched as the van exited the main entrance and turned left. She ran to the back of the containers to see if the vehicle had continued straight or turned. A Jeep pulled up. She ran for the Jeep, the door flew open, she hopped in, and Jacob took off after the van.

As she kept an eye on the van, she called Quinn. "We're following a utility van." She read off the license and told him in which direction they were headed. "We saw two men place either a drugged or dead woman into the van."

"Stay with them. I'll contact my agents and have them contact you to help with the take down." Quinn ended the call.

Her phone buzzed. It was Heath.

As soon as she slid the answer icon, Heath said, "What the hell is going on?"

"We saw two men put either a drugged or dead woman in a van. We're following it and are in contact with two FBI agents. Please, I need to help Jacob keep an eye on the van."

"Call me when the FBI takes over."

"I will." She ended the call and glanced at Jacob.

"I thought you said you told him what you are doing?" Jacob said as he followed the van onto the Interstate headed east toward Pendleton.

"I left a message when he didn't answer the phone. Then I was talking to him when I saw the van pull up to the warehouse." She shrugged. "He knows I'm with you and that the feds are on the way. We'll be fine. We just need to keep them in our sights and tell the agents where to meet up with us."

Her phone buzzed. It was a restricted number, meaning it was the feds Quinn told her about. "Dela here." She told the agent that they were following the van headed east on Interstate 84 and the milepost they were at.

"Keep them in your sights, we're about an hour from Umatilla on the interstate. We'll pick up the pace and try to catch up."

"Okay." Dela glanced at Jacob and said, "They're about an hour behind us."

He nodded, keeping his gaze on the van.

Dela wondered why they were going east. At Pendleton, she discovered why. The van took Exit 210 toward Milton-Freewater. "Where are they going?" she asked, as they followed the van through the east side of Pendleton and onto Highway 11 which would take them through the north end of the reservation. "They're going to dump her body on the reservation. It has to be Kaydee."

Jacob pressed down on the accelerator, and they shot up behind the van. "What should we do?"

Dela called Heath. "The van with the woman is on reservation land. They just turned off on Spring Hollow Road. We aren't keeping our distance anymore."

"I'm headed that way along with another officer. Don't engage if you don't have to. Keep this line open and tell me exactly where they go."

Dela described where they were and when the van stopped beside some bushes. A man on the passenger side stepped out of his door, acting like he was taking a leak. Jacob drove past, slammed it into park, and he and Dela jumped out with their guns drawn as the two men were pulling the woman out of the van.

"Police, put her back in the van and step away with your hands in the air!" Jacob shouted.

The man holding the woman's feet dropped them and went for his gun. Jacob shot him in the shoulder, sending him backward.

The screech of tires alerted them to reinforcements.

"Get your hands in the air," Heath shouted as another tribal officer cuffed the man who was shot.

As soon as they pulled the other man away from the woman, Dela shoved her gun in her fanny pack and ran forward. It was Kaydee. She was barely conscious and had been beaten so badly, she was barely recognizable. Dela held her head in her lap. "It's okay. It's Dela, we have you. You'll be fine." She looked up into Heath and Jacob's faces as tears trickled down her face. "Call an ambulance."

Chapter Nineteen

Dela rode in the ambulance with Kaydee to St. Anthony's in Pendleton. She stayed with the unconscious woman in the ER room until the doctors came to examine her.

Slumped on a chair in the waiting area, she hoped Heath and Quinn were grilling the two men who dumped Kaydee alongside the road like garbage. Every time she thought of how they were dragging her out of the van, anger exploded in her head. She stood up and strode the length of the waiting area when her mind wouldn't let go of the image.

She was thinking about Kaydee and her children when two people walked up. Dela glanced up into the confident faces of Mimi and Marion. She stood, and they both hugged her.

"You have saved another woman," Mimi said.

Dela shook her head. "It wasn't just me. Jacob Red Bear was with me."

"But you figured it out," Marion said, pulling Dela

down into a chair beside her as she talked quietly. "Quinn called and told me you'd found Kaydee and were a part of the arrest of the two men who had her."

Dela shook her head. "Those two men were only doing what they were told. We still have to get the head of the organization and that woman who sells her sisters."

Mimi frowned. "You mean it is one of us who is taking the women?"

"No. Just that it is a woman who is running the trafficking. I'm pretty sure of it. She decides who is kidnapped, and I think even helps in the kidnapping. She had to be the reason Kaydee walked close to the van parked on her jogging route." Dela peered into Marion's eyes. "We have to find a way to get that woman put in prison. Even though she deserves worse."

Marion gave her a slight nod.

Heath walked into the waiting area. "Any news?" he asked.

"They know I came in with her, and no one has been out to talk to me." Dela peered down the hall toward the ER rooms. "Has anyone called her sister or parents?"

The emergency doors swished open. Duke and Sonny's mom walked in. Dela stood up, her arm pulled back as if ready to throw a punch.

Heath put an arm around her shoulders. "Mimi, stay with me, please. Marion, take Dela to the cafeteria while I speak to Mrs. Wadass."

Dela couldn't stop her mouth from opening and her thoughts from spilling out. "She had to know what her sons were up to and possibly was in on the abduction and beating of Kaydee."

Marion tugged on her arm, leading her down the hallway toward the small cafeteria. "You have to control your anger if you are going to take down the traffickers."

Dela planted her feet and stared at Marion.

"Yes, I said if you are going to stop these traffickers, you need to control your anger." Marion released her arm. They stood in the hallway, staring at each other.

"Let's get something to eat and discuss how to go about helping Quinn and Heath put these people where they belong." Marion strode down the hall. Dela jogged after her.

"You're planning to help?" Dela asked when they stepped into the cafeteria.

"Get some lunch, and we'll talk." Marion grabbed a tray and started down the line, snatching a premade salad and drink.

Dela put chips, a salad, a cookie, and a drink on her tray.

They sat in a corner with their backs to the wall, watching the door.

"How did you figure out where Kaydee was?" Marion started.

"I used my sources to discover what properties the head of the Cartel owned. I decided the one closest to Pendleton would be where they'd take her. Jacob and I were staking it out to see if there were any women there so we could call in Quinn and crew." Dela felt the anger growing. She added, "The woman I was talking about earlier directed the men to put Kaydee in the van and get rid of her. I saw her poking one in the chest with her finger."

Marion frowned. "Why hasn't Quinn arrested her?"

"I don't know, but I can't wait for him to come take my statement. It should be damning enough to get that woman picked up." Dela wondered if that was why Heath had arrived. To get her statement.

"What is the woman's name?" Marion pulled out a small notebook.

"Julia Rivera. Quinn said she was Dillon Travers' girlfriend."

Marion's gaze shot up to Dela's face. "You said Dillon Travers?"

"Yeah. Why?" Dela could tell Marion either knew the man or knew something about him.

"What's he look like?"

Dela described the man.

"He came to one of the talks I gave at Tamasklikts and said he'd like to support the work we've been doing with regards to keeping tribal women safe." A glare furrowed her brow. "I thought he honestly cared. It was just his way to learn more about the program and perhaps how to get away with what he was doing."

"Didn't you mention him to Quinn? He would have recognized the name."

"No, I just said a philanthropic man was giving our program much-needed financial support." Horror widened her eyes and mouth. "He's using drug money, isn't he?"

Dela nodded. "More than likely, he's using the same money he gets for selling our women."

Marion's face darkened. "We are going to bring him and his organization down. That is the lowest thing I've ever heard. I'll make sure the money will go into the funds for drug rehabilitation, not our program."

Heath, Quinn, and Mimi walked into the cafeteria. They all three filled trays and sat at the table with Dela and Marion.

"Did you send Mrs. Wadass packing and get a guard for Kaydee?" Dela asked.

"I asked her why she was here. She said she'd heard that Kaydee was brought here." Heath studied her.

"How did she know before Kaydee's family?" Dela asked and continued, "Because she is a part of the group who took her daughter-in-law, that's why. I bet Julia called her to come to the hospital and see if Kaydee was alive enough to tell us what happened and where she was."

Quinn nodded. "I have an agent guarding Kaydee. She's in surgery for internal bleeding. When she comes out, there will be a guard on her at all times. She is our best witness to the whole operation."

Marion nodded toward Dela. "She's a pretty good witness, too."

"How so?" Quinn asked.

Dela told him everything she saw while watching the warehouse. Including Julia giving the orders to dump Kaydee.

"We're going to need that information. The two you apprehended aren't talking and they lawyered up." Heath put a hand on Dela's. "You need to be careful. I'm sure they are going to tell Julia and Travers that you and some guy stopped them."

"Which is part of my plan," Dela said, glancing at each person at the table. She'd thought about this while sitting in the waiting room alone. "I would like to blackmail Julia. Tell her I saw her at the warehouse giving orders to dump the woman. But I have an expensive wedding coming up and I'd like some money to fund it. Which I could do by not telling anyone I saw her."

"No!" Heath said, his face darkening.

"That's not a bad idea," Quinn said.

Both Marion and Mimi were shaking their heads.

"That would put you in the crosshairs of anyone Dillon hired to kill you," Marion said.

Quinn turned his attention to Marion. "Dillon? How did you know Travers' first name?"

"Remember that philanthropic man I told you about? I just learned from Dela, he is the man you've been trying to take down. And he offered money he made selling women and drugs to fund my organization."

"What?" Mimi said in a horrified voice.

"Exactly," Marion said.

Heath waved his hands. "It sounds like we have more than enough reasons to get the cartel and their leader off the reservation." He held Dela's gaze. "But we are not going to blackmail the girlfriend, or take on the head of the gang. We'll work through the minions, arresting them one by one and seeing if we can get some to crumble and roll on the rest."

"That will take too long," Dela said. "The feds can't keep Kaydee under surveillance as long as it will take to arrest the members of the gang one by one. I'm sure the feds know of undercover people in the gang that haven't been able to get what they need."

Quinn nodded.

"The only way to get them quicker is to shake them up," Dela said. "If I had incriminating evidence on

Travers, I'd try blackmailing him to get him to slip up." She saw Marion's face light up, but the woman didn't say anything.

"I don't like it," Heath said. "It's too dangerous."

"The feds can put a wire on me." Dela jumped to a thought. "Is there someone checking out the warehouse?"

Quinn nodded. "Milo and four other agents are there now. I should hear from them soon."

"Having a woman who is still alive to testify against them and any others the feds pick up, we should be able to get enough against Julia and Travers to get them locked up," Heath said.

"If they'll testify," Dela said. She was pretty sure with support from her and Marion, Kaydee would testify. After all, the gang killed her husband.

Quinn studied Dela. "If we don't go along with this blackmail scheme of yours, you're going to do it anyway, aren't you?"

"I haven't run through all of my options." She didn't glance at Heath. She knew he was scowling at her.

"What about the guard from the casino? We know he was selling drugs, maybe we can tell him if he helps us get them for trafficking, we'd drop the charges against him." Heath held her gaze.

Dela stared at him. That he was willing to let someone else go to keep her from walking into danger surprised her. He liked to make sure all the criminals paid.

"Do you think he would be convincing enough?" Quinn asked.

"He wouldn't," Dela said. "He could barely keep it

together when I caught him picking up the product at the casino."

"We can pull Julia in for the trafficking and make her think she could cut a deal if she gives us Travers," Quinn said.

A nurse walked into the cafeteria and walked straight to their table. "The woman you brought in is in stable condition. Her sister is here and would like to talk to you." She was staring at Dela as she talked.

"Thank you. I'll come with you." Dela stood.

As she walked away from the table, Heath grabbed her wrist. "We'll talk about this more later. No heroics alone."

She glanced at the other faces and nodded. "I couldn't do it alone."

Chapter Twenty

Tawii Talman, Kaydee's sister, stood beside a
hospital room door. A man in a suit stood on the other
side.

Dela walked up and hugged the woman. "We
found her, but she'd been beaten. It's hard to tell it's
her."

"I know. I stepped inside for a minute and had to
come back out and gather myself. Luckily, she's still
sedated." Tawii led them over to a pair of chairs across
the hall from the room. "What happened? I know you
found her, and I know you'll tell me the truth." She
nodded toward the fed. "He wouldn't tell me anything.
Only that she was to be guarded."

Dela started from the beginning. Her suspicions of
Kaydee being abused. The trip she and Marion took to
the house that turned out to be the same day she went
missing. Then Sonny coming to her for help in finding
his wife, only to go to Mimi and end up dead.

"I did some digging and discovered a warehouse in

Umatilla that is owned by the head of the cartel, Duke, and possibly Sonny, were selling for. Jacob Red Bear and I were staking it out when we saw two men put a woman into the back of a van. We were lucky to be there and see it to intervene when they were dumping her body on the reservation."

Tears flowed down Tawii's cheeks. "My family has been praying to the Creator to bring Kaydee home. Her children miss her."

Dela nodded and swiped at the tears burning the corners of her eyes. "Did you know anything about Sonny abusing your sister or that he was selling drugs?"

"I saw the bruises. She told me stories about falling down or being clumsy, but I could tell they weren't from that. She said that Sonny was doing something illegal with his brother and thought the whole Wadass family was involved. She'd overheard something Duke was telling his mom." Tawii shook her head. "And I'm not sure, but I think Kaydee was taking small amounts of money from Sonny. She commented a couple of weeks back that she just about had enough to leave him. When I asked where she got it, she said from the basket weaving classes, but I know she hasn't had enough people participate to have the money to leave."

Dela wondered if that was why Kaydee had been taken. To discover where she hid the money she'd stolen from not only Sonny, but his employers.

A nurse came out of the room. "You can go in now. She's starting to come around. I think some friendly faces would be a comfort for her."

Dela and Tawii stood and walked into the room.

Kaydee's purple and blue face looked like a balloon. It was round with slits for eyes. Her nose was bandaged as well as her head, and one arm was in a cast.

"I thought I would never see you again," Tawii said, walking up to the bed and taking Kaydee's hand that wasn't in a cast.

"The kids?" Kaydee whispered.

"At home with Leo and Mom. They keep asking for you. We told them you were at a basket-weaving workshop."

"Glad Sonny isn't taking care of them." She swallowed and grimaced.

Dela stepped forward with a glass of water and a straw. She let Kaydee sip until she pulled her head away. "Kaydee, Sonny was killed the morning after you were taken."

The woman's eyes barely widened. Dela couldn't tell what she was thinking.

"Were the kids there when it happened?" she asked, peering at her sister.

"No. He'd brought them to our house the night before, saying he was going to look for you," Tawii said.

"He didn't look," Kaydee said, swallowing again. "He had them take me."

Dela had wondered about that. "Why did you get into that van?" she asked, knowing that she should have a law enforcement person here taking notes.

"I'd met the woman online through a group for women with abusive husbands. When I went for my jog, she was going to meet me and give me a new identity to use when I left Sonny. Instead, the guy with her grabbed me, put something over my mouth, and tossed me into the van." Her body shuddered.

"She was one of the people Sonny was working for." Dela moved closer to the bed. "Did they beat you to learn about the money you took from Sonny?"

Again, the woman's eyes opened a bit wider before becoming slits in her purple flesh. "How did you know that?"

"I guessed from things you said." Tawii patted Kaydee's hand. "I don't blame you for doing what you thought would get you away from him. But all you had to do was tell me, and I would have gotten help."

"Marion Shumack and I were at your house the morning you were kidnapped to talk to you about your options." Dela added, "Rosie and I didn't believe your stories about being clumsy. And neither did your friends."

Tears slipped out the slits hiding her eyes. "I was ashamed that I'd married a man who would beat his wife. I thought I'd chosen well."

"For what it's worth, I think Sonny was being pressured by his family to sell drugs. That probably made him feel helpless. He turned his anger and frustration on you." Dela had surmised that from the little bit she'd been around Sonny and his family.

There was a knock.

"Come in," Tawii called out.

Quinn, followed by Heath, entered the room. "If you're up to it, we'd like to take your statement so we can put the people who did this to you in prison."

Dela met Heath's gaze as Quinn moved toward the bed.

"I'd prefer it if Dela stayed while I talk to you," Kaydee said.

"I'll be outside," Tawii said.

"Marion and her mom are out there. They'd like to visit with you," Heath said.

Tawii nodded, squeezed her sister's hand, and walked to the door. "I'll call and tell Mom and Leo you're going to be okay."

"Thank you." Kaydee raised her hand as if she wanted more water.

Dela grabbed the glass and held it for her. The woman drank and then leaned her head back against the pillows.

"Mrs. Wadass—" Quinn started.

"Call me Kaydee. I don't want to be connected to that family," Kaydee said.

Dela glanced at Heath. He had his phone out. She assumed he was recording the conversation.

"Kaydee," Quinn started over. "Tell me what happened the day you were abducted."

"Tell them everything you told me," Dela said, watching Quinn give her a narrow-eyed stare.

Kaydee told them about the online group, thinking the woman was bringing her new I.D. and then being gagged, tied up, and driven to a warehouse.

"Were you the only woman in the warehouse?" Quinn asked.

"No. I'd say about a dozen were led through the room I was in." She shivered and said, "They kept me tied to a chair in the middle of a room. When they weren't trying to get me to tell them where the money was, they had me gagged and left the room dark."

"What money did they want?" Quinn asked.

Kaydee glanced at Dela. She nodded, hoping the woman understood to tell them everything.

"A couple months ago, I found a lot of money in a

metal box under the hood of Sonny's truck. I had to use the truck to take Emily to the doctor. It died alongside the road on the way. I popped the hood to see if the spark plugs had come loose again from driving on all the gravel roads. I saw the box and opened it to see if that was the problem. There sat more money than I'd ever seen. I took two hundred out and put it in my purse. After that, I would go to the truck and pull out a couple of hundreds every night when Sonny was sleeping. I had over two thousand dollars saved up from doing that. I was hoping to get to five thousand. Then I planned to go to my auntie in Colville and pay for a divorce. I knew I wouldn't be able to get one staying here. One of Sonny's cousins works in the legal department at the Governance Center."

"They beat you to get you to tell them about two thousand dollars?" Quinn said it as if he didn't believe her. "That's nothing to them. You have to know something."

Kaydee moved her head back and forth slowly a couple of times and then stopped, peering at Dela. "Unless it was the conversation I overheard between Duke and his mom."

Dela picked up the water glass and handed it to Kaydee. She sipped and then handed it back.

"I overheard them talking about needing to get rid of a woman, but the boss was attached to her."

Dela's brain pulled up the video of Celia going into Travers' room at the casino. "When was this?"

"About two-three weeks ago. About the time I discovered the money."

"Who do you think it is?" Heath asked Dela.

"About that time, a dealer at the casino stopped

coming to work. It was after Travers handed her his room key and she took him up on his offer." Dela held Heath's gaze, then flicked over to Quinn. "You might want to look up Celia Storm and see if she moved on or disappeared."

"I don't have to look her up. She was an agent who was trying to get close to Travers. And you're right. She disappeared about that time." He stared at Kaydee, making the woman squirm.

"Just ask the question and stop scaring her," Dela said, moving closer to Kaydee for support.

"Did they mention a name or anything that could help us determine if it was our agent?"

"Not before I bumped something and had to get away from where I was." Kaydee touched her head. "Are you about finished? My head's starting to hurt."

"Yeah. Thanks. We have a guard stationed outside your room. No one but your family and law enforcement are allowed in here," Quinn said, before turning to the door.

Heath walked up, said a prayer in Cayuse, and headed to the door.

"I'll send Tawii in to sit with you. I need to talk to those two." Dela walked away from the bed.

"Please put these people where they belong. Now that Sonny won't be beating on me, I want to stay here with my family."

Dela nodded. "I'll try my best."

In the hall, Quinn was talking to the guard. Heath stood on the other side of the hall waiting for her. When she walked up, he wrapped his arms around her.

"You gave me a scare today. I wish you wouldn't rush into things without talking it over first." Heath released her when she pushed out of his arms.

Dela took a step back to peer into his eyes. "I couldn't have done things any differently. If Jacob and I hadn't been there to see them hauling Kaydee away, she would have been dead by the time anyone found her under that bush."

"I know why you had to find her. Save her. But please, think about the people who care about you before you do something like that again."

She knew he could have been arguing or yelling at her, but he kept his tone low, almost intimate, as he admonished her. "I'll try, but I can't guarantee."

Quinn walked over, watching the two of them. "Did I give you two enough time?"

"Do you think Celia was in the warehouse?" Dela asked. "Have you heard from Milo?"

"They did find women in the warehouse, but not Celia. Julia also got away. They only found four men who were inside the building with the women. So far, the men aren't talking. The agents took the women to the Portland office to be checked out and interviewed."

"We have to find Julia and nail Travers," Dela said, her desire to take the two down heightened by hearing Kaydee's account of things. "We need to get the Wadass family to turn on Travers."

That was the answer. She studied Heath and Quinn. They didn't say anything for nearly a minute. She assumed they were running all they'd heard through their minds and trying to figure out the best way to bring them down.

"Let me get some feelers out in my agency and see what we can come up with that might make them talk." Quinn started to walk away and then turned back.

"Dela, next time, wait for me to get back to you." He spun on his heel and walked down the hall.

She glared at his back and spotted Heath watching her. "Don't you have people to interview?"

"We locked them up until they want to talk. Let's go for a drive." Heath put his arm around her shoulders and led her down the hall, through the waiting area, and out to his tribal vehicle. He opened the passenger door and waited for her to get in before he closed the door and rounded the front of the vehicle.

She hated it when he was so calm. It meant he'd been thinking a lot about something. She worried this little escapade had him changing his mind about the wedding and possibly marrying her at all. Now that she'd decided it was what she wanted, she desired it to happen.

He slid in behind the steering wheel and cranked the ignition.

"Where are we going?" Dela asked in a softer tone of voice.

"To gather evidence." He pulled out of the hospital parking lot and headed toward the freeway. But instead of entering the freeway, he went under it and through Pendleton, heading to Highway 11.

"Do you think they left evidence near the bushes where they were dumping Kaydee?" she asked.

"Nope. We already went over that." He continued driving.

What was in this direction? It dawned on her. "We're going to Kaydee's house. What makes you think we'll find something there?" Dela leaned forward, watching the side roads for any vehicles she thought might be part of the drug dealing.

"If the cartel is looking for the money Kaydee took or possibly the money Sonny had, they might have gone back to look for it after we took Sonny's body away."

A light clicked in Dela's brain. "Did you go through his truck? Kaydee said the money was kept in a metal box under the hood of his truck."

"No one looked under the hood that I know of. I found the body on the ground next to the truck. Like he was getting in to go somewhere when he was killed. We can pop the hood and take a look."

As they drove past Horace Running Bear's house, the old man was standing outside.

"Can you turn around, so I can tell Horace we found Kaydee. His information helped me piece things together."

Heath turned the vehicle around, and they drove up to the man's house. He sat on the top step of the porch.

"Did you find her?" he asked when Dela stepped out of the tribal vehicle.

"We did. She's going to need to mend, but she's alive and her children will have their mother." Dela sat on the step next to the man. "Your information helped us find her. Thank you for talking to me."

"It was the right thing to do. We can't have outsiders coming in here and trying to kill us from the inside. We have to remain strong and survive as our ancestors did. It is up to us to heal the earth. We can't do that if we let others make us sick."

"*K*ʷ*yáam*," Heath said. "We must work together to keep our people strong."

"Have you seen anything else unusual on this road?" Dela asked.

"Two men went by about thirty minutes ago in a

van. Not the camper type I've been seeing. This was like a utility van. No windows except in the front."

"Which way were they going?" Heath asked.

"Toward Duke's place."

"Thanks," Heath said, motioning for Dela to stand.

She thanked Horace again for his help and walked over to the tribal vehicle.

"Cloud of dust coming. That might be them!" Horace called out.

Dela hopped into the SUV as Heath turned it around and managed to get to the end of the driveway before the van came around a corner. The van slowed as if it caught sight of the tribal vehicle.

As the white van passed, two men sat in the bucket seats.

"Those look like the two that were at the warehouse this morning and with Travers at Hamley," Dela said.

"Let's follow them," Heath said, pulling out behind the van.

Chapter Twenty-one

The vehicle continued at a normal speed for five miles before taking a bridge across the Umatilla River. They made a quick right, and at the next fork, made a left.

"That's all dirt roads out there," Dela said, wondering what the two were doing driving roads on the reservation as if they knew them as well as a local.

"Yeah, it is. They have to know we're behind them. Out here, it isn't easy to lose a tail." Heath dropped back a bit. "We can see them easily. Let's give them a bit of wiggle room."

Dela couldn't believe Heath was being so laid back. "Why don't you just pull them over?"

"For what? They'd just say I was harassing them. If they are up to no good, we'll find out soon enough."

They followed the vehicle across ridgelines heading southeast.

"This is Kanine Road," Heath said. "It comes out at Deadman's Pass Wayside."

"Why would they go there?" Dela sat back in her seat. "Do you think this is the road they are using to bring in the drugs? It would keep them from being seen going through Mission."

"That's a good guess. But with us following them, they'll have to change their route."

Trees started popping up on both sides of the road. "You need to get closer or we'll lose them in these trees," Dela said, trying to catch sight of the van ahead of them.

"Look for dust," Heath said.

"It's too early for dust here. There are still small patches of snow in the shaded areas." Dela peered through the trees as the road curved up the ridge and over the top.

When they pulled into the wayside parking area, she didn't see the van. "We missed it. They're probably headed back to Pendleton on the freeway." Disappointment vibrated in her body. She'd wanted to get the two men who seemed to be Travers' right-hand goons.

They pulled over behind the restroom building, and Heath made a call to Quinn. When he finished, he shifted in his seat to face Dela. She took her eyes off the parking lot long enough to listen. "Quinn said he went back through the last things they learned about Celia Storm before she went missing. He'd like you to call Marty and tell him to release the video you have of Celia to the FBI."

Dela pulled out her phone. She texted Marty, telling him to give the Celia Storm video to the FBI. Then she asked him to pull up all the video footage he could find on both Julia Rivera and Dillon Travers.

Specifically, who they met and talked to.

The white van appeared out of the trees from Kanine Road. "There they are. What were they up to while we sat here?" she asked.

The van sped through the parking area and onto the interstate, headed west.

Heath started his vehicle and drove over to Kanine Road. "They had to have met someone or deposited something in the trees."

Dela's heart sped up. "They were coming from Duke's place. Do you think they had Celia and dumped her like the other two tried to do with Kaydee?"

"Maybe we can see where they came out of the trees." Heath drove slowly with them both hanging out the windows, staring at the dirt alongside the road.

Dela spotted the tracks coming onto the road. "Here!" she exclaimed and opened the door before Heath stopped the vehicle.

"Careful, we don't know if that's someone who went in to pick up what they dumped off." Heath put a hand on her arm, slowing her pace. They walked side by side along the tracks. A hundred yards in, they saw what looked like a pile of garbage. As they approached, something slipped out from under a bag.

"It's a foot," Dela said, and hurried forward. She and Heath pulled the garbage bags back.

Mrs. Wadass lay on the ground, her body in an odd shape. Blood covered her torso, and her face had bruises. Dela knelt to check for a pulse as Heath called it in.

"She's alive. But they better hurry." Dela glanced at Heath, who knelt beside her, checking the woman's wounds. He was a certified Medicolegal Death

Investigator.

"I need a first aid kit. Her wounds are severe." He stood and took off running back the way they had walked in.

Waiting for Heath and the kit, Dela ripped the bottom of Mrs. Wadass's long shirt and folded it to hold against the wound in the woman's abdomen. She didn't understand why they didn't shoot her in the head or straight through the heart. They would have known she was dead. Leaving her like this made it likely she could live to point a finger at them.

The woman's eyes fluttered and her eyelids rose halfway.

Dela couldn't tell if the woman was coherent or not. "Mrs. Wadass, I'm Dela Alvaro. Detective Seaver went to his vehicle to get a first aid kit. An ambulance is on the way."

The woman made a noise so faint that Dela couldn't hear it. She leaned down. "What did you say?"

"Don't. I must die for my sins." A gurgling sound followed the words.

"You can relieve your conscience by telling me where to find Celia Storm." Dela hoped they would find the FBI agent alive.

"Too late. Duke…Duke…" Her voice faded, and her breathing stopped. The blood no longer gushed out of her wound.

Dela sat back on her haunches and stared at the woman. Such a loss. So many losses. All because of the drug cartel. Anger knotted her body.

"Here's the kit." Heath stopped beside her, breathing hard. He put a hand on her shoulder and knelt, slowly unfisting her hands. "What happened?"

"She didn't make it. Why didn't they outright kill her and not make her suffer?" Dela stared at the woman's unseeing eyes.

"Cartels are like that. They prefer to have their victims suffer. The good news is we can arrest those two because we know they dumped this body."

Dela held her hand out to Heath to help her to her feet. He stood and pulled her up beside him. She wrapped her arms around his waist and leaned against him. "She didn't want help. She believed she deserved to die for her sins."

"Did she say anything else?"

"I asked about Celia. She said 'too late' and kept repeating Duke's name. She sounded like she was drowning."

"The shot to the chest could have put a hole in her lungs which would have sucked in blood from the body cavity." Heath hugged her then held her away from him. "Are you good now? We need to work the scene so once the others get here, we can go after the two in the van."

"Did you call it in, so a state or county officer could detain them?" Dela had the license plate memorized.

"Call Quinn and tell him what we know while I take photos and check her out."

Dela pulled out her phone and scrolled through her contacts for Quinn.

He answered right away. "What do you have?"

"We followed a white van license," she recited the plate number and letters, "we lost it and backtracked its tire tracks and found Mrs. Wadass with a bullet hole and bruises as if they'd beaten her. She has expired since we found her. Heath is gathering evidence while we wait for a team to show up."

"Where are you?"

She told him their location and what the woman said. "It sounds like Celia is most likely dead and disposed of."

"Damn! I was afraid of that. Few agents make it out of a cartel alive if they have been compromised."

"Mrs. Wadass seemed to be worried about Duke. Do you have anyone keeping an eye on him?" Dela asked.

"We do. I'll check in with him." Quinn cleared his throat and said, "Good news. All but one of the women we found at the warehouse are willing to testify against Julia and the six men they saw while being held. They were angriest at Julia. It seemed she was the meanest to them and the one who lured them into the trap."

"If you catch her first, don't give her any incentives to give up Travers. She is lower than he is and doesn't deserve anything less than the maximum for what she's done." Dela also knew if she found Julia first, the woman would regret ever laying eyes on her.

"What do you mean if I catch her first? You better not be going after her. This is strictly FBI business."

Changing the subject, she asked, "Are you sending any agents up here?"

"No. I think tribal and county can take care of it."

"Then get out there and find Julia. She needs to be off the streets before more people are killed." Dela ended the call as a county deputy and the sheriff walked out of the trees.

They walked up to Heath, shook hands with him, and nodded to her.

"We weren't sure if we should drive in or not," the sheriff said.

"Have your deputy make a casting of the tire tracks. Then vehicles can get closer," Heath said, and turned to her. "Sheriff Walters, this is Dela Alvaro, head of security at the casino."

"Pleased to meet you, but I don't understand what you're doing here." The sheriff's gaze traveled from her to Heath and back to her.

Dela decided to let Heath do the talking.

"Dela has been helping both the tribal police and the FBI to take down a drug and trafficking ring on the reservation. She was with me when we spotted the van." Heath went on to explain how they'd followed the van, lost it, and then found the tracks that led to the woman.

"Sounds like you have quite the mess going on here," Sheriff Walters said. "What can I do to help?"

"If I'm gone when forensics arrives, make sure they take all the garbage bags, just in case there is something in them that could help us with the case."

As Heath talked, Dela began wandering around, looking for anything that was out of place. When she couldn't see anything and felt her body losing energy from the adrenaline blasts she'd experienced today, she walked over to Heath's vehicle and sat in the passenger seat with the door open.

The Tribal Police Chief and Jacob arrived. Heath filled them in as a forensic team arrived, along with a van to take the body to the state pathologist. Once everyone was busy doing their jobs, Heath walked over to his vehicle and slid behind the steering wheel. He grasped her hand and squeezed. "How are you doing?

You've had a busy day."

"I'm hungry and want to go home and soak in the bathtub." The longer she sat, the more exhausted she felt.

"I'll take you home. Call Molly and see if she can bring you a pizza." He started the vehicle.

"What are you going to do?" Dela asked, thinking he'd had a busy day as well.

"I need to go to the police station and finish my report on the two who dumped Kaydee, type up her interview, and then catch up with what Quinn has found out." He drove with one hand while still holding her hand.

She loved how he knew when she needed his strength and when she wanted to be alone.

"Go ahead, call Molly. You need to tell her about the wedding date anyway." He kissed the back of her hand before he released it.

Dela pulled out her phone, scrolled for Molly's number, and touched the icon.

"Hey, Dela. How's the bride to be?" Molly answered.

A grin tugged at Dela's mouth. "Exhausted. I'll tell you all about it when you bring a pizza over. Heath and I picked a date, and I want you and Rosie to help me with the wedding."

"What about your mom? She has done nothing but talk about this wedding for years. How will she feel about us taking over?"

Dela glanced at Heath and smiled. "Heath told her that I wanted you and Rosie to help me. It will be in her backyard, so she can still help, just only with that part. You and Rosie know me well. I don't want anything big or fancy."

"We would be happy to help. And yes, we know exactly what you like. When do you want me there?"

"Give me an hour. I want a bath first."

"What happened?" Molly's voice held concern.

"I'll tell you later, but we found Kaydee. See you in an hour."

Heath had taken the exit off the freeway and was driving toward their house. She smiled. Until he proposed, she'd always thought of the house as hers. She bought it, remodeled it, and asked him to move in as a roommate when he returned to Nixyáawii. But his being in the house with her made it a home. Whether they were married or not.

He parked in the driveway and hurried around to her side of the vehicle.

"You don't need to escort me to the door, I can make it," she said, slapping his hand as he tried to slip it under her arm.

"You look exhausted. Don't fall asleep in the bathtub." He kissed her cheek. "I'll try not to be too late."

"You do what you have to do to bring peace to the reservation." She meant it. They had to rid the reservation of fear.

"Enjoy the pizza and time with Molly." He kissed her cheek again and headed back to his vehicle.

Dela laughed at the happy barks and brays coming from the pasture. She unlocked the door and let herself inside, locking the door behind her. She knew better than to leave any door unlocked. Two people had broken into her house and tried to kill her. One she'd killed and the other managed to get away, but was brought to justice later.

She walked straight through to the French doors. Unlocked those and then across the yard to open the gate and let Mugshot and Jethro into the yard. They were the best security system. They always let her know if there was a stranger around.

She scratched both of them behind the ears and gave Jethro some grain and Mugshot dog food. "You two hang out here in the yard while I take a bath."

Closing and locking the French doors, she walked down the hall to her bedroom and bathroom. She started the water running into the bathtub and stood in front of the bathroom mirror. She noticed dark and glistening stains on her shirt. The darker dried blood was from Kaydee, and the still-wet blood from Mrs. Wadass. She took off her shirt and shoved it in the trash can. Back in her bedroom, she stripped and removed her prosthesis.

Using crutches, she carried a fresh set of sweats and a t-shirt into the bathroom. She placed the crutches against the wall beside the towel bar and used the grab bars to get in and lower her body into the hot, bubbly bath water.

Chapter Twenty-two

Mugshot barking and pounding on the door brought Dela out of the trance she'd been in. The cool water around her body caused her to gasp. She splashed, trying to grasp the grab bar and pull her body up out of the tub.

Footsteps hurrying down the hall had her grabbing for a towel.

"Dela! Dela!" Molly called.

"I'm fine! I'm in the tub," she called back.

The door flew open, and Molly's and Rosie's heads appeared. The concern on their faces brought tears to her eyes.

"I'm okay. I must have dozed off. Go set things up in the kitchen, I'll be out as soon as I get some clothes on."

Rosie smiled and disappeared. Molly studied her for a few more seconds before she backed up and closed the door.

Breathing a sigh of relief that it had been her

friends, she finished getting out of the tub, dried off, and put her sweats and t-shirt on. Using her crutches, she swung down the hall to the kitchen.

The aroma of pepperoni, pizza sauce, and cheese filled the air. One spot had iced tea and a plate, another had a large soda and a plate, and another place had juice and a plate. Beside that plate was a notepad and pen.

Rosie was in the living room petting Mugshot. Molly stood by the window looking out.

"Thank you for coming and bringing pizza," Dela said, taking the chair with the iced tea.

Rosie walked to the sink and washed her hands before sitting in front of the large soda. That left Molly to sit at the juice and notepad.

"I'm glad I had the spare key you gave me. When you weren't answering the door, we both thought something had happened to you," Molly said.

"I'm sorry. I didn't realize how exhausted I was." Dela sipped her iced tea.

"That's okay. We know you're safe now. So, when's the date?" Molly asked.

"Where did you find Kaydee?" Rosie asked. Which got her a glare from Molly.

Dela pulled a large piece of pizza onto her plate and met both women's gazes. "We picked September sixth as the date for the wedding. You'll have to help me decide on the time, then we can pick invitations and address them. That way we can keep a cap on the size."

Both women nodded. Molly wrote down the date.

Dela peered into Rosie's eyes and told her about discovering the warehouse, taking Jacob with her, and then following the van and finding Kaydee.

"Oh! No wonder you are exhausted and needed a

bath," Molly said.

Dela shook her head. "That wasn't all of it." She told them about her and Heath heading to look for evidence and spotting the van. And what they found.

"Mrs. Wadass? Why?" Rosie asked.

"She was in as deep as her sons in the drug dealing on the reservation," Dela said.

"No! Really?" Rosie shook her head. "She seemed like a good woman. One who would want to honor her ancestors."

"She seemed worried about Duke before she died." Dela couldn't get the woman's plaintive call to her son out of her head.

Molly pulled another piece of pizza onto her plate and said, "Let's talk about happier things. Like the wedding."

The rest of the evening was spent discussing a theme for the wedding, which Dela hadn't thought was necessary, but according to Molly, it would help them pull things together if they had a theme.

"You could do a western theme. Heath looks good in a western shirt," Rosie said and giggled.

Dela rolled her eyes. "Let me ask him what he wants to wear. He likes traditional clothing." She thought he looked handsome in his deerskin shirt and the leggings his mom made for him when he returned to the reservation.

"But if he wears traditional clothes, what will you wear?" Molly asked.

Rosie gave Dela's leg a nudge under the table. Rosie knew Dela believed she was related to the Thunder family, but Molly didn't know that. Dela and Heath were keeping it quiet until they had proof.

"Whatever I wear has to be either pants, a long skirt, or a dress that covers my prosthesis."

"I bet my mom could make a jumpsuit that would look darling on you," Rosie said. "She loves coming up with fun clothing."

Dela liked that idea. A jumpsuit would be practical from the standpoint that no one would see her prosthesis, and she'd seen some nice ones in magazines. "Do I need to give her some pictures of ones I like?"

"That would help."

"You're sure you want a jumpsuit? That's not very sexy," Molly said.

Dela studied her friend. "I don't want to be sexy when I get married. I just want to make our commitment binding, to make everyone around us happy."

"Is that the only reason you're marrying Heath? To make us happy?" Molly looked disappointed.

"We've been living together for the last few years, and nothing, not even my being a suspect in a murder, has separated us. Why do we need a ceremony to show we belong together?" Dela had tried to get that across to her mom, but she didn't understand it. And Heath, while he agreed, was also traditional and felt they should marry.

"Okay, let's move on. You said the wedding will be in Deborah and Lance's backyard. That means we won't need any extra flowers except for the tables at the reception."

"Mom said the only flowers to worry about were the bridal bouquet and what you two carry. She'll take care of the rest. I'm thinking, she'll have cut flowers from the flower beds for the tables and anywhere else you think they are needed." She hoped they all didn't go overboard with flowers. While Dela liked the color and the scents, she didn't like being bathed in them.

"That will help your budget," Molly said.

"Oh! I don't know what a good budget is for a wedding or what Heath is willing to help pay for." Dela hadn't thought about the cost. She'd been so busy putting it off, she hadn't thought about any of that.

"We'll keep it low. What about the reception? Depending on the time of day, it can be just cake and punch, or it can be dinner," Rosie said. "And I can guarantee if you want to do dinner, the casino will help cater it."

"But the price?" Dela said.

"All the casino employees will pay a little bit into the cost as your wedding gift. I'm sure it will be manageable for you and Heath to pick up the rest."

"But will they all want to come if they help with the cost?" Dela didn't like the idea of all the casino employees at her wedding and reception. She'd already told her mom that it would be a limited number. "Let's do cake and punch."

"They won't come. They'll be at work." Rosie shook her head. "They all want to be a part of your happiness, even if they aren't there in person. Don't you understand? You mean a lot to this reservation. The women you've found and the murders you've solved have made you a part of us. The way you treat the casino employees like family, they all see that and want to give you something in return."

Dela couldn't wrap her head around what Rosie was saying. She figured it was due to her exhaustion. "Do you have enough to get started? I'm finding it hard to keep my eyes open. I think I need to go to bed."

Rosie picked up the dishes and put them in the sink. Molly flipped over the sheets on her notepad and slipped it into her purse.

"We get the message. You need sleep and are tired of talking about the wedding." Molly hugged her. "I'll talk to you tomorrow."

"Sounds good." Dela let Molly out the door and turned to find Rosie watching her.

"How's Kaydee?" Rosie asked.

"She was beaten up pretty bad. You wouldn't recognize her. But she's alive and she is willing to testify against the woman who lured her to the van and her in-laws that she figured out were selling drugs as well as her husband."

Tears glistened in Rosie's eyes. "She is a sweet woman who didn't deserve that."

"No one deserves what they did to her. They were putting her under a bush beside the road like garbage." Dela felt her anger growing. "It made me furious then, and it still makes me want to hit something when I think about it. No one deserves to be treated like that. They even threw bags of garbage on top of Mrs. Wadass to keep people from noticing an old lady's body in the woods."

"That's horrible! Can I help?"

Dela thought about Rosie saying she'd talked to Celia. "Remember the dealer, Celia, I asked you about?"

"Yeah."

"She's missing, and she's an FBI agent who was undercover."

"No wonder she asked so many questions. What

did you want to know?"

"Did she ever say anything that might give us a clue as to where to find her? Did she talk about a favorite place or meeting anyone, like a boyfriend somewhere special?"

Rosie sat down on the couch and stared at the blank television. "She mentioned falling hard for someone she shouldn't have. And her eyes lit up like there were stars in them." Rosie snapped her fingers. "She mentioned the two of them going skiing and staying at his place."

Dela smiled. That would give her something to check out. See if Travers had a house near a ski lodge. If Travers was as infatuated with Celia as she was with him, he may have hidden her away from the feds and Julia.

Chapter Twenty-three

Excited barking woke Dela from a deep sleep. She glanced at the clock and saw it was eleven. She'd been asleep for three hours.

"Shhh. We don't want to wake—"

"I'm awake," she said, rolling to face the door and turn on the bedside lamp.

"I didn't want to wake you, but Mugshot had other ideas." Heath patted the dog's large head and sat on the bed beside her. "Did you get some sleep?"

"Yeah. How did your reports go?" She yawned and rolled onto her back.

"Slow progress, but they are finished until we can get the suspects we pulled in to talk. State Police picked up the two in the van."

Dela perked up. "That's good news. I suppose they lawyered up."

"They did. But forensics found traces of blood in the van they were driving and that we believe dumped the body. They can see if it matches Mrs. Wadass."

"That's really good news." Dela decided to tell Heath what she'd learned from Rosie. She sat up against the headboard. "Rosie came over with Molly. After we had hashed out some of the wedding stuff, she stayed and asked about Kaydee. I asked her if she could remember anything Celia might have said when they visited at the deli. Rosie said she was definitely in love with the person she talked about and that he had taken her skiing near where he lived."

Heath had stood to take off his clothes. He stopped and stared at her. "What are you thinking?"

"That maybe Travers has Celia hidden away from the FBI and Julia. From the way they couldn't keep their eyes off each other in the video I watched, I think he fell as hard for her as she did for him. He may be protecting her from Julia." Dela watched as Heath continued undressing and walked into the bathroom to shower. The water went on, and he stuck his head back out. "That's a good idea. You should run it by Quinn in the morning." His head disappeared, and Dela slid down in bed. She had till morning to decide if Quinn would take her seriously, or not.

The following morning, Dela called Quinn while Heath watched. They had been sitting at the table eating breakfast when Heath told her to call Quinn and mention what she'd learned.

"Dela, we are still working on finding Celia and Julia," Quinn answered.

"Good to hear you're looking for them."

Heath shook his head as if to say, don't taunt the man.

"I'm driving to see if we can get more out of the

two you told us about yesterday. The blood in the van came back as a match to the Wadass woman. It should be enough to get them to talk about something."

"That's good to know. I was talking to Rosie last night. She said Celia had mentioned the man she was head over heels in love with had taken her skiing near his house. You might—"

"Celia wasn't seeing anyone when she accepted the assignment. She was just telling that to Rosie because she learned how nosey she was. I have to go." The call went silent.

Dela held the phone out in front of her and glared at it.

"What did he say?"

"That Celia didn't have a boyfriend when she accepted the assignment, and she just told that to Rosie because she was nosey. He didn't even give me time to tell him what I observed." Anger boiled in her chest. She slammed her phone down too hard on the table and regretted it. "Sorry." Then she studied Heath. "That is why I end up doing things myself. He doesn't listen or thinks he knows more than he does."

Heath reached across the table and gave her hand a squeeze. "I listen, and I think you might be on to something. I have to find Duke. Since he was released, no one has seen him. The cartel may have been cleaning up loose ends after we started pulling in their members." He released her hand and touched her chin. "When you discover this place you believe Travers is keeping Celia, call me. We'll figure out how to get there. Don't pull anyone else into going with you because I may not be ready to go as soon as you find out."

She stared into his eyes and knew he believed in her and wanted to protect her. Dela pressed her hands on the table, leaned across, and kissed him, then said, "I will wait for you to go with me. I trust you with my life."

He smiled, kissed her back, and pushed away from the table. "Now that that's settled, I can get on with my day. Call me as soon as you figure it out. I'll have to find someone to cover for me."

"I will. Thank you." It was a heady feeling knowing the man she was binding herself to for the rest of her life listened to her and believed in her.

Heath walked down the hall to grab his gun and jacket. As much as she liked him in uniform, she appreciated the way he wore civilian clothes. He'd dressed in civies to get answers about Duke and figured that by being out of uniform, more people would respond to his questions than if he wore his uniform. Many on the reservation still had trouble believing not everyone on the tribal police was dirty. After dealing with a crooked tribal detective, she understood their mistrust.

Dela cleaned up the kitchen and swung down the hall to get dressed for her meeting with Farley at the Cayuse Conference room at nine. She'd texted him as soon as she woke to make the meeting. She'd put him to work looking for residences owned by Travers that were near ski resorts.

After about two hours of Farley tapping away on his laptop, he had three possibilities. It appeared the head of the cartel used his money to purchase properties near resort areas. "Some of these have the woman's name as owner as well," he said, sliding a printout across the table to Dela.

She noted he'd highlighted the ones that only had Travers' name. "He must have purchased these without Julia knowing. Which would make them a great place to hide a lover." Dela was impressed that the man would step out on a vicious woman like Julia.

"Thank you for doing this after Marty had you work overtime to put those videos together for me." Dela stood. She was ready to head to work and ask Rosie if any of the places had been mentioned by Celia. Luckily, two places had a management company taking care of them. She could call and pretend she was told to contact Travers, and he wasn't responding. Did they know if he was at that residence?

"No problem, I'm going home to sleep now." Farley picked up his laptop and walked her down the hall to the entrance. "You aren't planning on going to those places alone, are you?"

"No. Heath said when I figured out which one, he'd go with me."

"Good. You've done too many heroic things. After a while, even those with the best of luck can get unlucky." He walked to his vehicle and dropped into the driver's seat.

Dela waved and walked over to her car. She spotted the van on the opposite side of her car moments before a man leaped out of the vehicle. Pivoting on her good foot, she took off at a run for the front of the Cayuse building. She spotted two men coming out through the glass front. Not slowing, she burst between them as they opened the double doors. She stopped at the reception desk, out of breath and her stub complaining. "Call… security…, please." She managed between gulps of air.

The woman picked up the phone, and Dela glanced out the front windows. The two men who exited the building were out front, confronting the man. One had him by the arm. The van peeled out of the parking lot.

Two men in blazers and wearing earbuds appeared at the desk.

"That man, those two are detaining, tried to take me." She knew everyone on the reservation was tired of women and children being abducted.

The security guards jogged out the door and took over, pulling the man into the building.

"Is this the man?" one of them asked Dela.

"Yes. He was parked by my car and came after me when I was leaving." She hid the smug smile she wanted to give the man.

"We'll call the tribal police. Stay here so they can get your statement." They both forced the man ahead of them through a set of doors.

Dela pulled out her phone and texted Heath. *Someone from the cartel tried to grab me at Cayuse. They will be calling to have a tribal arrest the man. The van took off.*

Are you okay? Heath replied.

I'm fine. Noticed the van and as soon as the door opened, I ran for the building. I have the information we need. Well, part of it. Tell you if you come here, otherwise, you'll hear from me later.

I doubt I'll be the one coming. I've been at Sonny and Duke's houses looking for evidence to tie them to the cartel and anything that might tell me where Duke is.

Ok. Good luck.

Dela ended the texting as a tribal police vehicle pulled up to the front of the building. A smile spread across her face. It was Tabitha Shaw. The newest tribal officer, who had lots of grit and determination.

"Hey, Dela, what are you doing here?" Tabitha asked, entering the building.

"I'm the reason you're here." Dela led her over to the two chairs in the lobby and told her what had happened. "I've seen enough of those vans lately to know that it was someone from the cartel and that they aren't happy with me."

Tabitha had written down all she was told. "And for good reason. You've been getting them arrested like crazy and catching them doing illegal things. I was so happy to hear that Kaydee was found by you and Jacob. Not that I can't work with the feds, but I like it when the tribals kick butt."

Dela nodded and smiled. "Now that you have my statement, can I go?"

"Yes, if I have any questions, I know where to find you." She waved her hand up and down.

Dela had dressed for work. She hadn't been sure if she'd make it back home before she had to go in for her shift. "Yes, I'll be at the casino most of the rest of the day. Thanks." She stood and walked out the door, keeping a lookout for the van.

Not seeing one, she slipped into her car, locked the doors, and drove out of the parking lot and over to the casino employee parking lot. She made two circles around the parking lot to make sure there weren't any vans lurking close by before she parked, exited her vehicle, and hurried to the employee's entrance.

Margie was at the podium checking in a new hire.

Dela walked by, smiled, and headed to her desk. She pulled out her phone and scrolled for Marty's number. Tapping it, she waited for his voicemail to say he was busy and the ding.

"I was checking in to see what you did with the videos I requested." After leaving the message, she sat in her chair, thinking. She was a few hours early to take over for Kenny. She had planned to be here early to review the videos. But since she didn't know where to find them, she decided to see if Rosie was at work and run the names of the places by her.

"Are you here officially?" Margie asked as the new hire walked up to Dela.

"Not yet. I have a few things to do. I'll contact Kenny shortly." She turned her attention to the new security guard. Kenny must have passed the names of the people she'd starred from past interviews. HR would have gone down the list and hired people to replace Kurt and Phil. However, this person didn't look familiar. She usually remembered the people she interviewed. Especially, the ones that she put a star by their names.

She held out her hand. "Dela Alvaro, I'm head of security. You'll be working under me."

The man's eyebrows shot up. "You don't remember me, do you?"

She studied him for several seconds. His face was angular, his lips full, his eyes were a soft gray, and his hair was military short. "I'm sorry. I don't."

"Private Henderson, quit playing cards and get this cell cleaned out!" he shouted.

Dela took a step back and looked him up and

down. "No way…" Then she studied the eyes and the man smiled. "Spencer Henderson, you have grown into a man. You were a boy when you were sent to be part of our detail." Her thoughts were churning. She remembered the young recruit who had arrived at her detention center a week before her Humvee was hit. How he remembered her was remarkable. And that he would end up here, working for the casino, was even more so.

The man standing before her in a security uniform grinned. "I wasn't sure what to do with myself when my second tour ended. Then I read something about a head of security for a casino who had found a kidnapped child, and thought, I wanted to work for someone who had that much dedication to a job. Then I found out it was you, and I knew I had to get hired."

The reunion was sweet and sad. She knew the only reason Spencer hadn't been in that Humvee with the rest of them was something he'd eaten. He'd been in the latrine all night throwing up his guts. She'd replaced him at the last minute with Sanchez. Who took the brunt of the explosion.

"I'm glad to have someone on the team I know I can trust. You're taking the place of someone who was caught in illegal activities while on duty." She studied him. "We'll catch up another time. I have some things to do. Margie, call Kenny and have him give Spencer a tour of the casino and show him what his job will be."

"Yes, Ma'am," Margie said.

Dela glanced at the woman who gave her a wink. Shaking her head, she said, "See you around," to Spencer and headed to the deli.

Her mind was still whirling with the sight of

Spencer and how he'd come here to work for her. All she could remember of the man was he'd been fresh out of high school and from the looks of him now, hadn't grown to his full height or musculature.

Stepping into the deli, she was pleased to see Rosie visiting with a customer.

Dela stepped into line and waited for her turn to get to the counter.

Rosie smiled when Dela stepped in front of her. "Iced tea, please, and do you have a minute?"

"I do. It's time for a break." She told the woman beside her she was going on break, and then she filled a cup with iced tea and one with soda and motioned for Dela to find a table.

They chose one at the back of the seating area, away from the noise of the casino. Most people were seated closer to the opening.

"What's up?" Rosie asked.

"I have some places I'm going to read. Tell me if one of them might have been mentioned by Celia." Dela pulled the folded piece of paper out of her pocket. She read the three names she had.

"The last one sounds familiar, but I couldn't swear it's because Celia mentioned it." Rosie shrugged. "Sorry."

"That's okay. I thought that might make it faster to find it." Dela sipped her tea. Spencer was still floating around in the back of her mind.

"You look distracted. You aren't planning a way to go check out all those places by yourself, are you?" Rosie said.

"No. Heath told me when I whittled it down, he'd go with me since Quinn won't even listen to me." She

spun her straw back and forth between two fingers.
"I'm not sure how I feel about a new hire in the security
department."

"Did they have a bad background check?" Rosie
asked.

"No. I was his superior in the Army." Dela peered
into Rosie's eyes. "I need to get over it. He'll be great. I
can see him working his way up to Kenny's position,
and then I will have two people I can count on to take
over when I want some time off."

Rosie put her hand on Dela's arm. "Get over what?
Were you and he…"

Dela stared into her friend's eyes. "Were we
what?"

"You know. Were you close, and you're worried
your feelings will come up and Heath—"

"Oh, hell no!" Dela laughed. "He was straight out
of high school. He hadn't moved up the ladder any
farther than cleaning up the detention cells and working
in the mess hall." She stopped and saw the whole
conversation she'd had with him the morning they were
to head out on a detail. "He'd been throwing up in the
latrine all night and was supposed to go on my last
detail. I told him to stay behind and get well. The
person I replaced him with…" She swallowed and
stared at the straw she was now squeezing between her
fingers. "That person flew in a thousand pieces
when…" she released her straw and tried to take a
drink, but the plastic was so mangled she couldn't suck
anything up. She ripped the lid off the cup and gulped,
shoving down the fear and horror she'd felt watching
the Humvee explode and her comrades going all
different directions.

"It's okay. You're not there anymore. You're about to get married." Rosie's soft voice broke through the memories.

Dela shook her head. "You're right, I'm here and I'm about to get married." But what about the ones who didn't make it home or were too disabled to ever have the chance to marry? Her heart felt heavy with grief for those who weren't as lucky.

"Speaking of the wedding. I did send out a memo to everyone that if they wished to contribute to your wedding reception, they could give money to Brenda in accounting. She'll keep a tally and has a card for contributors to sign. You'll know how much will be covered by those wishing you a wonderful wedding." Rosie smiled broadly.

"Thank you for doing that. I need to start making calls to see if I can narrow down which of these places Travers could be. Thanks for being such a good friend." Dela meant it. Rosie might be able to get strangers to tell her secrets, but she would never tell her friends' secrets to anyone.

"Let me know if you have any luck." Rosie stood, then she narrowed her eyes. "You aren't going there alone, are you?"

Dela laughed. "No. Heath told me he'd go with me. He'd take time off to go, since Quinn isn't taking me seriously."

"That's good! I was worried for a minute. Please, take Heath. Don't be impatient." Rosie studied her.

"I promised Heath I would wait for him."

Rosie nodded and went back to work. Dela decided the deli was as quiet as she'd get, other than the office, to make her calls.

Chapter Twenty-four

After making her phone calls, Dela narrowed the places Travers and Celia could be to McCall, Idaho or Bozeman, Montana. McCall was only 5 hours away, while Bozeman was nearly twice that.

She texted Heath. *Do you have time to meet for lunch?*

Yes. Did you find out something? He replied.

Yes.

I'll be there in twenty.

She sent him a thumbs-up and wandered to the security office. She needed to see who to put in charge if Heath was willing to make the trip tomorrow.

Kenny was sitting at his desk when she entered. "You're here early," he said.

She remembered she'd told Margie she was going to contact Kenny. With Spencer's appearance and talking to Rosie, she'd forgotten. "Yeah, I'm not officially working yet." She glanced at Margie and then nodded to the room they used to interview and hold people they found doing illegal things in the casino.

Dela walked into the room.

Kenny followed, closing the door behind him. "What's up?"

"I'm sure you've heard that we found Kaydee, and Mrs. Wadass was murdered." She watched the man to see if any of it was a surprise.

He nodded. "When I heard Kaydee was found, I figured that's why you had me work for you last night."

"It was. I had a hunch and it paid off." She glanced at the door and then sat down. "I have another hunch and I need you to fill in for me."

He sat across from her. "Another missing sister?"

"Yes, and no. An FBI agent is missing, and I think I know where she is. Heath is going with me, but I'll need you to cover my shift. Do like you did yesterday, have Nadine fill in for you. Until I tell you otherwise."

His tall brow on his round face wrinkled. "How long will you be gone?"

"If it's the first place I think, two days max. If it's the second place, three days, possibly four."

"Let's hope it's the first place." He smiled.

"That's what I'm hoping. But don't tell anyone what I'm doing. I already had someone from the cartel try to abduct me today."

He glared. "Do we need to walk you to your car?"

"I think I'll ask the new hire to return and walk me to my car."

Kenny studied her. "He said you two were in the Army together. You know him well?"

"Not well, he came just shortly before I was shipped home. But I trust him." She didn't know why but because the young recruit had listened to her and followed all of her orders, she'd seen that he was willing to do the grunt work to get the chance to do more, unlike some who arrived wanting to go out on patrol when they didn't have a clue which way was north or east.

"Do you want me to let him know you'll be talking to him?"

"No. I can do that when I clock on. Right now, I'm headed to have lunch with Heath. After that, I'll be ready to relieve you if you'd like to go home early. It was a lot to ask you to work last night and come in this morning."

"My wife would be happy if I came home early," he said and smiled.

"Then plan on leaving after I get back from lunch."

"Sounds good." Kenny stood, opened the door for her, and then followed her back into the office.

Curiosity had heightened Margie's coloring and her eyes watched Dela closely.

"I'm headed to lunch with Heath. I'll take over from Kenny when I'm done," Dela walked out of the office, down the hall to the door to the casino floor, and her phone buzzed.

She glanced down and saw Marty's name. She slid the icon over.

"Hey, did you get my message?" she asked.

"That's what I'm calling about. I'll be in around two and can set it all up for you," Marty said.

"Sounds good. I'm headed to have lunch with Heath. We should be done by the time you come in. Text me when you get here." She ended the call as Heath walked through the main entrance.

"That's good timing. I was going to text you when I entered." Heath walked up to her and put a hand on her arm. "Where did you want to eat?"

She glanced in the direction of the Pony Grill. Spencer stood on the edge of the slot machine floor near the grill. "Let's go to the Pony. I have someone I want you to meet."

"Sounds good to me." Heath put a hand on her back and they walked toward the Pony.

Dela veered to the right, walking up to Spencer. He smiled and his gaze landed on Heath.

"Spencer, I'd like you to meet my fiancé, Heath Seaver. He's a detective with the tribal police. Heath, this is Spencer Henderson. He was a new recruit with my detachment shortly before I came home. He's now working for casino security."

The two shook hands.

"Welcome to the casino and the reservation," Heath said.

"Thank you, sir."

"You can call me Heath."

"I'll be back to talk to you before your shift is over. I hope this first day hasn't been too boring," Dela said.

Spencer grinned. "I'm figuring out my granny isn't the only crazy old lady."

Dela and Heath laughed.

"I'll talk to you later." Dela headed to the grill.

When they were seated, Heath said, "How long have you known Spencer?"

She told him all what she'd already told Rosie.

"He seems like a good guy," Heath said as the waitress arrived at their table to take their order.

When the waitress left, Dela leaned close to Heath.

"Because of what happened at the Cayuse today, I'm going to have Spencer stay after his shift and walk me to my car when I'm finished tonight."

"That's a good idea. Tabitha filled me in on what you said in your statement. The van was sitting there waiting for you to come out of the Cayuse?"

"Yes. They had to have followed me either from home or were waiting for me at the casino and saw me drive by." This had been running through her head along with all the other stuff going on.

"I also want you to text me when you leave the casino, when you get in your car, and if I'm not home, when you get home." Heath picked up her hand. "Promise me?"

"I will. I don't like the idea I have the cartel waiting to get me any more than you do. I think I've narrowed down the places Travers could have Celia. Either in McCall, Idaho or Bozeman, Montana. When can you be ready to go with me?" Dela sipped her tea and watched Heath.

He appeared to be doing some calculations in his head and asked, "What time do you get off?"

"I planned on midnight. Do you want me to leave earlier?" Dela was ready to hit the road and find Celia.

"Can you get off at nine or ten? That will be a different time than the cartel would suspect, since they have probably worked out your usual schedule. And that would put us in McCall late enough that if we find them there, we can call Quinn and stay there until the Feds arrive and still get back home and only miss one day of work."

Dela studied him. "You had that figured out fast. What if they aren't there?"

"Then we spend the night and head out early for Bozeman. If we can discover them there, we call Quinn, wait for the Feds, and only miss two days of work."

"That works for me."

The waitress arrived with their sandwiches and fries.

Dela nibbled on a fry and said, "I just have to tell Kenny to come back in to finish out the night. I told him he could go home early because I was here early."

"Will he mind?" Heath asked.

"No. He likes overtime. He has three kids."

They finished their meal. "I'll be waiting out front for you at nine. It's more likely the cartel will be looking for you at the employee entrance and not the front. Text me when you're headed out the door, and I'll pull right up in the valet spot."

"Okay. Are you going to pack my clothes? And who will take care of the animals?" Dela asked.

"I'll call Travis and see if he can stay at our place until we get back." Heath finished off his food and leaned back. "I'll go home and pack everything we'll need."

"Like my Sig, crutches, and stub socks?"

"I've lived with you long enough to know exactly what you need." He kissed her cheek. "See you at nine."

She nodded and slid off the chair. Time to clock in and tell Kenny he'd need to come back and that she would for sure not be around tomorrow and possibly the next day.

After clocking in, Dela headed for surveillance. She wanted to see more of the videos of the interaction between Travers and Celia, and see everyone Julia visited.

"Hey, good job finding Kaydee and the dead woman," Marty said when she entered the surveillance office.

"Thanks. I wish Mrs. Wadass had said more than her son's name before she died." Saying the words lit an idea. That was why the cartel wanted her. They were afraid of what the woman might have said before she died. Which meant someone told them she'd spoken before she died.

"I need to send a couple of texts while you set things up." She walked over to a chair and sat. First, she texted Heath. *I think the cartel was after me to see what Mrs. Wadass said to me. You might have a leak in the tribal police.*

Then she sent a text to Quinn. *You might have a leak in your agency. Someone from the cartel tried to grab me this morning. I think it's because they think Mrs. Wadass said something to me before she died.*

Her phone pinged back from Heath. *I'll check on it.*

Her phone rang. It was Quinn. She slid the answer icon.

"What do you mean the cartel almost grabbed you? Why didn't someone call me?" he answered.

"It happened this morning on the reservation. I walked out of the Cayuse building and saw a white van parked on the opposite side of my car. A man jumped out of the van. I ran back into the building, and their security caught him. He's at the Tribal Police Station if you want to talk to him." She glanced at Marty, who was scowling.

"Where are you now?" Quinn asked.

"At work."

"You need to be careful when you leave."

"Heath is picking me up. And you need to see who in your agency is working for the cartel. I have to go." She ended the call.

"Why would the cartel want you?" Marty asked.

"Because Mrs. Wadass was still alive when we found her. But the only thing she said to me was not to help her, she had sinned. I asked her about the missing agent, and she said, 'Too late,' and then just repeated Duke, Duke. She didn't tell me anything the cartel would care about. But they don't know that." She walked over and sat down in front of the monitors. "Let's watch some videos."

♠ ♣ ♥ ♦

It was 9:05 when Dela stepped up to the casino entrance and texted Heath. *Ready.*
She spotted headlights come on and a car driving into the valet lane.

"You're leaving early," Arthur said, from his stool on the left of the door.

"Heath's picking me up. Keep an eye on things. I'll be gone for a couple of days."

"This have anything to do with the Wadasses?" he asked.

"Yeah, a little." She knew Heath would get worried if she didn't step out. "But don't tell anyone."

Arthur made the zipping the lips motion, and she walked through the doors. The passenger door on Heath's truck opened, and she climbed in. By the time she had her seatbelt fastened, they were headed through the parking lot.

"What took so long to walk out the door?" Heath asked, turning left, heading toward the interstate.

"Arthur engaged me in conversation. I told him to keep a lookout while I was gone."

"He won't tell anyone." Heath settled back as they pulled onto the interstate. "You can tell me what plans you, Molly, and Rosie came up with for the wedding to make the time go quicker."

Dela told him what she could remember. "Oh, and do you want to wear a suit or traditional clothing?"

He glanced over at her. "What do you prefer?"

"I think you should wear your traditional clothing. At the very least, a ribbon shirt."

"What are you planning to wear?"

Dela told him about Rosie saying her mom could make her a jumpsuit. "I've been looking at some photos and there are a couple of designs that would make a pretty outfit to be married in."

"If that's what you want, I like it. You look good in jumpsuits."

They stopped in Ontario, Oregon, for fuel and snacks. It was the halfway point to McCall. After eating their snacks, Dela brought up what she'd watched on the videos.

"Marty had surveillance video of Travers and Julia set up for me to look at. Travers and Celia met weekly from the beginning of her job. Quinn might need to see if they had already known one another before she took the undercover assignment. They were all goo-goo eyes from the first meet-up at the casino." Dela slurped the last of her iced tea she'd purchased when they'd stopped.

"Do you think her getting the job was a way for her and Travers to make her disappear so they could be together?" Heath asked.

"I think so. But they weren't as clever as they thought. Julia was watching them in a couple of the videos. She knew what was going on. I think she ordered someone to kill Celia, and Travers found out. He probably whisked Celia away the last night they were together in his room. Since she wasn't seen after that." Dela didn't like repeating what else she'd seen. It made the casino, her, and HR look bad. She sighed.

"What else did you see?" Heath asked.

"Julia had Kurt working for her, picking up what she dropped. She also had two waitresses she visited and handed off small envelopes. But she also had two people in housekeeping who she handed envelopes large enough to hold money. She has eyes and ears all over the casino. I left a message for HR to fire the waitresses and housekeepers tomorrow. I gave them the reason why. And Marty was going to have Farley go back farther in the video and see if Julia had recruited anyone else before we knew about them turning up six months ago."

"It sounds like you had a busy afternoon and evening before I picked you up."

"You could say that."

After another hour and a half of driving, Dela put the coordinates for the house into her phone. At 2:30 in the morning, they found the residence. The log home was on the shoreline of Payette Lake set in a thick grove of pine trees.

Heath parked their vehicle fifty feet up the driveway off to the side. They went on foot from there. Hiding behind the trees, they stood alongside the circular driveway on the front of the house.

Faint lights glowed in a few windows. The type

you'd leave on at night so you could find your way around.

"Let's do a perimeter search. If we can't see anyone moving around, then we'll have to wait for them to wake up and move around to see who is in the house," Heath whispered next to her ear.

Dela nodded and grasped his hand as they used the trees to move to the left of the large and, in her mind, ostentatious home. On the shoreline side, there were massive windows on both floors. She pointed up at one of the windows. "I saw a movement up there."

She felt Heath turning. He stopped. "Someone is coming in a boat."

Dela leaned around him and stared out at the lake. Every few seconds, something glinted on the water. The movement was rhythmic, like someone dipping an oar in and out of the water. Then she heard the cadence of the oars. "You're right."

They slid back into the trees and waited.

The boat docked, and two people walked up the small pier and followed the path to the house. One was built and walked like a man. The other was a woman.

"This isn't good," Dela whispered to Heath. "I think that's Julia."

"The man could be Travers for all we know." Heath countered.

"But there is someone in that house. If it's not Travers, then it has to be Celia." Dela started to move forward. Heath held her back.

"Let's see what they do. If it's Travers, he'll unlock the door."

Dela didn't like waiting. She liked action. But she stood still, watching as the two took off their packs and pulled out a rope with a grappling hook. The man threw it up, hooking the railing around the upper deck.

They had a discussion before the woman climbed the rope.

Dela expected the man to go up too, but when he didn't, she ran around to the front of the house and turned over all the rocks near the entrance.

A hand grabbed her arm. "What are you doing?" Heath whispered.

"Looking for a key to get inside." Just as her hand touched what felt like a key, shouting and a gun went off.

Chapter Twenty-five

Heath grabbed the key from Dela's hand.

She pulled her Sig M11 out of her hoodie pocket and followed him into the house. The stairs to the second floor were directly in front of them. A small night light lit the bottom section. They started up the stairs, careful not to make too much noise.

Voices drifted down.

"I told you not to get involved with her!" Julia's voice held more menace than Dela had ever heard in a woman.

"Julia, we're through. We have been for a long time. We're just business partners." Travers' voice was strong, solid. He must not have taken a bullet.

Dela worried Julia had shot Celia. As they reached the top of the stairs, someone barreled up behind them, making lots of noise.

She turned to tell him to stop.

A large hand grabbed her gun and flung it down the stairs, as he shoved her up against Heath, knocking them both to the landing.

Dela cried out as the man's foot landed on her lower left arm, snapping it.

"Shit!" Heath hissed and reached toward her.

Pain shot up her arm. She willed herself not to blackout.

"What are you doing in here?" Julia shouted. "Get out!"

"There's two people on the stairs." A deep voice said.

Dela figured that was the man who'd just run over them.

"Who?" Julia asked.

Heath grabbed Dela's hurt arm.

She screamed.

He hooked her around the waist with an arm and carried her down the stairs.

"My gun," she managed to say even though her body was folded in half over his arm.

"Hold it or I'll start shooting!" Julia called from above them.

"This isn't good," Heath said quietly as he stopped. "What's wrong with your arm?" he asked, placing her on her feet next to him. The night light reflected that they were three stairs up from the bottom.

She wished he'd made a run for the door. There was more coverage out in the trees. "That giant stepped on it. I think the bones are broken."

The stairway lit up. Dela blinked and raised her good arm to shield her eyes from the brightness. When her eyes adjusted to the change, she peered up the stairs. Julia with a gun in her hand, the big guy, and Travers all stood shoulder to shoulder, looking at them.

"It's the head of security for the casino and her boyfriend," Julia said in a singsong voice. "This should be fun."

Dela glared at the woman. Now she wished she'd told someone where they were going. Only Rosie had the names of the places she'd asked her about.

With the light on, she spotted her weapon two steps up from where she was.

"Who did you shoot?" Heath asked.

"Oh, that. It was a warning shot." Julia glared at Travers.

"Where's Celia Storm?" Dela asked.

"She's dead," Julia smirked.

Dela watched Travers. She didn't think Celia was dead, and he knew it. He must have paid off the man who was supposed to kill her, then whisked her away as Dela had suspected.

"Where's Duke Wadass?" Heath asked.

"Why do you care? That's one less drug dealer on your reservation," Julia said. Her eyes narrowed. "Why are you looking for him?"

"He's a person of interest in our investigation," Heath said.

"You say that like you're a cop." Julia aimed the gun at Heath. "The only good cop is a dead one."

Adrenaline kicked in, and Dela ignored the screaming pain in her arm. She dived for her gun.

A bullet zinged over her, hitting a wall.

She wrapped her hand around the Sig's grip and raised it, shooting several rounds up the stairs as she ran down and out the door.

Heath grabbed her hand holding the gun, and they ran down the road to the truck.

He backed out and headed to town.

Dela drifted in and out of consciousness as the pain in her arm intensified from her flinging her body around and pumping blood to her legs as they ran from the house.

"Are you hit?" she finally asked Heath when the nausea lessened.

"Yeah. I'm headed to the hospital. They'll call the police and we'll give our statements." He sucked in air. "I'm sure we'll both be in hot water for having weapons and discharging them."

"Did I hit anyone?" Dela asked.

"I saw the big guy go down, not sure about anyone else." Heath pulled them up to the emergency room doors.

He got out and came around to open her door. By then staff were rolling wheelchairs out to help.

♠ ♣ ♥ ♦

Dela woke to beeping and hushed voices. It reminded her of when she woke up and found her leg missing. She reached down with her right arm to feel her leg and discovered her left arm was hanging and in a cast, keeping her from reaching very far.

"Heath?" she said, trying to look around the room.

"Honey, are you looking for the man who brought you in?" A nurse in her fifties appeared in front of Dela.

"Yes. He's my fiancé. Where is he? What happened to him?" Worried that his wound had been worse than hers, she tried to sit up.

"Rest. Your anesthesia hasn't worn off yet. Your guy is okay. He had a through shot in his shoulder. It missed the bones. He's talking to the police. I'll bring him in when he's done."

Relief flooded her in waves. Tears trickled down her cheeks. She swiped at them with her right hand. When she'd swallowed the lump of emotion, she asked, "How long will I be in here?"

"You'll have to ask the doctor who did the surgery to set your arm. He'll be along shortly, now that you're awake."

Dela leaned back, thankful they were both alive, but mad that they were injured.

She closed her eyes, and the next thing she felt was Heath kissing her cheek. Opening her eyes slowly, she smiled. "You're my hero."

He grinned and shook his head. "No. It was you going for your weapon that saved us both." He tipped his head back a little. "The local police would like to question you."

"Okay. I think enough of the anesthesia has worn off that I can think straight." She tried to move her body to a sitting position and remembered the cast dangling in the air. "Can you make this bed sit me up?"

Heath used his left hand to mess with different switches, causing a nurse to come hurrying in. His right arm was in a sling, and he had a bandage on his right shoulder.

"Is everything alright?" she asked.

"We can't figure out which one of these controls works the bed," Heath said.

The nurse found the control and sat Dela up.

"Thank you," she said. "Can I get something to drink?"

"I'll bring you some water."

As the nurse walked to the door, Heath said, "You can send the police in. She's ready to talk to them."

The nurse nodded.

Heath pulled a chair up beside Dela's bed on her right side. She reached out and he grasped her hand. They were sitting, just holding hands, when the local police walked in.

"I'm Sergeant Lane and this is Officer Evans," the oldest of the two said.

"Dela Alvaro."

"I understand from talking to your fiancé that you aren't law enforcement," the sergeant said, and the officer pulled out a notepad.

"No. I'm head of security for the Spotted Pony Casino on the Umatilla Reservation outside of Pendleton."

The nurse walked in, handed her a water bottle with a straw, and walked out.

"Why were you in McCall?" Sergeant Lane asked.

Dela knew they probably asked Heath the same questions. They wanted to get the story straight. Before she could answer, she had to ask, "Has anyone gone to Seventeen hundred, sixty-seven Warren Wagon Road? There could be someone there who is shot."

"I've dispatched a car to that address. I've yet to hear from them," Sergeant Lane said. "Who do you think is shot?"

"I don't know. After the woman shot at us, I returned four rounds before we got out of the house." Dela drew the straw into her mouth, drank, and handed the water bottle to Heath. "We came to McCall…" She finished telling the police why they came to McCall when the door opened and Quinn strode in.

"What did I tell you about going off half-cocked?" he said to Dela and then turned to Heath. "And you, coming with her when you should have made her stay put."

Heath stood up. "We wouldn't be here if you had listened to her. We found Travers and so did Julia and a goon."

"What about Celia?" Quinn asked.

"Excuse me," Sergeant Lane cut in. "Who are you?"

Quinn pulled out his badge. "Special Agent Quinn Pierce with the FBI Special Task Force. These two have been helping me with a case, but they weren't supposed to go after anyone alone." He ran a hand over his head. Peering down at Dela, he said, "When I got the call, Marion was with me. You better hope she's still talking to me when I get back."

Dela smiled. She wished she could have heard Marion lay into Quinn. It was worth having a broken arm. She winced. Maybe.

"You can sit over there while we finish our interview with Ms. Alvaro," the sergeant said, pointing to a stool by the door.

Heath sat back down and grasped Dela's hand.

She cleared her throat and told them exactly what happened from the time they parked in the driveway to running for their lives and ending up at the hospital.

Sergeant Lane nodded. "That pretty much sums up what Seaver had to say."

Dela smiled at Heath. It was good that their

stories matched.

"I'll need your weapons for ballistics. Depending on what the prosecutor decides, you might get them back before a trial. If the prosecutor determines there won't be a trial, then you'll get them sooner," Sergeant Lane said, studying them.

Heath released her hand and stood. "Officer Evans, you can come with me to my truck. They're locked in the glove compartment."

The sergeant and officer followed Heath out of the room, leaving Dela alone with Quinn.

He walked up to the bed. "Did you see Celia?"

"No. But when Julia talked about her, Travers had a smug look on his face. I think when Julia sent someone to kill Celia, he intervened and shipped her somewhere." Dela had thought about it on the drive from the house to the hospital. She'd learned when she lost her leg that keeping her mind on anything but the pain helped.

"Where do you suppose he has her?" Quinn asked, a bit sarcastically.

"Don't talk to her like that!" Heath said, stepping through the door. He looked as if he would hit the agent even though his strongest arm was in a sling. "You should have agents going through the house on Warren Wagon Road. Maybe there will be evidence there."

The two men stood toe to toe and practically nose to nose.

"Stop. Quinn, go check out the house and see if anyone was killed or injured besides us. I don't think the locals here will keep us in the loop." Dela closed her eyes. "I want to sleep for a while. Heath, stay with me."

He grasped her hand, and she felt him settle in the chair beside the bed.

She didn't open her eyes, but heard Quinn blow out a huff and walk out of the room.

"Is he gone?" she whispered.

"Yeah."

Opening her eyes, Dela turned her head and peered into Heath's concerned brown eyes. "I really want to know who was hit by our shooting and where they went."

"Relax. We aren't going anywhere until the doctor says you are ready to travel. Then we're going back to Nixyaawii."

Chapter Twenty-six

It wasn't until the following day that the doctor released Dela. Heath slept in the chair beside her bed the whole time.

Sergeant Lane did stop by and let them know there was blood from two different people at the top of the stairs, but they couldn't find anyone. He had officers asking at the marinas about someone renting a boat and had put out an all-points bulletin on Dillon Travers' vehicles registered in Idaho.

Heath helped Dela put her prosthesis on and dress. They were waiting for the nurse to return with a wheelchair to take Dela out of the hospital when Quinn showed up.

"Looks like you two are ready to go." He leaned against the doorjamb, his legs crossed at the ankle.

"We're heading back to Pendleton," Heath said, zipping Dela's backpack closed.

"Good to hear. We picked up Travers last night. He's not saying anything, but we did learn he has a house in Morocco. Two agents left this morning to see if that's where Celia could be hiding. If all she's done is fall in love with Travers and we can get her to tell us all she learned, she'll be let go from the FBI without any other charges."

"What about Julia?" Dela asked. That woman worried her more than Travers. She had a viciousness to her that was bordering on psychopathic.

"Not a trace of her anywhere."

"Did Travers have any wounds?" Dela asked.

"No. He came out of your gunfight unscathed." Quinn pushed away from the doorjamb as the nurse appeared with the wheelchair. "Safe trip home. Contact me when you're both settled in. I'd like to discuss your going rogue." He walked away.

Dela cursed under her breath.

"Ignore him. We're going home. That's all that matters. They have Travers, and hopefully soon, they'll have Celia and Julia." Heath picked up her pack with his left hand as the nurse helped her into the wheelchair.

They exited the hospital with Dela searching the hallway, and once outside, the vehicles nearby. She couldn't shake the feeling that they hadn't seen the last of Julia.

"Look at us. Am I going to have to sit in your lap so we have two hands on the steering wheel?" Dela asked as the nurse helped her into the truck.

"I don't think that would be any safer," the nurse said, glancing at Heath.

He laughed. "She's right. Thank you for helping us get to the truck."

The nurse smiled and nodded before heading

back into the hospital.

Heath closed Dela's door and walked around to the driver's side.

"At least we're only five hours from home," he said, using his left hand to start the car and put it in gear.

Dela leaned her head back against the seat. The doctor had given her a prescription for painkillers, but she preferred not to be that knocked out when there was a woman who wanted a piece of her.

"Be sure to keep an eye on all the vehicles around us," she said, before closing her eyes and letting the motion of the vehicle lull her to sleep.

Dela registered the vehicle slowing and coming to a stop. She opened her eyes and saw they were at the Farewell Bend truck stop along the Snake River past Ontario.

"Nice to see you're awake. Do you need to use a restroom or want anything to eat or drink?" Heath asked.

"Yes, to all the above."

"Let me fill the truck and then I'll park to the side and we'll both go in." Heath exited the vehicle.

She sat up straighter, scoping out the other vehicles and the stop. It was new. All the pumps were shiny. Even the building that housed the fast food, market, and restrooms was clean and inviting.

Heath returned, drove the truck to the side of the building, and they walked in. People stared at them. Her with her arm in a cast and sling, and Heath with his right arm in a sling and a bulge under his shirt at his right shoulder. They looked like they'd been in a vehicle accident together.

She walked away from him and into the women's restroom. She had her hand on the latch to lock the door when it was shoved in, hitting her in the forehead and knocking her down onto the toilet.

"What's wrong—" Her words stuck in her throat as she stared into the crazy eyes of Julia.

The woman had a long-sleeved shirt on, but there was no missing the bulge of a bandage and blood seeping through the sleeve. "You thought you'd just walk away after what you did?" The woman's voice echoed through the restroom like a shrill screech of a hawk.

"All I did was find Dillon. And the FBI has him, by the way." Even as fear made her heart race and clogged her throat, she managed to speak as if she weren't affected by the crazy woman blocking the stall door.

"They can have him. He's been so busy fooling around with that fed, he hasn't had his head in the business for nearly a year. I'm the one who's been bringing in the goods and making money. He's useless."

Dela realized the woman didn't have a weapon and the door swung inward. She reached up with her good arm and touched her head where the door had slammed into her head. She felt the stickiness of blood. Great, another thing to make everyone stare at her.

The door to the room creaked open. "Dela, are you okay?" Heath called.

"Julia!" she yelled and slammed the door into the woman's face.

She screamed and stepped backward.

Dela pulled the door toward her and found Heath

struggling to grasp the squirming woman with his one arm.

Julia swung around and slugged him in his injured shoulder and ran out of the restroom.

An older woman walked in. "Oh my!" she said, backing out.

Heath stood by the sink, holding his shoulder. "What did she do?"

"Slammed the door in my head when I was trying to close it." Dela waved to the outside door. "I still have to go. Wait for me outside the room, or they'll throw you out."

He nodded and walked to the door as the older woman returned with a man.

Dela closed the stall door and finished her business with shaky hands. After washing her hands and using a paper towel to clean up her head, she walked out and found Heath talking to an Oregon State Trooper.

The trooper faced her. "This man says you were assaulted by another woman?"

Dela nodded. "She assaulted him, too." The shoulder of Heath's shirt was darkening from blood seeping through his bandage. "Her name is Julia Rivera. She's part of a drug cartel." Dela told him what had happened in the restroom and that the woman had been in an altercation with them two nights ago. He could call the McCall police and ask for Sergeant Lane.

"Would you like me to escort you to your vehicle and keep an eye out to see if she follows you?" the trooper asked.

Dela held up her cast and pointed to Heath's sling. "We would appreciate it if you did."

The trooper nodded and followed them out to the

truck.

After they were in the truck and headed out of the parking lot, Dela noticed a bag of goodies on the console between them.

"When did you get these?" She dug into the bag and found all her favorite junk food.

"When you were taking so long in the bathroom, I decided to buy our snacks. When I came back in and you still weren't out, I started getting worried."

"I'm glad you opened the door and called to me. It distracted her long enough that I could slam the door in her face." Dela pulled out a bag of chips and opened it using her hand and teeth. "I should probably tell Quinn that Julia is out for my blood."

"What did she say to you?" Heath asked as he navigated the truck back onto the freeway.

"That I shouldn't have thought I could just walk away after what I did." Dela held a chip in her hand. "Did you see she had blood oozing on her left arm? I think I hit her."

"I saw that. I had blood on my hand because that was the arm I grabbed when I was trying to detain her."

"She said she'd been running everything ever since Travers started going out with Celia, and he was useless to her anyway. She basically told me that she is running the trafficking and the drugs." Dela put her chip bag on the dash and dug for her phone. "I'm going to tell Quinn. Maybe he'll work harder at finding her."

"Hang on. There's a car about five back that's driving like a lunatic. It might be Julia coming after you."

Dela held onto the grab handle and stared in the sideview mirror, watching the dark car coming their way.

The truck surged forward. Dela glanced at the speedometer and saw that Heath was going close to 100, moving around cars and semis in the right-hand lane.

She glanced ahead. "There's a State Trooper ahead."

"He can pull us over. The other trooper knows you were attacked earlier."

As they whizzed by the trooper, he turned on his lights and came after them. As soon as the lights went on, Heath slowed down and pulled over. He kept his gaze on his sideview mirror.

"Is she getting closer?" Dela asked, as they waited for the trooper to get out of his car and talk to them.

"The car slowed down when the trooper's lights went on. It's coming by… now. Get the license."

Dela watched the car drive by. It was a rental. She used one hand to type the license plate into her phone and then texted it to Quinn. *Crazy Julia is after us. This is what she is driving. More later.*

Her phone buzzed as the trooper walked up to the window. It was Quinn. She ignored it.

"Do you know how fast you were going?" the trooper asked.

"Yes, I do. You can check with Trooper Alvarez, and he'll confirm we were attacked by a woman at the truck stop about thirty miles back. When I spotted a car coming up behind me at a fast speed and swerving in and out of cars, I thought it was the same person. She tried to kill us two nights ago." Heath pulled out his driver's license and handed it to the trooper.

Heath's phone rang. He ignored it.

The trooper ducked down to look at Dela. She gave him a faint smile.

Dela's phone buzzed. She glanced down. Quinn. She ignored it.

"And your I.D., please," the trooper asked.

"It's in my backpack in the back seat. Do you want me to lean over the seat or come outside and get it? It's just there by the door near you." She pointed with her right hand.

"Why don't you both get out and stand by the back of the truck, and I'll get it." The trooper backed up to let Heath out. He motioned to his shoulder. "What happened there?"

"Two nights ago, the woman who attacked us in the truck stop shot me. You can verify that with the McCall City Police." Heath stood by the truck's tailgate.

Dela walked up behind him and then stood at his left side.

The trooper pointed to her cast. "And you?"

"Same incident, only the lady who shot him had a goon with her, and he stepped on my arm, breaking the two bones." Dela pointed to her forehead. "That's what she did to me at the truck stop. Slammed a stall door into my head. That's why we didn't want her to catch us. Our weapons were taken from us by the McCall Police."

He stared at them. "Your weapons? Concealed carry permits?"

"I'm Detective Heath Seaver with the Umatilla Tribal Police. Dela has a concealed carry permit. We were pretty sure we would need our weapons since we were dealing with a drug cartel."

The trooper stared at them and then told them to wait.

"Quinn keeps calling because I texted him about crazy Julia," Dela said when the trooper was in his car.

"Hopefully, he can get confirmation of the other night and the incident at the truck stop. I'd like to get home and rest. Though how we're going to rest until Julia is caught is beyond me." Heath ran his hand over his head and then reached over and grasped her hand. "As long as we stick together, we'll beat her."

Dela nodded and watched the trooper return.

"Everything you're saying checks out. But you have to keep the speed under control. And I have to write you a ticket."

"Trooper Smith, you are asked to detain Seaver and Alvaro for the FBI. Repeat. Detain Seaver and Alvaro for the FBI." Came across the trooper's radio.

"Arrest them?" the trooper asked into his shoulder mic.

"Negative. Just hold until an FBI Unit can pick them up. I've forwarded your location to them."

Dela sighed. "At least we know Julia can't get to us if Quinn sent an escort."

"Do you want us to sit in your vehicle or ours?" Heath asked.

The trooper glanced from one rig to the other. "You'd be more comfortable in yours, but I could see trouble coming easier if you were in mine."

"Can I get our snacks?" Dela asked.

"Get whatever you want, but you'll have to sit in the back of my car."

"That's fine." Dela walked on the passenger side of the truck, up to the door and opened it. She leaned in, grabbed the snack bag, dropped their phones in, and shut the door. She heard a zing and saw gravel dance about a foot from her.

"Get over here!" shouted Heath and the Trooper at the same time.

She ran as best she could, holding the bag in one hand and trying not to jiggle her left arm too much. Heath pulled her behind the truck as the Trooper aimed his gun in the direction the bullet must have come from.

"You weren't kidding, someone is after you," the trooper said. "I think the shot came from that overpass. Get in the back of my vehicle from the driver's side."

Heath ushered Dela ahead of him to the other side of the vehicles. He remained hunched over as he moved to the back door and pulled it open. Then he motioned for her to come to him.

Dela hunched down and scurried to Heath. Another bullet zinged over her head before she ducked behind the door and fell onto the back seat.

Heath shoved her over and slid in, closing the door. "If we had been sitting in the truck, we would have been direct targets."

Dela pushed up to sit and gasped in pain. This was too much. "I don't like being a sitting duck, and I don't like looking over my shoulder when I'm not the bad person."

They were sitting with their injured body parts together. Heath couldn't put an arm around her, and she couldn't grasp his hand.

The trooper was talking on his mic. She had a pretty good idea he was reporting the shooting.

She dug in the snack bag for her phone and saw that Quinn had tried to call four times. The fifth time, he left a message. She tapped message and then the speaker.

"Damnit, Dela, don't leave a message like that and then don't answer your phone. We saw that the State Police stopped you. I'm having them detain you so we can give you an escort home. Stay put and don't get all pissy with the trooper."

Heath chuckled. "He knows you pretty well."

She twisted to slug him and remembered it would hurt them both. "At least he's thinking about keeping us alive by sending Feds."

The trooper opened the driver's door and slid in. "There are more troopers on their way, and the FBI is only twenty minutes out. As long as that person doesn't start shooting at the car, we're good."

Chapter Twenty-seven

Two dark SUVs pulled up behind the state trooper's car. Another trooper had joined them about ten minutes after the shooting. He was parked in front of Heath's truck.

Dela smiled as she spotted Milo walking toward them from the first SUV. He and Quinn were partners in the office in Pendleton. She hadn't liked the man at first, but he'd come to grow on her.

The trooper was standing by his car, visiting with the other trooper. They both walked forward and requested to see the agents' I.D.s. Their asking made Dela feel safe, even though she knew Milo.

What she hadn't expected was Quinn's ex-wife, FBI HQ Supervisor Prescott, to step out of the second vehicle. "They sent in the big gun," Dela said.

"Milo?" Heath asked.

"No. The woman. She's HQ Supervisor Prescott and Quinn's ex. This should be good."

"How do you know who she is and that she's his

ex?" Heath asked, studying her.

"I met her when Quinn took me to the FBI headquarters in Seattle while we were working on a case at the casino. It was before you came back to the reservation. They argued, and she put him down several pegs. He reluctantly told me their connection."

Milo appeared at her side of the vehicle and opened the door. "Dela, I didn't think I'd ever be escorting you anywhere." He smiled and reached in to help her out.

She glanced over at Heath and saw another fed helping him out.

"What about my truck?" Heath asked as they were being led to the SUVs.

"We'll have an agent drive it between our two vehicles," Supervisor Prescott said. She nodded at Dela. "It seems you have really gotten yourself tangled up with bad guys this time."

Dela shrugged and wished she hadn't as pain radiated through her left arm.

"You are in this car and your pal is in the back car," the supervisor said.

Digging in her feet, Dela stopped and said, "No. We're riding together. He's my fiancé." She glared at the woman. "We aren't the ones doing anything wrong, and we won't be treated like criminals."

Heath had stopped beside her. "What she said."

"We can leave you alongside the road without an escort," the supervisor said.

"If that's how you treat civilians, I think I'd rather take that chance," Dela returned, glaring at the woman.

Milo tapped the supervisor on the shoulder and whispered in her ear. Anger flashed in her eyes, but she faced them and said, "Fine. You can both get in the last vehicle."

Dela and Heath clasped hands and walked with an agent to the second vehicle and climbed into the back seat.

The door closed, and she leaned into Heath. "She's even more of a witch than I remember."

Supervisor Prescott sat in the passenger seat, and an agent slid into the driver's seat.

"We'll take you to the Pendleton Office until we can get surveillance set up at your residence," the supervisor said.

"We both have jobs to do," Heath said.

"I'm sure both of your employers would appreciate not having someone in their midst who is a target." She shifted in her seat as the SUV pulled onto the freeway.

"You're going to use us as bait to catch Julia, who, by the way, has been running both the trafficking and the drugs for a year. At least that's what she told me while holding me captive in a bathroom stall." Dela didn't mind being holed up with Heath at home. But she feared for her family and friends. Julia was a vindictive woman. She might start taking her anger out on them.

She pulled her phone out of the snack bag she'd carried with her and texted her mom. *Something has come up that could put you in danger. Stay close to the farm and don't meet anyone anywhere if you don't know them. And if you do know them, call them back and make sure they made the call. Please do this. I'll tell you more later.*

Her phone rang. Mom. She sighed. She hadn't wanted to make this call while being escorted by the supervising agent, but she couldn't not answer.

"Hi Mom," she said cheerfully.

"What was that text about? Are you in danger again and bringing it on the rest of us?" It wasn't an accusation so much as a reprimand.

"It seems Heath and I ticked off a woman. She is crazy. I want you and all our family and friends to be safe. Can you spread that to everyone?" Dela hoped her mom got the gist so she wouldn't have to text everyone and have them call her. "Start with Mimi and Marion. They'll know what to do."

"You need the people on the reservation to keep an eye out for this person, and I need to be careful."

Tears burned the backs of her eyes, she was so relieved her mom understood. "Yes. This person has been causing all the trouble there."

"I'll get it done. When will you be home?"

"Later today, but stay away, please."

"Are you in trouble now? Does someone have you?" Mom's worried tone hurt Dela's heart. It seemed like all she did was give her mom worry.

"No, the FBI are with us. And will be until we catch the woman." At least she could give her mom that comfort.

"That's good. I'll let you go and take care of things."

"Thanks, Mom, love you." She ended the call and leaned her head on Heath's shoulder.

"You okay?" he asked,

"Yeah, I just bring her so much worry." Then she put her mouth to his ear and whispered, "She's going to tell everyone on the Rez to keep an eye out for Julia and to be more careful than ever."

He kissed her temple.

"Now that you're finished talking to your mom, I'd like to know what all you two have discovered about the trafficking and the drug dealing on the reservation," HQ Supervisor Prescott said.

Dela peered into Heath's eyes. It was all written up in Quinn's reports, so it didn't really matter. Though out of loyalty to Quinn, and because she didn't like his ex, she wouldn't mention that he didn't listen when she figured out where Travers could be.

Between her and Heath, they told everything they knew about both illegal activities to Prescott as they drove uneventfully to the Pendleton Office.

Dela paced back and forth. They'd been stuck in the Pendleton FBI Office for four hours. Milo had brought them takeout from Hamley, which was delicious, but she wanted to go home and make sure her animals were okay.

"It can't take this long to put surveillance in place. We already have a camera." Dela walked over to where the agent had set down Heath's truck keys. "Let's just go."

Heath ended his call to the Chief of the Tribal Police. "I'm in trouble for going after Travers when I was supposed to be looking for Duke." He picked up the keys. "We might as well go all in."

"Wait, you two can't leave," said the agent watching over them.

"We're tired of waiting around here. We have things to do." Heath nodded to their snack bag, and Dela picked it up.

"Tell Quinn I got tired of waiting. He'll understand," Dela said, following Heath to the elevator that took them to the bottom floor. They walked out into the last of the day's sunshine.

The truck was parked in front of the building. They hurried to it, scanning all around them. Once they were in the truck, Heath headed under the freeway to the south end of Pendleton and took Goad Road to Tutuilla Church Road. It was the back way to their place and a route that Julia wouldn't know or be waiting along.

While they were cooped up at the FBI Office, Dela had talked to Marty and told him to show all the photos they had of Julia to all the security guards and surveillance personnel. If the woman came into the casino, she was to be apprehended by any means and held for the FBI.

They parked in the driveway. Her car was still at the casino. She didn't see anyone around and wondered if the whole, 'going to set up surveillance at your house need you to stay away' had been the FBI's plan of keeping them in one place and out of their way.

Heath sat in the vehicle for a few minutes, scanning in all directions with all the mirrors. "If the feds are watching the house, they are well concealed." He opened his door. "Let me go first and unlock the door. You stay down, so there isn't a target for Julia to shoot at."

"What about you? You're a target." Dela said.

"She seems to be fixated on you. But yes, I am a target, too. Just please wait for me to get the door unlocked."

She nodded and was reassured when she heard barking and braying in the backyard. That's when it struck her: where was Travis? She pulled out her phone and texted him. *We're home. Where are you?*

He gave her a thumbs-up. *Working on Mom's house. Will be by for my stuff later.*

If you don't need it, wait. We have a crazy lady after us. Wouldn't want the feds to nab you thinking you work for her.

He sent her a surprised face emoji. *Are you two going to be okay?*

Feds are supposedly watching us.

He sent a laughing emoji. *You'll catch her first.*

Dela wasn't so sure about that when they were both injured.

"Come on. The door's open and the critters are about to knock down the French door." Heath grabbed both their backpacks and closed the back door of the truck.

Dela opened her door, slid out, slammed the door, and jogged to the door. Nothing but braying and barking. She heaved a sigh of relief, standing in the middle of her living room. Walking to the French doors, she let Mugshot in and gave Jethro a one-armed hug.

"I was texting Travis. Told him we were back and to stay away, there was a crazy lady after us."

Heath chuckled, "What did he say to that?"

"We'd get her before the feds." It made her happy to know their family and friends believed in their skills more than law enforcement did.

Heath tapped his sling and pointed to her cast. "Not sure if we'll be the dynamic duo with these injuries."

"I was thinking the same thing. But we can stay alive the best we know how." Dela packed her backpack to the bedroom and unpacked. All they could do was stay vigilant.

Chapter Twenty-eight

They'd been home about three hours when there was a knock on the door. Heath pulled the blind aside and said, "It's Quinn."

"Great…" Dela unlocked the door and let him in. He was followed by Marion, who hugged her.

"I was worried about you. When I found out you tried to get Quinn's help and he blew you off, I was so mad." Marion glared at Quinn.

"She's still mad and insisted she had to come see you. Though with a crazed woman like Julia after you, I didn't think it was such a good idea," Quinn said.

"Yeah, we're like a ticking bomb. No one knows when she'll come or what she'll do to try and rid her world of us." Dela shivered, and Marion rubbed her hands up and down her arm.

"Don't worry. Quinn won't let anything happen to you two." Marion smiled at Heath. "I heard you are engaged and the wedding is in September. That's wonderful."

Dela glanced at Heath. He nodded. "I finally

corralled her into marrying me."

"I'm glad you did. You two make a great team." Marion walked away from Dela and wandered into the kitchen. "How about a cup of tea?"

Dela followed, unsure what the woman and, for once, quiet Quinn, were up to.

Heath gave her a quizzical glance as she walked by. Dela shrugged and nodded for him to follow.

When they were all seated at the kitchen table, with the kettle on the stove, Quinn cleared his throat. "Marion told me that since you two were in trouble with your bosses—"

"How did you know that?" Dela asked Marion.

"Word was going around after you two left that you both took off all of a sudden, and no one, not Chief Steele or people at the casino, knew what was going on." Marion gave them both a pointed look. "You really need to keep someone in the loop."

Dela narrowed her eyes at Quinn. "I tried. He shut me down before I could tell him what I'd discovered."

Marion stood as the kettle whistled. "I had a long talk with him about that. He needs to heed your instincts."

"As I said, Marion felt that since you were in hot water with your jobs, I might as well be with mine. We have done an excellent job working together to solve murders before." He raised his hand and made a circling motion, causing Mugshot to stand up and bark.

"Shh. It's okay, he's just a crazy man," Dela said to the dog.

Quinn glared at her and said, "Supervisor Prescott didn't set up any surveillance for you. She wanted you out of her way while they tried to solve everything. She doesn't like that you two have been a step ahead of the FBI on these cases."

Dela slapped the table. "I knew it. I could tell by the way she treated us in the SUV that she didn't like us. And she asked us about everything we've learned and wanted to know everything we did." Dela tried to hide a smug grin.

"What didn't you tell her?" Quinn asked, smiling.

"We didn't tell her about our suspicions of Celia being alive. Did you tell her about Morocco?"

Quinn shook his head.

"I also didn't tell her I know who the other people at the casino are that Julia was in contact with." Dela leaned back in her chair. "I had HR fire them, but I have their names and addresses. One of them might give us a clue to how to find Julia. But my money is on Kurt. He seemed smitten with her, which leads me to believe the two of them might have been lovers." She glanced at Heath. "Do you know if he is still in jail?"

He shook his head. "Some expensive lawyer got him out on bail."

"I have the information about Kurt in my files." Quinn studied Heath. "You up to taking a ride with me? We can go knock on his door tonight and see what he has to say."

"Hey, he's my ex-employee. Why can't I go?" Dela asked.

"It would be better to have her with us, since she seems to be the target of Julia's rage," Heath said.

"I think you're safer here with the cameras and your animal security," Quinn said.

"It's a crapshoot whether or not I'm safe anywhere. She found me in a stall in a truck stop. What's to keep her from finding me here or walking into Kurt's house? I'd rather do something than sit here wondering." Dela looked to Marion for support.

"When she puts it like that, she is a target no matter where she is. Better she is with you two than here alone. I know you won't let me stay with her." Marion gave Quinn a pointed glance.

Both men sighed.

"True," Heath said. "It looks like you'll be coming with us."

Dela pushed the tea Marion had placed in front of her to the middle of the table. "I'll reheat this later. Thanks."

"Leave Mugshot in here and leave the lights on," Quinn said.

"Won't that make him a target?" Dela asked, petting Mugshot on the head.

"If he's inside barking his big bark, she'll be less likely to try to break in," Quinn said.

It kind of made sense. But Dela didn't want to return and find her pets dead.

"We'll all get in my vehicle," Quinn said. "I'll drop Marion off on our way to Kurt's."

"My weapon is in Idaho," Dela said.

"We shouldn't need weapons if all we're going to do is pay a surprise visit to Kurt." Quinn motioned for them to move to the front door.

"I have to pee," Dela said, hurrying down the hall. She slipped into the bathroom, dug to the back of her towel cabinet, and quickly turned the dial on the gun safe she had installed. Inside, she found her petite Sig P238 auto that she carried in her purse when she was going somewhere sketchy, and Heath's work Glock.

They'd confiscated his backup weapon in Idaho.

She shoved the weapons and magazines in her hoodie pocket, closed the safe, the door to the towel cabinet, and flushed the toilet.

At the door where everyone was waiting, she smiled and said, "Thank you."

Quinn studied her for a couple of seconds, opened the door, and scanned the area, then he sent them all out to the vehicle. Marion sat in the front as Dela had hoped.

When they were headed to the freeway, Dela slid Heath's gun across the seat toward him. He took the weapon, shoved it in the waistband of his pants, and pocketed the magazine.

"You two are quiet. Don't worry about Julia. There's no way she'll think you two would meet up with someone you fired." Quinn smiled at them in the rearview mirror.

Dela glanced at Heath. He looked about as convinced as she felt.

They dropped Marion off at Quinn's house in Pendleton.

"According to the information I have on Kurt, he lives along McKay Creek." Quinn headed south through Pendleton, going underneath the freeway and taking Highway 395 south.

At the hospital, he took the road to the right and drove slowly through the neighborhood, following a winding path to where he stopped.

"That house up there is Kurt's." Quinn pointed to a rundown, single-story house that appeared to have been in the area the longest. "According to my information, that's his car in the driveway. He isn't married, and as far as we know, he doesn't have a roommate."

Dela started to reach for the door, and the hair on the back of her neck tingled. "Be ready. I don't like this."

Heath put a hand on her cast. "We don't have to go with him. He can go talk to Kurt by himself."

"No. We have to go. Something doesn't feel right." She opened the door and went to stand by Quinn, who was already standing at the front of the vehicle. "You two took a while. Are you having second thoughts?"

"And third. But we can't let you go in there alone," Heath said, motioning for him to go first. "You follow Quinn, and I'll check our backs."

Dela nodded, put her left hand in her hoodie pocket to hold the gun as she used her right hand to find and shove the magazine in her Sig. Using her left hand put a strain on her arm, but she'd live with it. Luckily, this pocket Sig wouldn't require her to rack the slide to start shooting.

Quinn stopped on the porch and knocked on the door.

No one answered. "Kurt, it's the FBI. We have some questions for you."

There wasn't a sound coming from inside. Dela's senses were on high alert. She heard a car on the next street over, a dog barking, and the murmur of a television. Her nostrils flared as a breeze carried the fetid stench of death.

"If he's in there, I don't think he's alive," she whispered.

"The smell wouldn't be that strong if he were inside the house," Heath whispered a reply.

"We don't want Prescott to know we were here,"

Quinn said. "I'll call it in as a foul odor."

They all returned to the SUV. Quinn called the local police and said he was walking his dog past the address of Kurt's house and smelled something like a dead animal. When he ended the call, he shifted to peer into the back seat. "Who was one of the other people on the list?"

"Two waitresses and two housekeepers," Dela pulled out her phone and texted Marty. *Who were the waitresses and housekeepers who had contact with Julia?*

Are you two going to be safe? Marty texted.

Yes. The FBI is keeping tabs on us. But Quinn needs the names to talk to the four. We need to find Julia before she finds us.

Denise Ballard, Kesia Wapash, Earlene Rolle, Tamika Wolf. Do you need addresses?

If you have them handy. Dela recognized two of the names. Tamika was a cousin to Heath and Denise worked in the Pony Grill that Dela frequented.

Check your email.

Thanks.

"I have the names and addresses." She shifted to tell Heath. "One of them is Tamika Wolf."

"My cousin? Damn her. She knows better than to get tangled up with the likes of Julia. Let's go there first." Heath was leaning forward as if he could get Quinn to put the vehicle in motion.

"Denise Ballard lives in Pendleton. Let's talk to her first. The other three are in Riverside and Mission." Dela gave Denise's address to Quinn.

He started up the vehicle, moving down the street slowly as a city patrol car came around the corner.

"We almost sat there too long," Quinn commented, speeding up after they turned a corner and were out of the policeman's sight.

Denise lived on the hill in SE Pendleton. Quinn parked behind two cars on the street in front of the house that sat down the hill from the road.

Dela exited the SUV as soon as it stopped. She didn't fear running into Julia here. There wasn't the uneasy sensation she'd had at Kurt's. And with good reason, since the man was probably dead.

She didn't wait for Heath and Quinn to catch up. She knew they would be by her side when the door opened. Dela knocked on the door, and the sound of the television lowered.

"Did you hear something?" a man's voice asked.

She knocked again.

"There, see there's someone at the door," the male voice said.

The door opened, and Denise blinked at her. "W-what are you doing here?"

"We have some questions to ask you," Dela said, opening the screen door and pushing by Denise.

Heath and Quinn walked in behind her.

"Who are you?" Denise asked Quinn.

He held out his badge. "Special Agent Pierce with the FBI."

Denise's eyes widened, and she glanced at the man in the chair.

Dela studied the man. He was twice Denise's age and dressed in a t-shirt and plaid pajama pants.

"These friends of yours? I told you not to bring friends home this late."

"Dad, this is Dela Alvaro. She's head of security at

the casino, and that's her boyfriend, he's a Tribal Police Detective, and this guy is FBI. They aren't friends of mine."

"Damnit, Girl, what did you do this time?" The man clicked the television off and sat on the front of his chair.

"Mr. Ballard, we'd like to talk to Denise in private," Dela said.

"Private? She's my daughter, I ought to be able to hear what you have to say to her." The man stood up, swayed a bit, and sat back down.

"Let's go to the kitchen. Dad, stay put." Denise pointed to the man in the chair and then led them through a door into a small kitchen with a table large enough for four.

"Is this about why I was sacked?" Denise asked.

"Partially." Dela waited for the younger woman to sit, and then she sat across from her, leaving the two men to sit on either side of the square table. "Do you remember talking to this woman?" She held up her phone with the photo of Julia.

"Yeah, she'd come in the Pony and sit by herself. She seemed kind of lonely. I'd talk to her when I wasn't busy. She tipped good. What about her?" Denise flicked her gaze back to Dela.

"Did she ever ask you to do something for her or to spy on anyone?" Dela could see the woman was trying to decide what to say. "We have video of her handing you a small envelope. What was in it?"

The young woman cringed. "It was pills my boyfriend started selling to make money to get me out of this place. We can't afford a decent place to live with what we make. He met up with a guy who told him how to make easy money."

"So your boyfriend contacted this person to make the drop to you at the casino?" Dela didn't understand why her boyfriend didn't do the pick-up.

"No, the guy he talked to told her my boyfriend was interested and she said she'd drop it off at the casino to me." Denise's eyes widened. "I thought it was crazy that she knew I was his girlfriend. We had talked a couple of times about men, and I mentioned a boyfriend and wanting to get married, but I never said his name."

"When dealers are looking for more people to peddle their drugs, they learn everything about them," Heath said.

"So other than at the casino, you don't know anything about this woman?" Dela asked, studying Denise. "Did she say anything about where she liked to stay or the man she was upset with?"

"She only mentioned that she liked the wide-open spaces here. And she was through with her lover. That's about it."

"What's your boyfriend's name and address? I'd like to talk to him and see if he knows anything more about the guy who hooked him up to sell," Quinn said, pulling out a small notebook and pen.

Denise recited her boyfriend's name, address, and phone number. Then she stared at Dela. "Is taking those envelopes from her what got me fired?"

"Yes, we don't tolerate anyone who helps deal drugs on the reservation." Dela felt sorry for the young woman, but she shouldn't have helped with an illegal activity. "You're lucky I'm not turning you into these guys." Dela tipped her head toward Heath and Quinn.

"But they're sitting here listening." Tears glistened in Denise's eyes.

"I suggest you and your boyfriend find a better way to raise money to get married," Heath said. "Dela and I won't press charges against you. Agent Pierce will let it go as well. But he will be watching both you and your boyfriend, and if it happens again, you will both be prosecuted."

Denise nodded her head.

Dela stood. "I hope you can find another job, but we can't hire you back at the casino. Not after what you were a part of."

"I understand." Denise sat at the table. "Don't tell Dad. He already hates my boyfriend."

"We'll see ourselves out," Quinn said, leading the way to the front door.

Once they were seated in the SUV, Dela said, "I hate it when people like that resort to illegal dealings to get ahead."

"There are other ways. Take a second job or find a better job," Heath said.

"I know. That's why it doesn't make sense to me." Dela sighed and leaned back. "Now we can go to Tamika's."

Heath gave Quinn directions to his cousin's house. It was getting late but the lights were still on.

"I'll go first," Heath said, leading the way up the sidewalk to the front door. The long single-story house was dark outside until Heath was ten feet from the porch, and the light came on.

"I'll get you this time!" The door flew open, and a man stood on the porch in boxers holding a shotgun.

Chapter Twenty-nine

"Uncle, there is no reason to shoot us," Heath said.

Dela watched the man point the rifle at the porch roof and stare. He finally found his voice and said, "I didn't shoot. How come you're all bandaged up?"

"Altercation with someone else," Heath said. "Why are you jumping out the door with a shotgun?"

"I'm trying to get that damn racoon that's been getting into the garbage, sorry Nephew. Come on in."

Dela had yet to meet this uncle. She had a feeling he was the most interesting.

Heath motioned for her to step up beside him as they walked into the house. It smelled of fry bread and venison. The aromas reminded her of visiting her friends on the reservation as a child.

"What are you doing coming around so late?" Heath's uncle asked.

"Uncle Jack, this is Dela Alvaro, my fiancée, and this is FBI Agent Quinn Pierce," Heath said, making introductions.

"Pleased to meet you, young lady. The family is buzzing about the wedding." Jack smiled warmly at Dela, then turned narrowed eyes on Quinn. "What'cha bringing a fed in here for?"

"We're here to talk to Tamika. We think she might have some information that will help us find someone." Heath scanned the room. "Where's Auntie and Tamika?"

"Your aunt is off visiting her sister in Lapwai. Tamika went to bed about two hours ago. She's been layin' around the house like a tick-infested dog since getting fired." Jack studied Dela. "Hey, you work for the casino. Can you tell me what she did?"

"Maybe after we talk to Tamika," Heath said. "Can you go wake her up?"

"Sure, sure. Make me get my head bit off." The man leaned his shotgun in the corner near the door and walked down the hallway.

"I like him," Dela said to Heath.

"Yeah, he's a character. He's not a blood relation, it's his wife, Auntie Karen. She's my mom's cousin."

"I told you not to wake me!" shouted a woman's voice.

The man wandered back. "Good luck. I'm going for a walk." He picked up the shotgun. "I might run into that raccoon." He walked out the door and left them standing in the middle of the living room.

Dela studied Heath. "Want me to go see if I can get her up?"

"Yeah, and if that doesn't work, I'll pull her out," Heath said. "She's always been a brat."

"It's times like this that I'm glad I don't have

siblings or cousins." Dela walked down the hall and figured the door with a sign that said Princess was the room she was looking for.

Opening the door, she flipped on the light.

"I said go away, old man. I'm not helping you kill a raccoon," a muffled voice from under the covers said.

"Tamika, it's Dela from the casino. Heath and I need to talk to you," Dela said in her military command voice.

The covers flipped down and Tamika's hair stood out all around her head, and her eyes opened slowly. "What are you doing here? You're the one that got me fired."

"Come talk to us and we might be able to fix that."

"Really?" Tamika sat up and shoved the hair off her face.

"I want to know your side of what I saw on the video. It could be helpful to us." Dela picked up the robe lying across the end of the bed. "Put this on and come out to the living room, please."

The young woman nodded and slipped an arm into the robe.

Dela left the room and walked back to the living room. Heath and Quinn were sitting in chairs, waiting.

"She's coming." Dela sat down on the couch beside Heath. She was getting tired. It was eleven at night. It had been a long day after not sleeping the night they left Pendleton headed to McCall and then last night in the hospital.

Tamika appeared, her robe drawn tight and her hair slicked back in a ponytail. "Hiya, Cousin," she said to Heath.

"Hey, Tamika. We have some questions for you

about the woman who handed you an envelope." Heath pointed to a chair beside Quinn.

"Who's he?" Tamika asked. "He looks like a fed."

"He is. So answer all our questions truthfully," Heath said.

"What did you ask?" she hedged.

"Tell us why a woman gave you an envelope?" Dela said.

"What are you talking about?" Tamika asked, her gaze bouncing between Dela and Heath.

Dela pulled out her phone and scrolled to the video of Tamika taking an envelope from Julia in the hall outside of the room Travers used when he was at the casino.

"This." Dela held the phone in front of Tamika as the video played.

"Oh, that! She paid me to take a photo of the women who went into that room when Mr. Travers was there. She said she was his business partner and had to make sure he wasn't hanging out with the wrong type." Tamika smiled like there wasn't anything wrong with taking money for photos of guests in the hotel.

"That is an invasion of our guests' privacy," Dela said.

Tamika pointed to Dela's phone. "What is that then? That's an invasion of my privacy."

"No, it's keeping the guests at the casino and hotel safe. What you did was against our policies. Was this the only time the woman paid you?"

"Yeah."

"How did you get the photos to her?" Heath asked.

"I texted them to her."

"We need that number. Get your phone," Heath

said.

Tamika glared at him. "Why should I?"

"Because I can arrest you for colluding with a known drug dealer and member of a cartel," said Quinn in his bad ass voice.

Tamika's head swiveled. She stared at him as if she'd forgotten he was in the room.

"Go get your phone," Heath said in a tone that told Dela he wasn't happy with his cousin not only taking money but also being belligerent in helping the authorities.

As Tamika walked out of the room, Quinn's phone rang. He cringed and answered the phone.

"Special Agent Pierce," he answered. Then listened, he nodded, and listened.

Tamika came back into the room. She glanced at him, then handed the phone to Heath.

"Find the number for me," he said.

She messed with the phone, then handed it to him.

Dela put the number into her phone and wrote Julia as the contact.

"How many photos did you send her?" Dela asked, as Quinn rose out of the chair and went outside.

"Just the three times the same woman went into the room. You know, you should fire her ass. She's a dealer." Tamika glared at Dela.

"She can't be fired, she's missing," Dela said, staring back at Tamika.

"And she's a Federal Agent. You had evidence in a federal case that you have withheld. What was the date on the last photo you took of her going in or out of that room?" Heath asked.

Tamika snatched the phone back and started

scrolling. "There. I made sure the dates and times were on the photos when I sent them."

Dela stared at the photo of Celia. She was smiling up at Travers. They both were carrying suitcases. "Did they take the elevator or the stairs?"

"The stairs. How did you know that?" the young woman stared at her.

"That's the day she disappeared, and that woman who wanted the photos wanted her dead." Dela stood. "You're still fired because you don't seem to understand the necessity of our guests' privacy."

Heath handed the phone back to his cousin. "You knew better than this. Keep your nose clean."

They walked out of the house and found Quinn standing by his vehicle, staring up at the sky.

"Doing a little star gazing?" Heath asked as he opened the back door for Dela.

"That was Prescott on the phone. She wanted to know where the hell I was. And why I didn't respond to her request to check out the body found at Kurt's house." Quinn stood inside his open SUV door.

Heath slid into the passenger seat and closed the door. "What did you tell her?"

"That I was following up on some leads on Julia." Quinn shook his head. "I'm sure she's unhappy with me. She also mentioned that the agent told her you two left, and I was to tell you to stay put at your house."

Dela laughed and said, "I'm sorry you are in deep with your superior. We learned that the day Celia went missing, she left Travers' room at the hotel with luggage and was smiling up at him. They took the fire stairs."

"To avoid anyone seeing them leaving together,"

Quinn said.

"That's what I think." Dela clicked the seat belt. "Let's go talk to Kesia."

"It's getting late, shouldn't we call it a night?" Quinn said.

Heath chimed in. "Yeah, you and I can check out Kesia and Earlene tomorrow. I'm beat."

"Okay, then take us home, James," Dela said flippantly, but her heart was racing in her chest. She felt safe in Quinn's SUV. There was no way Julia would find them in one of the probably dozen Fed vehicles running around in the Pendleton area.

But the house…she could be lying in wait for them there.

Chapter Thirty

Dela was thankful Quinn had her wait in the car until Heath unlocked the door and cleared the house. Heath waved for her to enter. She opened her door, jogged to the house, closed the door behind her, and clicked the lock in place.

"It's okay," Heath said, holding her in his uninjured arm for a few minutes in the living room.

Mugshot whined and danced to the French doors. He either needed to pee or wanted to check on Jethro.

"Let Mugshot out, please. I want a shower." She headed down the hallway, hearing the French doors open and the clatter of Mugshot's toenails on the floor as he rushed out.

She clicked on the bedroom light and stared at the painting that Travis's friend Toby painted on her wall above her bed when they remodeled the house. She loved the brightly colored dreamcatcher with five feathers on either side above her bed.

Walking in and sitting on the end of the bed to take

off her prosthesis, she peered up at the serene setting Toby had painted on that wall above her closet. It was the Blue Mountains in spring. With wildflowers at the base of the pine trees and wildlife coming out to taste the fresh new grass. She loved the blended colors and images that felt like a dream as she took in the scene. A deep breath and a long exhale released the tension in her body.

She stood to drop her pants.

Jethro started braying as if he were announcing an intruder. Why wasn't Mugshot barking? And where was Heath?

She put her hand in her hoodie pocket, glad she hadn't taken it off, and walked into the hall.

A cool breeze told her a door was open. Heath should have been back in and the door closed by now.

She halted listening. Fear for Heath had her debating on calling out his name. But that would give away where she was.

A shadow flicked across the end of the hallway before the lights went out.

Her heart thudded in her chest and blood whooshed in her ears, blocking out Jethro's panicked braying. Dela calmed her breathing and racing heart as she slowly pulled out the Sig, aiming it down the hall. To backtrack would have her boxed in. Going forward gave her two doors to get out.

Easing her way down the hall, she continued to listen. She heard whining in between Jethro's braying. Mugshot was hurt. *Double frickin' shit*. She had to believe Heath was also hurt for Jethro to be carrying on, and because he hadn't come to her aid.

It's up to me to keep all of us alive. She heard a

movement to the left, in the dining area by the French doors.

Who was it? Heath or Julia?

Three more feet and she'd be out of the hall.

One more step and she listened, drawing her arm holding the gun back closer to her body so it wasn't the first thing that whoever was out there saw. She didn't need it knocked out of her hand.

"Go get her!" she heard Julia whisper.

Double frickin' shit. Two people were waiting to grab her. She concentrated on the sound. It came from the living room. Were they both on that side and Heath was on the left? Or had they split up, one on each side of the hallway?

She decided to wait for one of them to make a move. Her eyes were becoming accustomed to the darkness. She knew the shapes of her furniture and where they were. But she wasn't walking out of this hall. She'd let them come at her. She'd have clear shots staying in the hall.

"Go on!" whispered Julia.

Dela raised her uninjured arm, ready to shoot whoever stepped into the hall.

A large, dark shadow stepped into the hall.

She pulled the trigger three times.

The body dropped.

The sounds of a person pleading for help were hard to ignore, but she knew Julia would have a gun and wasn't afraid to use it.

"You bitch. You've ruined everything. Everything!" Julia screamed and stepped into the opening, firing her gun. Dela dropped to her belly and shot three rounds into Julia. As soon as the body landed on top of the first one, she hurried to the bedroom, found a flashlight in her bedside table, and flicked it on. She found her phone and called Quinn.

"What's happened?" he asked.

"Julia is lying in my hallway with a man. I just shot them. They turned off my power. I'm going to look for Heath." She ended the call and walked down the hallway, her light on the two bodies. She kicked the weapons down the hall toward the bedroom and then checked them for pulses. The man had a faint pulse. Julia was dead.

Dela stepped around them and headed to the French doors. She found Heath on the ground at the edge of the patio. Mugshot sat beside him, licking Heath's face and whining.

"Good boy. Are you okay?" Then to quiet Jethro, she called, "We're okay!"

To herself, she said, *I hope*. And felt Heath's pulse. It pumped beneath her fingers.

She used the flashlight and her fingers to figure out what was wrong. He was bleeding from his head and shoulder. She dialed 911 and recited what she knew of the wounds and the address.

By the time she hung up, sirens pierced the air and tears trickled down her face.

She knew she needed to get up and unlock the front door, but she didn't want to leave Heath. She continued to hold his hand and tell him he would be fine.

The sirens stopped, and she called out, "Come around back!"

The back gate opened. A flashlight beam blinded her.

"God, Dela! What happened?" Tabitha's voice

unwound Dela's fear. The light dropped from her face, and the officer hurried over.

"Can you see if you can get the electricity back on. There are two bodies in my hall." Dela was surprised her voice was so strong. She kept holding Heath's hand and willing him to wake up.

"Dela! Dela!" Quinn shouted.

"In back!" she called back as more sirens sounded.

He burst through the gate, shining a flashlight across her and Heath.

"Is he?"

"He's alive, but unconscious. They must have caught him when he was letting Mugshot out and checking on Jethro. Could you show the ambulance around here and unlock the door for whoever needs to get in? Also, see if you can help Tabitha—"

The house lit up, as well as the backyard lights.

"Never mind, she got the lights on." She leaned down and kissed Heath's cheek. "Hang in there. Help is here." Then she did a more thorough search for wounds on him.

Quinn disappeared, and the EMTs from the reservation arrived. They asked her to step back as they checked him out. Heath's eyes fluttered open, and his head started to move back and forth.

Dela stepped forward and grasped his hand. "I'm here. I'm not going anywhere."

Her voice calmed him, and his eyes closed. His hand gripped hers.

Quinn came back out. "Go with Heath. I'll deal with this. Someone will find you at the hospital and get your statement. But it's pretty clear by where the bodies are that you had no alternative but to shoot to save yourself."

"Yeah."

"We're taking him now," the EMT said.

Dela nodded, with Heath still holding her hand, she climbed into the ambulance to ride with him.

The ride was a blur, as was the doctor in the ER telling her that Heath had a hard knock to the head and the stitches on his shoulder wound had been ripped open. They planned to keep him in the hospital for a couple of days. She should go home.

Even though she was dead on her feet, she shook her head. "I have to be here when he comes to. He doesn't know if I was killed or alive." Once Heath was settled in a hospital bed and all the medical staff had cleared out of the room, Dela climbed into the bed next to Heath and fell asleep.

Chapter Thirty-one

A hand was moving up and down Dela's back. She liked the feel of it. Then she remembered where she was and opened her eyes. She gazed into Heath's eyes. He was smiling.

"I'm surprised they let you sleep here," he said.

"I didn't give them much choice, I just climbed up here and fell asleep." She moved up and kissed his lips, then settled with her head on his good shoulder. "I thought they'd killed you."

"I wasn't paying attention when I walked out onto the patio with Mugshot. He looked behind him and growled. By the time I started to pull out my gun and turn, something hit me in the head. I came too once and tried to stand up, but then blacked out." He raised her chin to look up at him. "Did they hurt you?"

She peered into his eyes, so glad to see them open and staring at her with the love she knew was meant only for her. "Only my heart when I thought they'd killed you."

He pulled her up and kissed her.

"Ahem."

Dela rolled in Heath's arm and found the doctor, Quinn, and Marion standing inside the door.

"I thought I only put one patient in this bed last night," the doctor said.

Heath chuckled and Dela slipped off the bed.

"Sorry, I was tired. It's been a long three days with little sleep." Dela stepped away from the bed and Marion pulled her into a hug.

"I'm so glad you're okay and Heath will be alright." Marion released her and peered into her eyes. "Quinn told me what happened. You are the bravest person I know."

Dela shook her head. "No, I'm not. I was scared to death, but I had to get to Heath and see if he was okay." She glanced at the bed as the doctor examined him. "Luckily, he has a hard head."

There was commotion outside the door. Her mom came through, followed by Lance, Molly, and Rosie. They all hugged her and checked out Heath.

"That's a hard way to get out of a wedding," Lance said to Heath.

"There is no way I'm missing my wedding to Dela," Heath said.

The doctor left, and Quinn motioned to Dela. She walked over to him. "Glad to see he's doing well. I've been tasked with taking your statement."

She nodded. "Let's go to the cafeteria." She walked over and took Heath's hand. "I have to go give my statement to Quinn. We're going to go where it's a little quieter."

Heath glanced at Quinn. "What about my

statement?"

"I'll get it when I'm done with Dela." Quinn motioned to the door.

"Do you need a ride home?" Mom asked.

Dela started to say, 'Yes,' then remembered her house was a crime scene and she'd have to have someone come in and clean up the blood. "Actually, Heath and I will need a place to stay until my house is cleaned up."

"We can take you to your house for clothes, and you can stay with Lance and me," Mom said.

Dela glanced at Lance. "Are you sure you want us?"

"Your mother has been complaining she doesn't get to see enough of you. I'm happy with you two staying for as long as you need." Lance waved his hand to Heath.

Dela met Heath's gaze. "Is that what you want?"

"It's your mom or mine. I'd rather stay with your mom."

"Okay. When I'm ready to leave, I'll text and let you know." Dela touched Heath's hand and walked out of the room with Quinn.

She was tired of always making statements about people trying to kill her. She'd thought Afghanistan was dangerous. It was nothing compared to the corruption that seemed to ooze out of the cracks in Pendleton and spill over to the reservation.

In the cafeteria, she filled up a tray and poured herself a large iced tea before sitting at the table with Quinn.

"If you need to eat first, that's okay," he said.

She nodded and as she ate, asked him, "After you

dropped us off, did you go home or did you have to go talk to HQ Supervisor Prescott?"

"I talked to Milo. I'm not sure why you got her panties in a bunch, but she was acting so out of character that it made me suspicious. I asked Milo to do whatever she asked and let me know what she was up to. I guess she is being audited for some of her recent actions. She wanted to arrest Travers and Julia to regain the favor of her superiors. You figuring out everything before she even knew what was happening made her look bad." He smiled. "I don't think she'll have her job for very much longer."

He slid a photo across the table. "You were also right about Celia. Agents found her lounging by a pool in a fancy resort in the same town where Travers has a home in Morocco. They are transporting her and Duke back now."

Dela's gaze shot from where she was placing her fork on the tray to Quinn's face. "Celia and Duke? Were they the item, not Travers and Celia?"

"No. You were right about Travers and Celia. Duke was the person sent to kill Celia. Instead, he bargained with Travers, who put him on the payroll as Celia's bodyguard."

Dela smiled as she slid her empty tray to the middle of the table. "I'm glad she was still alive. This was a good investigation."

"Why do you say that?" Quinn studied her.

"Because we were able to find and bring back both women who were missing, and we know Duke didn't become a casualty of the cartel. There isn't usually a happy ending when they are discovered." She thought of her friend Robin. If she'd been a better friend and not been in such a hurry to get to practice, Robin would still be alive.

Sighing, she said, "I'm ready." Dela answered Quinn's questions about what he'd found at her house. Then she told him everything that happened from the time he dropped her and Heath off to when he arrived back at the house.

"That was smart of you to stay hidden in the dark hallway," Quinn said.

"I had to stay alive to make sure Heath lived." She stared into his eyes. "His people and I need him. I couldn't let someone out for vengeance on me take him away."

"You and Heath are a good team, in love and life." Quinn closed his notebook. "I know we've had some rocky times, and I don't always treat you like anything other than that tough, sassy Military Police Sergeant that I butted heads with in Afghanistan, but I do think of you as a friend."

Dela couldn't believe those words came out of Quinn's mouth. She smiled and said, "Could you repeat that? There was too much noise for me to hear it all."

Quinn grinned and shook his head. "You'll only hear that from me once. Go take care of that man of yours."

Dela stood, slid her tray over to Quinn, and walked out of the cafeteria smiling.

Thank you for reading book seven in the Spotted Pony Casino Mystery series. If you enjoyed the book, please leave a review where you purchased *Crapshoot*. And if you are a reader who uses Goodreads and Bookbub, please leave reviews there. Reviews are the best way of letting an author know you enjoyed the book and it puts the book into the world of other readers.

As I continue this series you will see major changes in Dela and Heath's life as well as the past meeting the present.

Paty

Other books in the Spotted Pony Casino Mystery series:
Poker Face
House Edge
Double Down
The Squeeze
The Pinch
Down and Dirty

If you enjoyed this series, you might enjoy my other mystery series:

Shandra Higheagle Mysteries

Double Duplicity	*Haunting Corpse*
Tarnished Remains	*Artful Murder*
Deadly Aim	*Dangerous Dance*
Murderous Secrets	*Homicide Hideaway*
Killer Descent	*Toxic Trigger-point*
Reservation Revenge	*Abstract Casualty*
Yuletide slaying	*Capricious Demise*
Fatal Fall	*Vanishing Dream*

Gabriel Hawke Novels
Murder of Ravens
Mouse Trail Ends
Rattlesnake Brother
Chattering Blue Jay
Fox Goes Hunting
Turkey's Fiery Demise
Stolen Butterfly
Churlish Badger
Owl's Silent Strike
Bear Stalker
Damning Firefly
Cougar's Cache
Wolverine Instincts
Wolf Moon

About the Author

Paty Jager grew up in Wallowa County in NE Oregon and has always been amazed by it's beauty, history, and ruralness. She has always had an interest in the Indigenous people and their culture and enjoys learning more every time she writes a book.

Paty is an award-winning author of 63 novels of murder mystery and western romance. All her work has Western or native American elements in them along with hints of humor and engaging characters. She and her husband raise alfalfa hay in rural eastern Oregon. Riding horses and battling rattlesnakes, she not only writes the western lifestyle, she lives it.

By following me at one of these places you will always know when the next book is releasing and where you can meet me in person.

Website: https://www.patyjager.net
Blog: https://writingintothesunset.net
Windtree Press: https://windtreepress.com/paty-jager/
Facebook Author Page: Author Paty Jager
Goodreads:
http://www.goodreads.com/author/show/1005334.Paty_Jager
Newsletter: https://bit.ly/2IhmWcm
Bookbub: https://www.bookbub.com/authors/paty-jager

Windtree
Press

Thank you for purchasing this Windtree Press publication. For other books of the heart, please visit our website at www.windtreepress.com.

For questions or more information contact us at info@windtreepress.com

Windtree Press

www.windtreepress.com